£1.50

CONTINUUM 1

Edited by
Roger Elwood

A STAR BOOK
published by
WYNDHAM PUBLICATIONS

A Star Book
Published in 1977
by Wyndham Publications Ltd.
A Howard & Wyndham Company
123, King Street, London W6 9JG

First published in Great Britain by
W. H. Allen & Co. Ltd. 1975

Printed in Great Britain by
Richard Clay (The Chaucer Press), Ltd., Bungay, Suffolk

ISBN 0 352 39664 4

CONTINUUM 1

INTRODUCTION

There are several excellent anthology series available today: Damon Knight edits one, Bob Silverberg has another, and so does Terry Carr. Each is based upon a single premise, fashioned by the editor's individual tastes: namely, the best science fiction written in an atmosphere of creative freedom.

But – and it's not a shortcoming, just a fact – there is no *other* connection between, say, *New Dimensions 1* and *New Dimensions 2*; or *Universe 1* and *Universe 2*. All present solid, top-notch science fiction by well-known and beginning authors . . . period. Considering the quality of these books, that's a strong *raison d'être*.

But the *Continuum* anthologies are, frankly, based upon an *additional* premise: a tightly woven series of threads will ultimately tie all four books closely together.

What does this premise mean?

That each story in each anthology is part of a series written by the author in question. There are eight stories in *Continuum 1*; eight in *Continuum 2*; and so on. That means, also, eight *series*. Thus, with all four books, there will be a total of thirty-two episodes – four episodes per series.

Now, each story is, in theory and actuality, a separate entity. We're not fostering Flash Gordon cliff-hangers here. You don't *have* to buy the second book to enjoy the first; and vice versa.

Yet, with the four *Continuum* anthologies, the series format reaches its full potential, with each series a minimum of 25,000 words all told; there is only one exception: Gene Wolfe's delightful short-shorts.

Since each story was written by the author as a separate entity, able to stand on its own, there was no sacrifice of artistic quality; no subsequent story was written *simply* to fulfil the series format. Thus, in several instances, authors discarded initial creations because after one or two stories, to add the remaining number would have meant sheer padding, and by the time the fourth story was written, well, it would have been just an assembly-line job. *Only* stories that naturally fit the series guidelines, *and* are valid separately, have been accepted for *Continuum.*

It is awkward for an editor to praise stories in books that he puts together because these comments usually seem self-serving. I run that risk here but to be able to note how much I think of these stories, well, it's worth the risk, in my opinion.

I doubt very much that any of the authors herein have done material that is significantly better than that which is represented in this *Continuum* or in the others comprising this series. A number are breathtaking *tours de force* which I have re-read several times since accepting them for publication.

I would very much like to extend thanks to George Ernsberger, Editor-in-Chief of Berkley Books, for his patience and his help in a variety of ways. George is one of those rare editors who possess boundless degrees of creative insight yet who permit their authors/anthologists to express *themselves* in the best way possible. Deep thanks also to Virginia Kidd, someone else whose relationship I value highly and who has been both a friend and a strong impetus in the aim to settle for nothing less than the very best.

Continuum is a new concept in anthologies. We sincerely hope that, as far as you, the reader, are concerned, it is also a satisfying one.

Roger Elwood

Margate, N.J.

Philip José Farmer

STATIONS
OF THE NIGHTMARE

Part 1: THE TWO-EDGED GIFT

1

Paul Eyre shot a flying saucer.

On this bright morning, he was walking through a farmer's field. Ahead of him was the edge of a wood bisected by a small creek. Riley, the setter, had just stiffened. Nose down, crouched low, seeming to vibrate, he pointed toward the magnet, the invisible quail. Paul Eyre's heart pumped a little faster. Ahead of Riley, a few yards away, was a bush. Behind it should be the covey.

They broke loose with that racket that had made him jump so when he was a novice. It was as if the earth had given violent birth to several tiny planets. But there was not the dozen or so he had expected. Only two. The lead one was much larger than the other, so much larger that he did jump then. He knew as the shotgun roared and kicked that it was not a bird.

The concentrated pattern of his modified choke must have hit the thing squarely. It fell away at a forty-five degree angle instead of dropping as a dead bird drops, and it crashed through the lower branches of a tree on the outskirts of the wood.

Automatically, he had fired the second barrel at the trailing bird. And he had missed it.

The thing had rocketed up like a quail. But it had been dark and about two feet long. Or two feet wide. His finger had squeezed on the trigger even as his mind had squeezed on the revelation that it was not a winged creature.

It wasn't a creature, he thought, but a made thing. More like a huge clay pigeon than anything else.

He looked around. Riley was a white and black streak, run-

9

ning as if a cougar were after him. He made no noise. He seemed to be conserving his breath as if he knew he'd need every atom of oxygen he could get. Behind him was a trail of excrement. Ahead of him, over half a mile up the slope, was a white farmhouse and two dark-red barns.

Roger, Paul's son, had spoken of mines which flew up into the air before exploding. This thing had not been attached to a chain nor had it blown up. It could be a dud. But there had been no blast as it soared up. Perhaps the noise of his shotgun had covered it.

He shook his head. It could not have been anything like that. Unless ... Had some vicious person put it in the field just to kill hunters? Senseless violence was on the increase in this God-forsaking country.

The situation was much like that of a car that refused to run. You could think about it all you wanted to and make mental images of what was wrong. But until you opened the hood and looked at the engine, you would not be able to make a definite analysis. So he would open the hood.

He walked forward. The only sound was the northwest wind, gentle here because the woods broke it. The bluejay and the crows that had been so noisy before he had fired were quiet. There was the bluejay, sitting on a tree branch. It seemed frozen with shock.

He was cautious but not afraid, he told himself. He had been afraid only three times in his life. When his father had deserted him, when his mother had died, and when Mavice had said she was leaving him. And these three events had taught him that nothing was as bad as he'd thought it at the time and that it was stupid, illogical to fear. He and his brothers and sisters and mother had gotten along without his father. His mother's death had actually made his life easier. And Mavice had not left him.

'Only the unimaginative, of whom you are the king, have no fear,' Tincrowdor had told him. But what did that effete egg-head know of real life or real men?

Nevertheless, he hesitated. He could just walk away, round up the dog, and hunt elsewhere. Or, better, tell Smith that someone had planted a strange mechanical device in his field.

Perhaps, though he did not like to admit it, his sight had betrayed him. Behind his glasses were fifty-four-year-old eyes. He was in good shape, better than most men twenty years

10

younger. Much better than that Tincrowdor, who sat on his tocus all day while he typed away on his crazy stories.

Still, he had been informed by the optometrist that he needed a new prescription. He had not told anyone about this. He hated to admit to anyone that he had a weakness, and that any-one included himself. When he had a chance to get fitted with new lenses, with no one except the doctor the wiser, he'd go. Perhaps he should not have put it off so long.

He resumed walking slowly across the field. Once, he looked toward the farmhouse. Riley, his pace undiminished, was still headed toward it. When he caught Riley, he'd rap him a few on the nose and shame him. If he were ruined by this, he'd get rid of him. He couldn't see feeding something that was useless. The hound ate more than he was worth as it was.

He could imagine what Mavice would say about that. 'You're going to retire in eleven years. Would you want us to give you away or send you to the gas chamber because you're useless?'

And he'd say, 'But I won't be. I'll be working as hard as ever on my own business after I've retired.'

He was ten feet from the wood when the yellow haze drifted out from it.

2

He stopped. It couldn't be pollen at this time of the year. And no pollen ever glowed.

Moreover, it was coming with too much force to be driven by the wind. For the second time, he hesitated. The thick yellow luminance looked so much like gas. He thought about the sheep that had been killed in Nevada or Utah when the army nerve gas had escaped. Could – But no ... that was ridicu-lous.

The shimmering haze spread out, and he was in it. For a few seconds, he held his breath. Then he released it and laughed. The stuff blew away from his face and closed in again. Here and there, some bits sparkled. Before he reached the trees, he saw tiny blobs form on the grass, on his hands, and on the gun barrels. They looked like gold-colored mercury. When he ran his hand over the barrels, the stuff accumulated at the ends into two large drops. They ran like mercury into the cup formed by

11

his palm.

Its odor made him wrinkle his nose and snap it to the ground. It smelled like spermatic fluid.

It was then that he noticed that he had not reloaded. He was mildly shocked. He had never missed reloading immediately after firing. In fact, he did it so automatically that he never even thought about it. He was more upset than he had realized.

Abruptly, the haze or fog, or whatever it was, disappeared. He looked around. The grass for about twenty feet behind him was faintly yellow.

He went on. A branch, broken off by the thing, lay before him. Ahead was the dense and silent wood. He pushed through the tangles of thorn bushes, from which he had flushed out so many rabbits. And there was one now, a big buck behind the thorns. It saw him, saw that it was seen, but it did not move. He crouched down to look at it. Its black eyes looked glazed, and its brown fur scintillated here and there with yellowness. It was in the shade, so the sun could not be responsible for the glints.

He poked at it, but it did not move. And now he could see that it was trembling violently.

A few minutes later, he was at the place where the thing would have landed if it had continued its angle of descent. The bushes were undisturbed; the grass unbent.

An hour passed. He had thoroughly covered the woods on this side of the creek and found nothing. He waded through the waters, which were nowhere deeper than two feet, and started his search through the woods on that side. He saw no yellow mercury, which meant one of two things. Either the thing had not come here or else it had quit expelling the stuff. That is, if the stuff *had* been expelled from it. It might just be a coincidence that the stuff had appeared at the same time the thing had disappeared. A coincidence, however, did not seem likely.

Then he saw a single drop of the mercury, and he knew that it was still . . . bleeding? He shook his head. Why would he think of that word? Only living creatures could be *wounded*. He had *damaged* it.

He whirled. Something had splashed behind him. Through a small break in the vegetation, he could see something round, flat, and black shooting from the middle of the creek. He had seen it before at a distance and had thought it was the top of a slightly rounded boulder just covered by the creek. His eyes *were* going bad.

12

He recrossed the creek and followed a trail of water which dwindled away suddenly. He looked up, and something – it – dropped down behind a bush. There was a crashing noise, then silence.

So it was alive. No machine moved like that, unless ...

What would Tincrowdor say if he told him that he had seen a flying saucer?

Common sense told him to say nothing to anybody about this. He'd be laughed at, and people would think he was going insane. Or suffering from premature senility, like his father.

The thought seemed to drive him crazy for a minute. Shouting, he plunged through the bushes and the thorn tangles. When he was under the tree from which the thing had dropped, he stopped. His heart was hammering, and he was sweating. There was no impression in the soft moisture-laden ground; nothing indicated that a large heavy object had fallen onto it.

Something moved to the right at the corner of his eye. He turned and shot once, then again. Pieces of bushes flew up, and bits of bark showered. He reloaded – he wasn't about to forget this time – and moved slowly toward the base of the bush at which the thing seemed to have been. But it wasn't there anymore, if it had ever been there.

A few feet further, he suddenly got dizzy. He leaned against a tree. His blood was thrumming in his ears, and the trees and bushes were melting. Perhaps the yellow stuff *was* some kind of nerve gas.

He decided to get out of the woods. It wasn't fear but logic that had made him change his mind. And no one had seen him retreat.

Near the edge of the woods, he stopped. He no longer felt dizzy, and the world had regained its hardness. It was true that only he would know he had quit, but he wouldn't ever again be able to think of himself as a real man. No, by God – and he told himself he wasn't swearing when he said that – he would see this out.

He turned and saw through the screen of bushes something white move out from behind a tree. It looked like the back of a woman's torso. She wore nothing; he could see the soft white skin and the indentation of the spine. The hips were not visible. Then the back of the head, black hair down to the white shoulders, appeared.

He shouted at the woman, but she paid no attention. When

he got to the tree where she had first appeared, he could no longer see her. Some of the grass was still rising, and some leaves had been distorted.

An hour later, Paul Eyre gave up. Had he just thought he'd seen a woman? What would a woman be doing naked in these woods? She couldn't have been with a lover, because she and the man would have gotten out of the woods the first time he'd fired his shotgun.

On the way back, he thought he saw something big and tawny at a distance. He crouched down and opened the bush in front of him. About thirty yards off, going behind an almost solid tangle, was the back of an animal. It was yellowish brown and had a long tufted tail. And if he hadn't known it was impossible, he would have said that it was the rear end of an African lion. No, a lioness.

A moment later, he saw the head of the woman.

She was where the lion would be if it stood up on its hind legs and presented its head.

The woman was in profile, and she was the most beautiful he had ever seen.

He must be suffering from some insidious form of Asiatic flu. That would explain everything. In fact, it was the only explanation.

He was sure of it when he got to the edge of the trees. The field was covered with red flowers and at the other side, which seemed to be miles away, was a glittering green city.

The vision lasted only three or four seconds. The flowers and the city disappeared, and the field, as if it were a rubber band, snapped back to its real dimensions.

He could hear it snap.

Ten minutes later, he was at the farmhouse.

Riley greeted him by biting him.

3

Eyre parked the car in front of his house. The driveway was blocked with a car to which was hitched a boat trailer, a motorcycle lacking a motor, and a Land-Rover on top of which was a half-built camper. Behind it was a large garage crammed with machines, tools, supplies, old tires, and outboard motors in the process of being repaired.

Thirteen-thirty-one Wizman Court was in an area which once had been all residential. Now the huge old mansion across the street was a nursing home; the houses next to it had been torn down and buildings for a veterinarian and his kennels were almost completed. Eyre's own house had looked large enough and smart enough when he and Mavice had moved into it twenty years ago. It looked tiny, mean, and decaying now and had looked so for ten years.

Paul Eyre, until this moment, had never noticed that. Though he felt crowded at times, he attributed this to too many people, not the smallness of the house. Once he got rid of his son and daughter, the house would again become comfortable. And the house was paid for. Besides taxes, maintenance, and the utilities, it cost him nothing. If the neighborhood was run down somewhat, so much the better. His neighbors did not complain because he was conducting his own repair business here.

Until now, he had not thought anything about its appearance. It was just a house. But now he noticed that the grass on the tiny lawn was uncut, the wooden shutters needed painting, the driveway was a mess, and the sidewalk was cracked.

He got out of the car and picked up his shotgun and bag with his left hand. The right hand was heavily bandaged. The old ladies sitting on the side porch waved and called out to him, and he waved back at them. They sat like a bunch of ancient crows on a branch. Time was shooting them down, one by one. There was an empty chair at the end of the row, but it would be occupied by a newcomer soon enough. Mr Ridgley had sat there until last week when he had been observed one afternoon urinating over the railings into the rosebushes below. He was, according to the old ladies, now locked up in his room on the third floor. Eyre looked up and saw a white face with tobacco-stained moustaches pressed against the bars over the window.

He waved. Mr Ridgley stared. The mouth below the moustache drooled. Angry, Paul Eyre turned away. His mother had stared out of that window for several weeks, and then she had disappeared. But she had lived to be eighty-six before she had become senile. That was forgivable. What he could not forgive, nor forget, was that his father had only been sixty when his brain had hardened and his reason had slid off it.

He went up the wooden unpainted steps off the side of the

15

front porch. It was no longer just a porch. He had enclosed it and Roger now used it for a bedroom. Roger, as usual, had neglected to make up the bed-couch. Four years in the Marines, including a hitch in Viet Nam, had not made him tidy.

Eyre growled at Roger as he entered the front room. Roger, a tall thin blond youth, was sitting on the sofa and reading a college textbook. He said, 'Oh, Mom said she'd do it.' He stared at his father's hand. 'What happened?'

'Riley went mad, and I had to shoot him.'

Mavice, coming in from the kitchen, said, 'Oh, my God! You *shot* him!'

Tears ran down Roger's cheeks.

'Why would you do that?'

Paul waved his right hand. 'Didn't you hear me? He bit me! He was trying for my throat!'

'Why would he do that?' Mavice said.

'You sound like you don't believe me!' Paul said. 'For God's sake, isn't anyone going to ask me how badly he bit me? Or worry that I might get rabies?'

Roger wiped away the tears and looked at the bandages. 'You've been to a doctor,' he said. 'What'd he say about it?'

'Riley's head has been shipped to the state lab,' Paul said. 'Do you have any idea what it's going to be like if I have to have rabies shots? Anyway, it's fatal! Nobody ever survived rabies!'

Mavice's hand shot to her mouth and from behind it came strangled sounds. Her light blue eyes were enormous.

'Yeah, and horseshoes hung over the door bring good luck,' Roger said. 'Why don't you come out of the nineteenth century, Dad? Look at something besides outboard motors and the TV. The rate of recovery from rabies is very high.'

'So I only had one year of college,' Paul said. 'Is that any reason for my smartass son to sneer at me? Where would you be if it wasn't for the G.I. Bill?'

'You go to college to get a degree, not an education,' Roger said. 'You have to educate yourself, all your life.'

'For Heaven's sake, you two,' Mavice said. 'Quit this eternal bickering. And sit down, Paul. Take it easy. You look terrible!'

He jerked his arm away and said, 'I'm all right.' But he sat down. The mirror behind the sofa had showed him a short, thin but broad-shouldered man with smooth pale-brown hair, a high forehead, bushy sandy eyebrows, blue eyes behind

16

octagonal rimless spectacles, a long nose, a thick brown moustache, and a round cleft chin.

His face did look like a mask. Tincrowdor had said that anyone who wore glasses should never sport a moustache. Together, these gave a false-face appearance. That remark had angered him then. Now it reminded him that he was looking forward to seeing Tincrowdor. Maybe he had some answers.

'What about a beer, Dad?' Roger said. He looked contrite.

'That'd help, thanks,' Paul said. Roger hurried off to the kitchen while Mavice stood looking down at him. Even when both were standing up, she was still looking down on him. She was at least four inches taller.

'You don't really think Riley had rabies?' she said. 'He seemed all right this morning.'

'Not really. He wasn't foaming at the mouth or anything like that. Something scared him in the woods, scared him witless, and he attacked me. He didn't know what he was doing.'

Mavice sat down in a chair across the room. Roger brought in the beer. Paul drank it gratefully, though its amber color reminded him of the yellow stuff. He looked at Mavice over the glass. He had always thought she was very good-looking, even if her face was somewhat long. But, remembering the profile of the woman in the woods, he saw that she was very plain indeed, if not ugly. Any woman's face would look bad now that he had seen that glory among the trees.

The front door slammed, and Glenda walked in from the porch. He felt vaguely angry. He always did when he saw her. She had a beautiful face, a feminization of his, and a body which might have matched the face but never would. It was thin and nearly breastless, though she was seventeen. The spine was shaped like a question mark; one shoulder was lower than the other; the legs looked as thin as piston rods.

She stopped and said, 'What happened?' Her voice was deep and husky, sexy to those who heard it without seeing her.

Mavice and Roger told her what had taken place. Paul braced himself for a storm of tears and accusations, since she loved Riley dearly. But she said nothing about him. She seemed concerned only about her father. This not only surprised him. It angered him.

Why was he angry? he thought.

And he understood, then, that it was because she was a living reproach. If it weren't for him, she would not be twisted; she'd

17

be a tall straight and beautiful girl. His anger had been his way of keeping this knowledge from himself.

He was amazed that he had not known this before. How could he have been so blind?

He began sweating. He shifted on the sofa as if he could move his body away from the revelation. He felt the beginning of a panic. What had opened his eyes so suddenly? Why had he only now, today, noticed how ugly and mean the house was, how frightened and repulsed he was by the old people across the street, and why Glenda had angered him when he should have shown her nothing but tenderness?

He knew why. Something had happened to him in the woods, and it was probably the stuff which had fallen on him, the stuff expelled by the thing. But how could it have given him this insight? It scared him. It made him feel as if he were losing something very dear.

He almost yielded to the desire to tell them everything. No, they would not believe him. Oh, they'd believe that he had seen those things. But they would think that he was going crazy, and they would be frightened. If he would shoot Riley while in a fit, he might shoot them.

He became even more frightened. Many times, he had imagined doing just this. What if he lost control and the image shifted gears into reality?

He stood up. 'I think I'll wash up and then go to bed for a while. I don't feel so good.'

This seemed to astonish everybody.

'What's so strange about that?' he said loudly.

'Why, Dad, you've always had to be forced to bed when you've been sick,' Glenda said. 'You just won't admit that you can get ill, like other people. You act as if you were made of stone, as if microbes bounced off of you.'

'That's because I'm not a hyper— a hyper— a what-you-call-it, a goldbricker, like some people,' he said.

'A hypochondriac,' Glenda and Roger said at the same time.

'Don't look at me when you say that,' Mavice said, glaring at him. 'You know I have a chronic bladder infection. I'm not faking it. Dr Wells told you that himself when you called him to find out if I was lying. I was never so embarrassed in all my life.'

The shrill voice was coming from a long way off. Glenda was becoming even more crooked, and Roger was getting

18

thinner and taller.

The doorway to the bedroom moved to one side as he tried to get through it. He couldn't make it on two legs, so he got down on all fours. If he was a dog, he'd have a more solid footing, and maybe the doorway would be so confused by the sudden change of identities it would hold still long enough for him to get through it.

He heard Mavice's scream and barked an assurance that he was all right. Then he was protesting to Mavice and Roger that he didn't want to stand up, but they had hoisted him up and were guiding him toward the bed. It didn't matter then, since he had gotten through. Let the doorway move around all it wanted now; he had fooled it. You could teach an old dog new tricks.

Later, he heard Mavice's voice drilling through the closed door. Here he was, trying to sleep off whatever was ailing him, and she was screaming like a parrot. Nothing would ever get her to lower that voice. Too many decibels from a unibelle, he thought. Which was a strange thought, even if he was an engineer. But he wished she would tone down or, even better, shut up. Forever. He knew that it wasn't her fault, since both her parents had been somewhat deaf during her childhood. But they were dead now, and she had no logical reason to keep on screaming as if she were trying to wake the dead.

Why hadn't he ever said anything about it? Because he nourished the resentment, fed it with other resentments. And then, when the anger became too great, he in turn screamed at her. But it was always about other things. He had never told her how grating her voice was.

He sat up suddenly and then got out of bed. He was stronger now, and the doorway was no longer alive. He walked out into the little hall and said, 'What are you saying to Morna?'

Mavice looked at him in surprise and put her hand over the receiver. 'I'm calling off tonight. You're too sick to have company.'

'No, I'm not,' he said. 'I'm all right. You tell her to come on over as planned.'

Mavice's penciled eyebrows rose. 'All right, but if I'd insisted they come, you would have gotten mad at me.'

'I got work to do,' he said, and headed toward the rear exit.

'With that bandage on your hand?' Mavice said.

He threw both hands up into the air and went into the living room. Roger was sitting in a chair and holding a textbook while

19

watching TV.

'How can you study freshman calculus while Matt Dillon is shooting up the place?' Paul Eyre said.

'Every time a gun goes off and a redskin bites the dust, another equation becomes clear,' Roger said.

'What the hell does that mean?'

'I don't know what it means,' Roger said calmly. 'I just know it works.'

'I don't understand you,' Paul said. 'When I was studying I had to have absolute quiet.'

'Didn't you listen to the radio while you were hitting the books?'

Paul seemed surprised.

'No.'

'Well, I was raised this way,' Roger said. 'All my friends were. Maybe we learned how to handle two or more things simultaneously. Maybe that's where the generation gap is. We take in many different things at once and see the connections among them. But you only saw one thing at a time.'

'So that makes you better than us?'

'Different, anyway,' Roger said. 'Dad, you ought to read MacLuhan. But then . . .'

'But then what?'

'But you never read anything but the local newspaper, sports magazines, and stuff connected with your work.'

'I don't have time,' Paul said. 'I'm holding down a job at Trackless and working eight hours a day on my own business. You know that.'

'Leo Tincrowdor used to do that, and he read three books a week. But then he wants to know.'

'Yeah, he knows so much, but if his car breaks down, can he fix it himself? No, he has to call in an expensive mechanic. Or get me to do it for him for nothing.'

'Nobody's perfect,' Roger said. 'Anyway, he's more interested in finding out how the universe works and why our society is breaking down and what can be done to repair it.'

'It wouldn't be breaking down if people like him weren't trying to break it down!'

'You would have said the same thing a hundred years ago,' Roger said. 'You think things are in a mess now; you should read about the world in 1874. The good old days. My history professor –'

Paul strode from the room and into the kitchen. He never drank more than two beers a day, but today was different. And *how* it was different. The top of the can popped open, reminding him of the sound when the field had snapped back to normalcy. Now *there* was a connection which Roger, anybody else in the world, in fact, would not have made. He wished he had stayed home to catch up on his work instead of indulging himself in a quail hunt.

4

At seven, the Tincrowdors walked in. Usually Paul kept them waiting, since he always had to finish up on a motor in the garage. By the time he had washed up, Leo had had several drinks and Morna and Mavice were engaged in one of their fast-moving female conversations. Leo was happy enough talking to Roger or Glenda or, if neither were there, happy to be silent. He did not seem to resent Paul's always showing up late. Paul suspected that he would have been content if he never showed up. Yet, he always greeted him with a smile. If he had been drinking much, he also had some comment which sounded funny but which concealed a joke at Paul's expense.

Tonight, however, Paul was in the living room when they arrived. He jumped up and kissed Morna enthusiastically. He always kissed good-looking women if they would let him; it gave him a sense of innocent infidelity, outside of the sheer pleasure of kissing. Morna had to bend down a little, like Mavice, but she put more warmth into it than Mavice. Yet she was always, well, often, chewing him out in defence of her friend, Mavice.

Leo Queequeg Tincrowdor enclosed Paul's hand with his over-sized one and squeezed. He was a six-footer with heavy bones and a body that had once been muscular but now was turning to fat. His once auburn hair was white and thinning. Below protruding bars of bone, his strange leaf-green eyes, the balls bloodshot, looked at and through Paul. His cheeks were high and red. His beard was a mixture of gray, black, and red. He had a deep voice the effect of which was lessened by a tendency to slur when drinking. And Paul had only seen him twice when he hadn't been drinking. He pushed ahead of him a balloon of bourbon. When he had money, it was Waller's Special Reserve. When he was broke, it was cheap whiskey cut with lemon juice. Evidently he had recently received a story check. The balloon had an expensive odor.

'Sit down, Leo.' Ritualistically, Eyre asked, 'What'll it be? Beer or whiskey?'

Ritualistically, Tincrowdor answered, 'Bourbon. I only drink beer when I can't get anything better.'

When Paul returned with six ounces of Old Kentucky Delight on ice, he found Tincrowdor handing out two of his latest soft-covers to Roger and Glenda. He felt a thrust of jealousy as they exclaimed over the gifts. How could the kids enjoy that trash?

'What's this?' he said, handing Leo his drink and then taking the book from Glenda. The cover showed a white man in a cage surrounded by some green-skinned women, all naked, reaching through the bars for the man. In the background was a mountain vaguely resembling a lion with a woman's head. On top of the head was a white Grecian temple with small figures holding knives around another figure stretched out on an altar.

'*Sphinxes Without Secrets,*' Leo said. 'It's about a spaceman who lands on a planet inhabited by women. The males died off centuries before, mostly from heartbreak. A chemist, a women's lib type, had put a substance in the central food plant which made the men unable to have erections.'

'What?' Mavice said. She laughed, but her face was red.

'It's an old idea,' Leo said. He sipped the bourbon and shuddered. 'But I extrapolate to a degree nobody else has ever done before. Or is capable of doing. It's very realistic. Too much so for the *Busiris Journal-Star*. Their reviewer not only refused to write a review, he sent me a nasty letter. Nothing libelous. Old Potts doesn't have the guts for that.'

'If there weren't any men, how could they have babies?' Paul said.

'Chemically induced parthenogenesis. Virgin birth caused by chemicals. It's been done with rabbits and theoretically could be done with humans. I don't doubt that the Swedes have done it, but they're keeping quiet about it. They have no desire to be martyrs.'

'That's blasphemy!' Paul said. His face felt hot, and he had a momentary image of himself throwing Tincrowdor out on his rear. 'There's only been one virgin birth, and that was divinely inspired.'

22

'Inspired? That sounds like a blow job,' Tincrowdor said. 'No, I apologize for that remark. When among the aborigines, respect their religion. However, I will point out that if Jesus was the result of parthenogenesis, he should have been a woman. All parthenogenetically stimulated offspring are females. Females only carry the X chromosome, you know. Or do you? It's the male's Y chromosome that determines that the baby be a male.'

'But God is, by the definition of God, all-powerful,' Glenda said. 'So why couldn't He have, uh, inserted a sort of spiritual Y chromosome?'

Tincrowdor laughed and said, 'Very good, Glenda. You'd make an excellent science-fiction author, God help you.

'Anyway, every culture has its deviates, and this lesbian society was no exception. So a few perverts were not repulsed by the spaceman. Instead, he was to them a most desirable sex object.'

'How could a woman who wanted a man instead of a woman be a deviate?' Paul said.

'Deviation is determined by what the culture considers normal. When we were kids, going down was considered by almost everybody to be a perversion, and you could get put in jail for twenty years or more if caught doing it. But in our lifetime, we've seen this attitude change. By 2010, anything between consenting adults will be acceptable. But there are still millions in this country who think the only God-favored way is for the woman to lie on her back with the man on top. And would you believe it, there are millions who won't undress in front of each other or keep a light on during intercourse. The sexual dinosaurs, for that's what they are, will be extinct in another fifty years. Could I have another drink?'

Paul Eyre glared at his wife. She must have been confiding in Morna. Tincrowdor had made it obvious that he was talking about the Eyres. Was nothing sacred anymore?

Nor did he like this kind of talk before Glenda.

He said, 'Roger, will you get him another whiskey?'

Roger left reluctantly. Mavice said, 'So what happened to the spaceman?'

'He was a homosexual and wanted nothing to do with the woman who let him out of his cage. Scorned, she turned him in to the priestess, and they sacrificed him. However, he was stuffed and put in a museum alongside a gorilla-type ape. Due

23

to complaints from the Decency League, he was eventually fitted with a skirt to hide his nauseating genitals.'

'What does the title mean?' Mavice said.

'That's from Oscar Wilde, who said that women were sphinxes without secrets.'

'I like *that*!' Mavice said.

'Oscar Wilde was a queer,' Morna said. 'What would he know about women?'

'Being half-female, he knew more about them than most men,' Tincrowdor said.

Paul wanted to get away from that subject. He leaned over and took the other book from Glenda. '*Osiris On Crutches*. What does that mean? Or maybe I'm better off if I don't ask.'

'Osiris was an ancient Egyptian god. His evil brother, Set, tore him apart and scattered the pieces all over earth. But Osiris' wife, Isis, and his son, Horus, collected the pieces and put them back together again and revivified him. My book tells the story in detail. For a long time, Osiris was missing a leg, so he hopped around earth on crutches looking for it. That wasn't the only thing he was missing. His nose couldn't be found, either, so Isis stuck his penis over the nasal cavity. This explains why Osiris is sometimes depicted as being ibis-headed. The ibis was a bird with a long beak. An early Pharaoh thought this was obscene and so ordered all artists to change the penis into a beak.

'Anyway, after many adventures, Osiris found his leg but wished he hadn't. He got a lot more sympathy as a cripple. He found his nose, too, but the tribe that had it refused to give it up. Since it was a piece of a divine being, they'd made a god of it. It was giving them good crops, both of wheat and babies, and it was dispensing excellent, if somewhat nasal, oracles.

'Osiris blasted them with floods and lightning bolts, and so scared them into returning his nose. But he would have been better off if he hadn't interfered with their religious customs. His nose elongated and swelled when he was sexually excited, which was most of the time, since he was a god. And he breathed through his penis.'

'For heaven's sake!' Paul said. 'That's pornography? No wonder Potts won't review your books!'

'They said the same thing about Aristophanes, Rabelais, and Joyce,' Tincrowdor said.

'I'm just as glad that the paper won't review his books,'

24

Morna said. 'It would be so embarrassing. I'm on good terms with our neighbors, but if they found out what he wrote, we'd be ostracized. Fortunately, they don't read science-fiction.'

Leo was silent for a moment, and then he looked at Paul's bandaged hand. 'Morna said your dog bit you today. You had to shoot him.'

He made it sound like an accusation.

'It was terrible,' Mavice said. 'Roger cried.'

'Tears over a dog from a man who's booby-trapped cans of food to blow up infants?' Tincrowdor said.

Roger handed him his drink and said, 'Those same little kids were the ones tossing grenades in our trucks!'

'Yeah, I know,' Tincrowdor said. 'Don't criticize a man unless you've walked a mile in his G.I. boots. I shot some twelve-year-old kids in World War II. But they were shooting at me. I suppose the principle's the same. It's the practice I don't like. Did you ever see your victims, Roger? After the explosions, I mean.'

'No, I'm not morbid,' Roger said.

'I saw mine. I'll never forget them.'

'You better lay off the booze,' Morna said. 'You've been insulting and now you're going to get sloppy sentimental.'

'Advice from the world's champion insulter,' Tincrowdor said. 'She calls it being frank. Does it hurt, Paul? The bite, I mean.'

'You're the first person who's asked me that,' Paul said. 'My family's more concerned about the dog than me.'

'That's not true!' Mavice said. 'I'm terribly worried about rabies!'

'If he starts foaming at the mouth, shoot him,' Tincrowdor said.

'That's not funny!' Morna said. 'I saw a kid that'd been bit by a dog when I was working in the hospital. He didn't get rabies, but the vaccination made him suffer terribly. Don't you worry, Paul. There's not much chance Riley had hydrophobia. He hadn't had any contact with other animals. Maybe the post-mortem will show he had a tumor on his brain. Or something.'

'Maybe he just didn't like Paul,' Tincrowdor said.

Paul understood that Tincrowdor was speaking not only for the dog but for himself.

'I once wrote a short story called *The Vaccinators from*

Vega. The Vegans appeared one day in a great fleet with weapons against which Earth was powerless. The Vegans were bipedal but hairy and had bad breaths because they ate only meat. They were, in fact, descended from dogs, not apes. They had big black eyes soft with love, and they were delighted because we had so many telephone poles. And they had come to save the universe, not to conquer our planet. They said a terrible disease would soon spread throughout the galaxy, but they would be able to immunize everybody. The Earthlings objected against forcible vaccination, but the Vegans pointed out that the Earthlings themselves had provided the precedent.

'After they had given everybody a shot, they departed, taking with them some of the terrestrial artifacts they thought valuable. These weren't our great works or art or sports cars or atom bombs. They took fire hydrants and flea powder. Ten weeks later all members of homo sapiens dropped dead. The Vegans hadn't told us that *we* were the dreaded disease. Mankind was too close to interstellar travel.'

'Don't you ever write anything good about people?' Paul said.

'The people get the kind of science-fiction writer they deserve.'

At least, that's what Paul thought he said. Tincrowdor was getting more unintelligible with every sip.

'Sure, I've written a number of stories about good people. They always get killed. Look at what happened to Jesus. Anyway, one of my stories is a glorification of mankind. It's entitled *The Hole in the Coolth*. God is walking around in the Garden in the coolth of the evening. He's just driven Adam and Eve out of Eden, and He's wondering if He shouldn't have killed them instead. You see, there are no animals in the world outside. They're all in the Garden, very contented. The Garden is a small place, but there's no worry about the beasts getting too numerous. God's ecosystem is perfect; the births just balance the deaths.

'But now there's nothing except accident, disease, and murder to check the growth of human population. No saber-tooth cats or poisonous snakes. No sheep, pigs, or cattle, either. That means that mankind will be vegetarians, and if they want protein they'll have to eat nuts. In a short time they'll have spread out over the earth, and since they won't discover agriculture for another two thousand years, they'll eat all the nuts.

Then they'll look over the fence around the Garden and see all those four-footed edibles there. There goes the neighborhood. The Garden will be ruined; the flowers all tromped flat; the animals exterminated in an orgy of carnivorousness. Maybe He should change His mind and burn them with a couple of lightning strokes. He needs the practice anyway.

'Another thing that bothers God is that He can't stop thinking about Eve. God receives the emotions of all his creatures, as if he's a sort of spiritual radio set. When an elephant is constipated, He feels its agony. When a baboon has been rejected by its pack, He feels its loneliness and sadness. When a wolf kills a fawn, he feels the horror of the little deer and the gladness of the wolf. He also tastes the deliciousness of the meat as it goes down the wolf's mouth. And he appreciates the animals' feelings for sex.

'But human beings have a higher form of sex. It involves psychology, too, and this is so much better. On the other hand, due to psychology, it's often much inferior. But Adam and Eve haven't existed long enough to get their psyches too messed up. So God, as a sort of mental peeping tom, enjoys Adam's and Eve's coupling. Qualitatively, Adam and Eve are so far ahead of the other creations, there's no comparison.

'When Adam takes Eve in his arms, God does too. But in this eternal triangle, no cuckolding is involved. Besides, God had made Eve first.

'But when Adam and Eve were run out of Eden, God decided to dampen the power of His reception from them. He'll stay tuned in, but He'll be getting only faint signals. That means He won't be getting full ecstasy of their mating. On the other hand, He won't be suffering so much because of their grief and loneliness. The two are deep in Africa and heading south, and the signals are getting weaker. About the only thing He can pick up is a feeling of sadness. Still, He sees Eve in His mind's eye, and He knows He's missing a lot. But He refuses to apply more of the divine juice. Better He should forget them for a while.

'He's walking along the fence, thinking these thoughts, when He feels a draft. The cold air of the world outside is blowing into the pleasant warm air of the Garden. This should not be, so God investigates. And he finds a hole dug under the golden, jewel-studded fence that rings Eden. He's astounded, because the hole has been dug from the Garden side. Somebody has gotten *out* of the Garden, and He doesn't understand this at all. He'd understand if somebody tried to get *in*. But *out*!

'A few minutes later, or maybe it was a thousand years later, since God, when deep in thought, isn't aware of the passage of time, he receives a change of feeling from Adam and Eve. They're joyous, and the grief at being kicked out of Eden is definitely less.

'God walks out of Eden and down into Africa to find out what's made the change. He could be there in a nanosecond, but He prefers to walk. He finds Adam and Eve in a cave and two dogs and their pups standing guard at the entrance. The dogs snarl and bark at Him before they recognize Him. God pets them, looks inside the cave, and sees Adam and Eve with their children, Cain, Abel and a couple of baby girls. It was their sisters who would become Cain and Abel's wives, you know. But that's another story.

'God was touched. If human beings could gain the affections of dogs so much that they would leave the delights of Eden, literally dig their way out just to be with humans, then humans must have something worthwhile. So He returned to the Garden and told the angel with the flaming sword to drive the other animals out.

' "It'll be a mess," the angel said.

' "Yes, I know," God said. "But if there aren't other animals around, those poor dogs will starve to death. They've got nothing but nuts to eat." '

Paul and Mavice were shocked by such blasphemy. Roger and Glenda laughed. There was a tinge of embarrassment in their laughter, but it was caused by their parents' reaction.

Morna had laughed, but she said, 'That's the man I have to live with! And when he's telling you about Osiris and God, he's telling you about himself!'

There was silence for a moment. Paul decided that now was his chance. 'Listen, Leo, I had a dream this afternoon. It may be a great idea for you.'

'O.K.,' Tincrowdor said. He looked weary.

'You didn't sleep this afternoon,' Mavice said. 'You weren't in bed for more than a few minutes.'

'I know if I slept or if I didn't. The dream must've been caused by what happened this morning. But it's wild. I dreamt I was hunting quail, just like I did this morning. I was on the

28

same field, and Riley had just taken a point, like he did this morning. But from then on . . .'

Leo said nothing until Paul was finished. He asked Roger to fill his glass again. For a moment he twiddled his thumbs, and then he said, 'The most amazing thing about your dream is that you dreamed it. It is too rich in imaginative details for you.'

Paul opened his mouth to protest, but Tincrowdor held up his hand for silence.

'Morna has related to me dreams which you told Mavice about. You don't have many – rather, you don't remember many, and those few you do seem to you remarkable. But they're not. They're very poor stuff. You see, the more creative and imaginative a person, the richer and more original his dreams. Yes, I know that you do have a flair for engineering creativity. You're always tinkering around on gadgets you've invented. In fact, you could have become fairly wealthy from some of them. But you either delayed too long applying for a patent, and so someone else beat you to it, or you never got around to building a model of your gadget or never finished it. Someone always got there ahead of you. Which is significant. You should look into why you dillydally and so fail. But then you don't believe in psychoanalysis, do you?'

'What's that got to do with this dream?' Paul said.

'Everything is connected, way down under, where the roots grope and the worms blind about and the gnomes tunnel through crap for gold. Even the silly chatter of Mavice and Morna about dress sizes and recipes and gossip about their friends is meaningful. You listen to them a while, if you can stand it, and you'll see they're not talking about what they seem to be talking about. Behind the mundane messages is a *secret* message, in a code which can be broken down if you work hard at it, and have the talent to understand it. Mostly they're S.O.S.'s, cryptic maydays.'

'I like *that*!' Mavice said.

'Up your cryptic!' Morna said.

'What about the dream?' Paul said.

'As a lay analyst, I'm more of a layer – of eggs, unfortunately – than an analyzer. I don't know what your dream *means*. You'd have to go to a psychoanalyst for that, and of course you'd never do that because, one, it costs a lot of money, and, two, you'd think people would think you were crazy.

'Well, you are, though suffering from that kind of insanity which is called *normalcy*. What I am interested in are the elements of your dream. The flying saucer, the gaseous golden blood from its wound, the sphinx, and the glittering green city.'

'The sphinx?' Paul asked. 'You mean the big statue by the pyramids? The lion with a woman's head?'

'Now, that's the Egyptian sphinx, and it's a he, not a she, by the way. I'm talking of the ancient Greek sphinx with a lion's body and lovely woman's breasts and face. Though the one you described seemed more like a leocentaur. It had a woman's trunk which joined the lion's body, lioness', to be exact, where the animal's neck should be.'

'I didn't see anything like that!'

'You didn't see the entirety. But it's obvious that she was a leocentaur. Nor did you give her a chance to ask you the question. *What is it that in the morning goes on four legs, in the afternoon on two, and in the evening on three?* Oedipus answered the question and then killed her. You wanted to shoot her before she could open her mouth.'

'What was the answer?' Mavice said.

'Man,' Glenda said. 'Typically anthropocentric and male chauvinistic.'

'But these are not ancient times, and I'm sure she had a question relevant to this contemporary age. But you must have read about her sometime, maybe in school. Otherwise, why the image? And about the green city? Have you ever read the Oz books?'

'No, but I had to take Glenda and Roger to see the movie when they were young. Mavice was sick.'

'He wouldn't let me see it on TV last month,' Glenda said. 'He said Judy Garland was an animal.'

'She used *drugs*!' Paul said. 'Besides, that picture is a lot of nonsense!'

'How like you to equate that poor suffering soul with vermin,' Tincrowdor said. 'And I suppose your favourite TV series, *Bonanza*, isn't fantasy? Or *The Music Man*, which you love so much? Or most of the stuff you read as the gospel truth in our right-wing rag, the *Busiris Journal-Star*?'

'You're not so smart,' Paul said. 'You haven't got the slightest idea what my dream means!'

'You're stung,' Tincrowdor said. 'No, if I was so smart, I'd be charging you twenty-five dollars an hour. However, I wonder if that *was* a dream. You didn't actually *see* all this out in that field? By the way, just where is it? I'd like to go out and investigate.'

'You *are* crazy!' Paul said.

'I think we'd better go,' Morna said. 'Paul has such an awful yellow color.'

Paul detested Tincrowdor at that moment and yet he did not want him to leave.

'Just a minute. Don't you think it'd make a great story?'

Tincrowdor sat back down. 'Maybe. Let's say the saucer isn't a mechanical vehicle but a living thing. It's from some planet of some far-off star, of course. Martians aren't *de rigeur* anymore. Let's say the saucerperson lands here because it's going to seed this planet. The yellow stuff wasn't its blood but its spores or its eggs. When it's ready to spawn, or lay, it's in a vulnerable position, like a mother sea-turtle when it lays its eggs in the sand of a beach. It's not as mobile as it should be. A hunter comes across it at the critical moment, and he shoots it. The wound opens its womb or whatever, and it prematurely releases the eggs. Then, unable to take off in full flight, it hides. The hunter is a brave man or lacking imagination or both. So he goes into the woods after the saucerperson. It's still capable of projecting false images of itself; its electromagnetic field or whatever it is that enables it to fly through space, stimulates the brain of the alien biped that's hunting it. Images deep in the hunter's unconscious are evoked. The hunter thinks he sees a sphinx and a glittering green city.

'And the hunter has breathed in some of the spore-eggs. This is what the saucerperson desires, since the reproductive cycle is dependent on living hosts. Like sheep liver flukes. The eggs develop into larvae which feed on the host. Or perhaps they're not parasitic but symbiotic. They give the host something beneficial in return for his temporarily housing them. Maybe the incubating stage is a long and complicated one. The host can transmit the eggs or the larvae to other hosts.

'Have you been sneezing yellow, Paul?

'In time, the larvae will mutate into something, maybe little saucers. Or another intermediate stage, something horrible and inimical. Maybe these take different forms, depending upon the chemistry of the hosts. In any event, in human beings the reaction is not just physical. It's psychosomatic. But the host is doomed, and he is highly infectious. Anybody who comes into

31

contact with him is going to be filled with, become rotten with, the larvae. There's no chance of quarantining the hosts. Not in this age of great mobility. Mankind has invented the locomotive, the automobile, the airplane solely to make the transmission of the deadly larvae easier. At least, that's the viewpoint of the saucerperson.

'Doom, doom, doom!'

'Dumb, dumb, dumb,' Morna said. 'Come on, Leo, let's go. You'll be snoring like a pig, and I won't be able to get a wink of sleep. He snores terribly when he's been drinking. I could kill him.'

'Wait for time to do its work,' Tincrowdor said. 'I'm slowly killing myself with whiskey. It's the curse of the Celtic race. Booze, not the British, beat us. With which alliteration, I bid you bon voyage. Or von voyage. I'm part German, too.'

'What are your Teutonic ancestors responsible for?' Morna said. 'Your arrogance?'

5

After the Tincrowdors had left, Mavice said, 'You really should get to bed, Paul. You do look peaked. And we have to get up early tomorrow for church.'

He didn't reply. His bowels felt as if an octopus had squeezed them in its death agony. He got to the bathroom just in time, but the pain almost yanked a scream from him. Then it was over. He became faint when he saw what was floating in the water. It was small, far too small to have caused such trouble. It was an ovoid about an inch long, and it was a dull yellow. For some reason, he thought of the story of the goose which laid golden eggs.

He began trembling. It was ten minutes or more before he could flush it down, wash, and leave the bathroom. He had a vision of the egg dissolving in the pipes, being treated in the sewage plant, spreading its evil parts throughout the sludge, being transported to farms for fertilizer, being sucked up by the roots of corn, wheat, soy beans, being eaten, being carried around in the bodies of men and animals, being . . .

In the bedroom, Mavice tried to kiss him goodnight. He turned away. Was he infectious? Had that madman accidentally hit on the truth?

'Don't kiss me then,' Mavice shrilled. 'You never want to kiss me unless you want to go to bed with me. That's the only time I get any tenderness from you, if you can call it tenderness. But I'm just as glad. I have a bladder infection and you'd hurt me. After all, it's my wifely duty, no matter how sick I am. According to you, anyway.'

'Shut up, Mavice,' he said. 'I'm sick. I don't want you to catch anything.'

'Catch what? You said you felt all right. You don't have the flu, do you?'

'I don't know what I got,' he said, and he groaned.

'Oh, Lord, I pray it's not the rabies,' she said.

'It couldn't be. Morna said rabies doesn't act that fast.'

'Then what is it?'

'I don't know,' he said, and groaned again. 'What is it Leo is so fond of quoting? *Whom the gods wish to destroy, they first make mad*?'

'What's that supposed to mean?' she said, but she softened. She kissed him on the cheek before he could object, and turned over away from him.

He lay awake a long time, and when he did sleep he had fitful dreams. They awoke him often, though he remembered few of them. But there was one of a glittering green city and a thing with a body which was part lioness and part woman advancing toward him over a field of scarlet flowers.

6

Roger Eyre stood up and looked at Leo Tincrowdor. They were standing near the edge of a cornfield just off the Little Rome Road.

'They're the tracks of a big cat all right,' he said. 'A very big cat. If I didn't know better, I'd say they were a lion's or a tiger's. One that could fly.'

'Your major is zoology, so you should know,' Tincrowdor said. He looked up at the sky. 'It's going to rain. I wish we had time to get casts. Do you think that if we went back to your house and got some plaster ... ?'

'It's going to be a heavy rain storm. No.'

'Damn it, I should have at least brought a camera. But I never dreamed of this. It's objective evidence. Your father isn't crazy, and that dream ... I thought he was telling more than a dream.'

'You can't be serious,' Roger said.

Tincrowdor pointed at the prints in the mud. 'Your father was driving to work when he suddenly pulled the car over just opposite here. Three men in a car a quarter of a mile behind him saw him do it. They knew him, since they work at Trackless, too. They stopped and asked him if his car had broken down. He mumbled a few unintelligible words and then became completely catatonic. Do you think that that and these tracks are just coincidence?'

Ten minutes later, they were in the Adler Sanitorium. As they walked down the hall, Tincrowdor said, 'I went to Shomi University with Doctor Croker, so I should be able to get more out of him than the average doctor would tell. He thinks my books are a lot of crap, but we're both members of The Baker Street Irregulars and he likes me, and we play poker twice a month. Let me do the talking. Don't say anything about any of this. He might want to lock us up, too.'

Mavice, Morna, and Glenda were just coming out of the doctor's office. Tincrowdor told them he would see them in a minute; he wanted a few words with the doctor. He entered and said, 'Hi, Jack. Anything cooking on the grange?'

Croker was six-feet three-inches tall, almost too handsome, and looked like a Tarzan who had lately been eating too many bananas. He shook hands with Tincrowdor and said, in a slight English accent, 'We can dispense with the private jokes.'

'Sorry. Laughter is my defense,' Tincrowdor said. 'You must really be worried about Paul.'

The door opened, and Morna entered. She said, 'You gave me the high sign to come back alone, Jack. What's wrong?'

'Promise me you won't say anything to the family. Or to anybody,' he said. He gestured at a microscope under which was a slide. 'Take a look at that. You first, Morna, since you're a lab tech. Leo wouldn't know what he was seeing.'

Morna bent over, made the necessary adjustments, looked for about ten seconds, and then said, 'Lord!'

'What is it?' Leo said.

Morna straightened. 'I don't know.'

'Neither do I,' Croker said. 'I've been ransacking my books,

34

and it's just as I suspected. There ain't no such thing.'

'Like the giraffe,' Leo said. 'Let me look. I'm not as ignorant as you think.'

A few minutes later, he straightened up. 'I don't know what those other things are, the orange, red, lilac, deep blue, and purple-blue cells. But I do know that there aren't any organisms shaped like a brick with rounded ends and colored a bright yellow.'

'They're not only in his blood; they're in other tissues, too,' Croker said. 'My tech found them while making a routine test. The things seem to be coated with a waxy substance which doesn't take a stain. I put some specimens in a blood agar culture, and they're thriving, though they're not multiplying. I stayed up all night running other tests. Eyre is a very healthy man, aside from a mental withdrawal. I don't know what to make of it, and to tell you the truth, I'm scared!

'That is why I had him put in isolation, and yet I don't want to alarm anybody. I've got no evidence that he's a danger to anybody. But he's swarming with something completely unknown. It's a hell of a situation, because there's no precedent to follow.'

Morna burst into tears. Leo Tincrowdor said, 'And if he recovers from his catatonia, there's nothing you can do to keep him here.'

'Nothing legal,' Croker said.

Morna snuffled, wiped her tears, blew her nose, and said, 'Maybe it'll just pass away. Those things will disappear, and it'll be just another of the medical mysteries.'

'I doubt it, Pollyanna,' Tincrowdor said. 'I think this is just the beginning.'

'There's more,' Croker said. 'Epples, the nurse assigned to him, has a face deeply scarred with acne. Had, I should say. She went into his room to check on him, and when she came out, her face was a smooth and as soft as a baby's.'

There was a long silence before Tincrowdor said, 'You mean, you actually mean, that Paul Eyre performed a miracle? But he wasn't conscious! And –'

'I was staggered, but I am a scientist,' Croker said. 'Shortly after Epples, near hysteria, told me what happened, I noticed that a wart on my finger had disappeared. I remember that I'd had it just before I examined Eyre . . .'

'Oh, come *on!*' Morna said.

35

'Yes, I know. But there's more. I've had to reprimand a male nurse, a sadistic apish-looking man named Backers, for unnecessary roughness a number of times. And I've suspected him, though I've had no proof, of outright cruelty in his treatment of some of the more obstreperous patients. I've been watching him for some time, and I would have fired him long ago if it weren't so hard to get help.

'Shortly after Epples had left Eyre and not knowing yet that her scars were gone, she returned to the room, She caught Backers sticking a needle in Eyre's thigh. He said later that he suspected Eyre of faking it, but he had no business being in the room or testing Eyre. Epples started to chew Backers out, but she didn't get a chance to say more than two words. Backers grabbed his heart and keeled over. Epples called me and then gave him mouth-to-mouth treatment until I arrived. I got his heart started with adrenalin. A half hour later, he was able to tell me what happened.

'Now Backers has no history of heart trouble, and the EKG I gave him indicated that his heart is normal. I –'

'Listen,' Tincrowdor said, 'are you telling me you think Eyre can both cure and kill? With thought projection?'

'I don't know how he does it or why. I'd have thought that Backer's attack was just a coincidence if it hadn't been for Epple's acne and my wart. I put two and two together and decided to try a little experiment. I felt foolish doing it, but a scientist rushes in where fools fear to tread. Or maybe it's the other way around.

'Anyway, I released some of my lab mosquitoes into Eyre's room. And behold, the six which settled on him expecting a free meal fell dead. Just keeled over, like Backers.'

There was another long silence. Finally, Morna said, 'But if he *can* cure people . . . ?'

'Not *he*,' Croker said. 'I think those mysterious yellow microorganisms in his tissues are somehow responsible. I know it seems fantastic, but –'

'But if he can cure,' Morna said, 'how wonderful!'

'Yes,' Leo said, 'but if he can also kill, and I say *if*, since he'll have to be tested further before such a power can be admitted as possible, if, I say, he can kill anybody that threatens him, then . . .'

'Yes?' Croker said.

'Imagine what would happen if he were released. You

36

can't let a man like that loose. Why, when I think of how often I've angered him! It'd be worse than uncaging a hungry tiger on Main Street.'

'Exactly,' Croker said. 'And as long as he's in catatonia, he can't be released. Meanwhile, he is to be in a strict quarantine. After all, he may have a deadly disease. And if you repeat any of this to anybody else, including his family, I'll deny everything. Epples won't say anything, and Backers won't either. I've had to keep him on so I can control him, but he'll keep silent. Do you understand?'

'I understand that he might be here the rest of his life,' Tincrowdor said. 'For the good of humanity.'

Poul Anderson

MY OWN,
MY NATIVE LAND

*The boy stood at sunrise on the edge of his world. Clouds tor-
rented up along the gap which clove it. They burned in the
light. Wind sang, cold and wholly pure.*

*A spearfowl broke from those mists to soar further aloft,
magnificence upon wings the hue of steel. For an instant the
boy did not move. He could not. Then he screamed, once,
before he fled.*

*He took shelter in a thicket until he had mastered both
tears and trembling. Boys do not tell anyone, least of all those
who love them, that they are haunted.*

'Coming in, now,' said Jack O'Malley over the radiophone,
and got to work at a difficult approach.

On its northeastern corner, that great tableland named High
America did not slope in mountains and valleys, to reach at last
the sea level which lay eight kilometers straight beneath. Here
the rim fell in cliffs and talus until vapors drowned vision. Only
at one place were the heights climbable: where a fault had
driven them apart to make the Cleft. And the drafts which it
channeled were treacherous.

As his aircar slanted toward ground, O'Malley had a clear
view across the dropoff and its immense gash. At evening, the
almost perpetual clouds that lapped around the plateau were
sinking. Rock heaved dark and wet above the ocean, which
billowed to the horizon. Their whiteness bore a fire-gold tinge
and shadows were long upon them; for the Eridani sun was low
in the west, barely above the sierra of the Centaurs. The illusion
of its hugeness could well-nigh overwhelm a man who remembered Earth – since in fact its disc showed more than half again
the width of Terrestrial Sol. Likewise the ruddier hue of its less
ardent G5 surface was more plain to see than at high noon.

Further up, O'Malley's gaze had savored a sweep of country from Centaurs to Cleft, from Hercules Mountains to Lake Olympus, and all the grasslands, woodlands, farmlands in between, nourished by the streams out of yonder snowpeaks. Where the Swift and Smoky Rivers joined to form the Emperor, he should have been able to make out Anchortown. But the rays blazed too molten off their waters.

Instead, he had enjoyed infinite subtleties of color, the emerald of man's plantings mingled in patchwork with the softer blue-greens of native growth. Spring was coming as explosively as always on Rustum.

Raksh, the larger moon, stood at half phase in a sky turning royal purple. About midway between the farthest and nearest points of its eccentric orbit, it showed a Lunar size, but coppery rather than silver. O'Malley scowled at the beautiful sight. It was headed in closer, to raise tides in the dense lowland air which could make for even heavier equinoctial storms than usual. And that was just when he wanted to go down there.

His pilot board beeped a warning and he gave his whole attention back to flight. It was tricky at best, in this changeable atmosphere, under a fourth more weight than Earth gives to things. Earth, where this vehicle was designed and made. He wondered if he'd ever see the day when the colony manufactured craft of its own, incorporating the results of experience. Three thousand people, isolated on a world for which nature had never intended them, couldn't produce much industrial plant very soon.

Nearing ground, he saw Joshua Coffin's farmstead outlined black against sky and some upsurgings from the cloud deck. The buildings stood low, but they looked as massive as they must be to withstand hurricanes. Gim trees and plume oak, left uncut for both shade and windbreak, were likewise silhouetted, save where the nest of bower phoenix phosphoresced in one of them.

O'Malley landed, set his brakes, and sprang out: a big, freckle-faced man, athletic in spite of middle age grizzling his red hair and thickening his waist. He wore a rather gaudy coverall which contrasted with the plainness of Coffin's. The latter was already, courteously, securing the aircar's safety cable to a bollard. He was himself tall, as well as gaunt and crag-featured, sun-leathered and iron-gray. 'Welcome,' he said. They gripped hands. 'What brings you here that you didn't want to discuss

39

on the phone?'

'I need help,' O'Malley answered. 'The matter may or may not be confidential.' He sighed. 'Lord, when'll we get proper laser beams, not these damn 'casts that every neighborhood gossip can listen in on?'.

'I don't believe our household needs to keep secrets,' said Coffin a bit sharply. Though he'd mellowed over the years, O'Malley was reminded that his host stayed a puritanical sort. Circumstance had forced this space captain to settle on Rustum – not any strong need to escape crowding, corruption, poverty, pollution, and tyranny on Earth. He'd never been part of the Constitutionalist movement. In fact, its rationalism, libertarianism, tendency toward hedonism, to this day doubtless jarred on his own austere religiousness.

'No, I didn't mean that,' O'Malley said in haste. 'The thing is – Well, could you and I talk alone for a few minutes?'

Coffin peered at him through the gathering dusk before he nodded. They walked from the parking strip, down a graveled path between ornamental bushes. The stellas were starting to flower, breathing a scent like mingled cinnamon and – something else, perhaps new hay – into coolness. O'Malley saw that Teresa Coffin had finally gotten her roses to flourish, too. How long had she worked on that, in what time she could spare from survival and raising their children and laying the groundwork of a future less stark than what she had known of Rustum? Besides science and ingenuity, you needed patience to make Terrestrial things grow. Life here might be basically the same kind as yours, but that didn't mean it, or its ecology, or the soil that that ecology had formed, were identical.

The small stones scrunched underfoot. 'This is new, this graveling,' O'Malley remarked.

'We laid it two years ago,' Coffin said.

O'Malley felt embarrassed. Was it that long since he'd had any contact with these people? But what had he in common with farmers like them, he, the professional adventurer? It struck him that the last time he'd trodden such a path was on an estate on Earth, in Ireland, an enclave of lawns and blossoms amidst rural bondage and megalopolitan misery. Memory spiraled backward. The sound of pebbles hadn't been so loud, had it? Of course not. His feet had come down upon them with only four-fifths the weight they did here. And even on High America, the air was thicker than it was along the seashores of Earth, carried sound better, made as simple an act as brewing a pot of tea into a different art –

A volant swooped across Raksh, warm-blooded, feathered, egg-laying, yet with too many strangenesses to be a bird in anything other than name. Somewhere a singing 'lizard' trilled.

'Well,' said Coffin, 'what is this business of yours?'

O'Malley reflected on how rude it would be to make Teresa wait, or the youngsters for that matter. He drew breath and plunged:

'Phil Herskowitz and I were running scientific survey in the deep lowlands, around the Gulf of Ardashir. Besides mapping and such, we were collecting instrument packages that'd completed their programs, laying down fresh ones elsewhere – oh, you know the routine. Except this trip didn't stay routine. A cyclops wind caught us at the intermediate altitude where that kind of thing can happen. Our car spun out of control. I was piloting, and tried for a pontoon landing on the sea but couldn't manage it. The best I could do was crash us in coastal jungle. At least that gave us some treetops to soften the impact. Even so, Phil has a couple of broken ribs where the fuselage got stove in against his chair.

'We didn't shear off much growth. It closed in again above the wreck. Nobody can land nearby. We put through a distress call, then had to struggle a good fifty kilometers on foot before we reached a meadow where a rescue car could safely settle.

'That was five days ago. In spite of not being hurt myself, I didn't recover from the shock and exhaustion overnight.'

'Hm.' Coffin tugged his chin and glanced sideways. 'Why hasn't the accident been on the news?'

'My request. You see, it occurred to me – what I mean to ask of you.'

'Which is?'

'I don't think a lot of the wreckage can be salvaged, damn it, but I'd like to try. You know what it'd be worth to the colony, just to recover a motor or something. Salvagers can't feasibly clear a landing area; they'd have no way of removing the felled trees, which'd pose too much of a hazard. But they can construct a wagon and slash a path for it. That'd at least enable them to bring out the instruments and tapes more readily – I think – than by trudging back and forth that long distance carrying them in packs.'

'Instruments and tapes,' Coffin said thoughtfully. 'You con-

41

sider that, whether or not repairable parts of the car can be recovered, the instruments and tapes must be?'

'Oh, heavens, yes,' O'Malley replied. 'Think how much skilled time was spent in the manufacture, then in planting and gathering the packages – in this labor-short, machine-poor economy of ours. The information's tremendously valuable in its own right, too. Stuff on soil bacteria, essential to further improvement of agriculture. Meteorology, seismology – Well, I needn't sell you on it, Josh. You know how little we know, how much we need to know, about Rustum. An entire *world!*'

'True. How can I help?'

'You can let your stepson Danny come along with me.'

Coffin halted. O'Malley did the same. They stared at each other. The slow dusking proceeded.

'Why him?' Coffin asked at last, most low. 'He's only a boy. We celebrated his nineteenth ... anniversary ... two tendays ago. If he were on Earth, that'd have been barely a couple of months past his fifteenth.'

'You know why, Josh. He's young, sure, but he's the oldest of the exogenes –'

Coffin stiffened. 'I don't like that word.'

'I'm sorry. I didn't mean –'

'Just because he was grown artificially instead of in a uterus, from donated cells instead of his parents coming here in person, he's not inferior.'

'Sure! Understood! How would three thousand people be a big enough gene pool for the future, cut off in an environment like this, if they didn't bring along –'

'– a potential million extra parents. When you marry, you'll also be required to have one of them brought to term for you to adopt.'

O'Malley winced. His Norah had died in the Year of Sickness. Somehow he'd never since had more than fleeting liaisons. Probably that was because he'd never stayed put long at a time. There was too much discovery to be made, by too few persons who were capable of it, if man on Rustum was to endure.

Yet he was still, in one way, shirking a duty to wed. Man in his billions was a blight on Earth, but on Rustum a very lonely creature whose hold on existence was precarious at best. His numbers must be expanded as fast as possible – and not merely to provide hands or even brains. There is a more subtle kind of underpopulation, that can be deadly to a species. Given

42

too few parents, too much of their biological heredity will be lost, as it fails to find embodiment in the children they can beget during their lifetimes. In the course of generations, individuals will become more and more like each other. And variability is the key to adaptability, which is the key to survival.

A partial, though vital solution to the problem lay in adoption. Spaceships had been overburdened with colonists; they would certainly not add a load of plants and animals. It sufficed to carry seeds – of both. Cold-stored, sperm and ovum could be kept indefinitely, until at last it was convenient to unite them and grow a new organism in an exogenetic tank. As easily as for dogs or cattle, it could be done for humans. Grown up, marrying and reproducing in normal fashion – for they would be perfectly normal people – they would contribute their own diverse chromosomes to the race.

This was, however, only a partial measure. The original settlers and their descendants must also do their part.

Coffin saw O'Malley's distress, and said more gently: 'Never mind. I get your point. You remembered how Danny can tolerate lowland conditions.'

The other man braced himself. 'Yes,' he replied. 'I realize the original cell donors were chosen with that in mind. Still, the way we lucked out with him, this early in the game – Look. The trip does involve a certain hazard. It always does, when you go down where everything's so unearthly and most of it unknown. That's why I've kept my idea secret, that Danny would be the best possible partner on this expedition. I don't think the risk is unduly great. Nevertheless, a lot of busybodies would object to exposing a boy to it, if they heard in advance. I thought, rather than create a public uproar ... I thought I'd leave the decision to you. And Teresa, naturally.'

Again Coffin bridled. 'Why not Danny?'

'Huh?' O'Malley was startled. 'Why, I, well, I took for granted he'd want to go. The adventure – a *real* springtime vacation from school ... After all, when he was a tyke, he wandered down the Cleft by himself –'

'And got lost,' Coffin said bleakly. 'Almost died. Was barely saved, found hanging onto the talons of a giant spearfowl that aimed to tear him apart.'

'But he *was* saved. And that was when proved he was, is, the first real Rustumite, a human who can live anywhere on the

43

planet. I've not forgotten what a celebrity it made him.'

'We've gone back to a decent obscurity, him and the rest of us,' Coffin said. 'I've seen no reason to publicize the fact that he's never since cared to go below the clouds. He's a good boy, no coward or sluggard, but whenever he's been offered a chance to join some excursion down, even a little ways, he's found an excuse to stay home. Teresa and I haven't pushed him. That was a terrible experience for a small child. In spite of being a ninety days' wonder, he had nightmares for a year afterward. I wouldn't be surprised if he does yet, now and then.'

'I see.' O'Malley bit his lip. They stood a while beneath a Raksh whose mottled brightness seemed to wax as heaven darkened. The evening star trembled forth. A breeze, the least bit chilly, made leaves sough. It was not bedtime; this close to equinox, better than thirty-one hours of night stretched before High America. But the men stood as if long-trained muscles, guts, blood vessels, bones felt anew the drag upon them.

'Well, he's got to outgrow his fears,' burst from O'Malley. 'He has a career ahead of him in the lowlands.'

'Why should he?' Coffin retorted. 'We'll take generations to fully settle this one plateau. Danny can find plenty of work. We could even argue that he ought to protect those valuable chromosomes of his, stay safe at home and found a large family. His descendants can move downward.'

O'Malley shook his head. 'You know that isn't true, Josh. We won't ever be safe up here on our little bit of lofty real estate – not till we understand a hell of a lot more about the continent, the entire planet that it's part of. Remember? We could've stopped the Sickness at its beginning, if we'd known the virus is carried from below by one kind of nebulo-plankton. We'll never get proper storm or quake warnings till we have adequate information about the general environment. And what other surprises is Rustum waiting to spring on us?'

'Yes –'

'Then there's the social importance of the lowlands. We came because it was our last hope of establishing a free society. In those several generations you speak of, High America can get as crowded as Earth. Freedom needs elbow room. We've got to start expanding our frontiers right away.'

'I'm not convinced that a political theory is worth a single human life,' Coffin said. His tone softened. 'However, the practical necessities you mention, you're right about those. Why do you need Danny?'

'Isn't it obvious? Well, maybe it isn't unless you've seen the territory. Take my word for it, men who have to wear reduction helmets are too handicapped to accomplish much in that wilderness. I told you, Phil and I barely made it to rendezvous with our rescue craft, and we had nothing more to do than hike. Salvagers will have to work harder.'

'Who'll accompany him?'

'Me. We haven't got anybody else who can be spared before weather ruins the stuff. I figure my experience and Danny's capabilities will mesh together pretty well.

'I've arranged about the wage, plus a nice payment for whatever we bring back. The College will be delighted to fill his pockets with gold. That equipment, that information represent too many manhours invested, maybe so many lives saved in future, that anybody would want to write it off.'

Coffin was quiet for another space, until he said, 'Let's go inside,' squared his shoulders and trudged toward the house.

Within lay firelit cheeriness, books and pictures, more room than any but the mightiest enjoyed on Earth. Teresa had tea and snacks ready; this household did not use alcohol or tobacco. (The latter was no loss, O'Malley reflected wryly. Grown in local soil, it got fierce!) Seven well-mannered youngsters greeted the visitor and settled back to listen to adult talk. (On Earth, they'd probably have been out in street gangs – or enslaved, under the name of 'contract,' to a Lowlevel robber baron – or barracked on some commune.) Six of them were slender, brown-haired, and fair-skinned where the sun had not scorched.

Danny differed in more than being the oldest. He was stocky, of medium height. Though his features were essentially caucasoid – straight nose, wide narrow mouth, rust-colored eyes – still, the high cheekbones, blue-black hair, and dark complexion bespoke more than a touch of Oriental. O'Malley wondered briefly, uselessly, what his gene-parents had been like, and what induced them to give cells for storage on a spaceship they would never board, and whether or not they had ever met. By now they were almost certainly dead.

Small talk bounced around the room. There was no lack of material. Three thousand pioneers didn't constitute a hamlet where everybody knew day by day what everybody else was doing, especially when they were scattered across an area the

45

size of Mindanao. To be sure, some were concentrated in Anchor; but on the whole, High American agriculture could not yet support a denser settlement.

Nonetheless, an underlying tension was undisguisable. O'Malley felt grateful when Teresa suddenly asked him why he had come. He told them. Their eyes swung about and locked upon Danny.

The boy did not cringe, he grew rigid, in the manner of his stepfather. But his answer could scarcely be heard: 'I'd rather not.'

'I admit we'll face a bit of risk,' O'Malley said. 'However' – he grinned – 'you tell me what isn't risky. I'm mighty fond of this battered hide of mine, son, and I'll be right beside you.'

Teresa strained her fingers together.

Danny's voice lifted and cracked. 'I don't *like* it down there!'

Coffin hardened his lips. 'Is that all?' he demanded. 'When you can carry out a duty?'

The boy stared at him, and away, and hunched in his chair. Finally he whispered, 'If you insist, Father.'

Hours passed before O'Malley left the house, to go home and prepare himself. Meanwhile full night had come upon the highland. The air was cold, silent, and altogether clear. Raksh, visibly grown in both size and phase, stood low above the cloud-sea, while tiny Sohrab hastened in pursuit; both moons crossed the sky widdershins. Elsewhere, darkness was thronged with stars. Their constellations weren't much changed by a score of light-years' remove. And though it was a trifle more tilted, Rustum's axis did not point far from Earth's. He could know the Bears, the Dragon – and near Boötes, a dim spark which was Sol –

More than forty years away by spaceship, he thought – human cargo cold-sleeping like the cells of their animals and plants and foster children, for four decades till they arrived and were wakened back to life. But did the spaceships still fare? It had been a nearly last-gasp effort which assembled the fleet that carried the pioneers here: an effort by which the government, with their own consent, rid itself of Constitutionalist troublemakers who kept muttering about foolishnesses like freedom. Had any of those vessels ever gone anywhere else again? Radio had not had time to bring an answer to questions beamed at Earth. Nor would man on Rustum be prepared to

46

build ships which could leave it for a much longer time to come. Quite possibly never ... O'Malley shivered and hastened to his car.

Roxana was a large continent, and this trip was from its middle to the southern edge. Time dragged for Danny. They were flying high, for the most part very little below the normal cloud deck. Hence transient nimbuses, further down, often cut them off from sight of land. But then they would pass over the patch of weather and come back into clear vision – as clear as vision ever got, here.

O'Malley made several attempts at cheerful conversation. Danny tried to respond, but words wouldn't come. At last talk died altogether. Only the hum of jets filled the cabin, or a hoot of wind and cannonade of thunder, borne by the thick atmosphere across enormous distances.

O'Malley puffed his pipe, whistled an occasional tune, sat alertly by to take over from the autopilot if there were any trouble. Danny squirmed in the seat beside him. *Why didn't I at least bring a book?* the boy thought, over and over. *Then I wouldn't have to just sit here and stare out at that.*

'Grand, isn't it?' O'Malley had said once. Danny barely kept from yelling back, 'No, it's horrible, can't you see how awful it is?'

Above, it was pearl-gray, except in the east where a blur of light marked the morning sun. Mountains reared beneath: so tall, as they climbed toward the homes of men, that their heads were lost in the skyroof. They tumbled sharply downward, though, in cliffs and crags and canyons, vast misty valleys, gorges where rivers gleamed dagger-bright, steeps whose black rock was slashed by waterfalls. Ahead were their foothills, and off to the west began a prairie which sprawled around the curve of the world. A storm raged there, swart bulks of cloud where lightning flared and glared, remorseless rains driven by the great slow winds of the lowlands. Hues were infinite, for vegetation crowded all but the stoniest heights. Yet those shades of blue-green, tawny, russet were as somber in Danny's eyes as the endless overcast above them; and the wings which passed by in million-membered flocks only drove into him how alien was the life that overswarmed these lands.

O'Malley's glance lingered upon him. 'What a shame you

47

don't like it here,' he murmured. 'It's your kind of country, you know. You're fitted for it in a way I'll never be.'

'I don't, that's all,' Danny forced out. 'Let's not talk about it. Please, sir.'

If we talk, I won't be able to hide the truth from him, I'll start shaking, I'll stammer, the sweat that's already cold in my hands and armpits, already sharp in my nose, it'll break out so he can see, and he'll know I'm afraid. Oh, God, how afraid! Maybe I'll cry. And Father will be ashamed of me.

Father, who followed me down into yonder horror and plucked me free of death.

Fear didn't make sense, Danny told himself. His mind had stated the same thing year after year, whenever a dream or a telepicture or a word in someone's mouth brought him back to the jungle. That was what had branded him. Not heat and wet and gloom. Not hunger and thirst (once his belly had lashed him into trying fruits which were unlike those he had been warned were poisonous). Not rustlings, croakings, chatterings, roar and howl and maniacal cackle, his sole changes from a monstrous silence. Not the tusked beast which pursued him, nor even – entirely – the gigantic bird of prey whose beak had gaped at him. It was the endlessness, Danny thought, the faceless friendless endlessness of jungle, through which he stumbled lost for hours that stretched into days and nights, nights.

Sometimes he thought a part of him had never come back again, would always grope weeping among the trees.

No, I'm being morbid, his mind scolded him before it sought shelter at home on High America.

Skies unutterably blue and clear by day, brilliant after dark with stars or aurora, the quick clean rains which washed them or the heart-shaking, somehow heart-uplifting might of a storm, the white peace which descended in winter. Grainfields rippling gold in the wind; flowers ablaze amidst birdsong. Wild hills to climb, and woods which were open to the sun. Rivers to swim in – a thousand cool caresses – or to row a boat on before drifting downstream in delicious laziness. The reach of Lake Olympus, two hours' airbus ride whenever he could get some free time from school or farm work, but worth it because of the sloop he and Toshiro Hirayama had built; and the dangers, when a couple of gales nearly brought them to grief, those were good too, a challenge, afterward a proof of being a skilled sailor and well on the way to manhood, though naturally it wouldn't be wise to let parents know how close the shave had been . . .

This I've had to leave. Because I've never had the courage to admit I'm haunted.

Am I really, anymore? That wasn't too bad a nightmare last sleep-time, and my first in years.

The eon ahead of him needn't be unbearable, he told himself. Honestly, it needn't. This trip, he had a strong, experienced boss, radio links to the human world, proper food and clothing and gear, a quick flit home as soon as the job was done, the promise of good pay and the chance of an even better bonus. *All I've got to do is get through some strenuous, uncomfortable days. No more than that. No more. Why, the experience ought to help me shake off what's left of my old terrors.*

Not that I'll ever return!

He settled into his chair and harness, and fought to relax.

The vehicle, a bulky cargo bus, almost filled the open space on which it had set down. Tall, finely fronded blue-green stalks – plants of that varied and ubiquitous family which the colonists misnamed 'grass' – hid the wheels and much of the pontoons. Trees made a wall around. They were mostly ruddy-barked goldwood, but among them stood slim feathery soartop, murky fakepine, crouched and thorny gnome. Between the trunks, brush and vines crowded like a mob waiting to attack. A few meters inward, the lightlessness amidst all those leaves seemed total, as if to make up for the lack of any noticeable shadows elsewhere. Insectoids glittered across that dusk. Wings beat overhead, some huge in this upbearing pressure. None of the life closely resembled what dwelt on High America, and much was altogether unlike it. Those environments were too foreign to each other.

The air hung windless, hot and heavy. It was full of odors, pungent, sweet, rank, bitter, none recalling home. Sounds came loud – a background of trills, whispers, buzzes, rustles, purling water; footfalls, above everything else, the first incautious words of human speech.

Danny took a breath, and another. His neck felt stiff, but he made himself stare around. *No matter how horrible a bush looks it won't jump out and bite me. I've got to remember that.* It helped a little, that they'd let their craft pressurize gradually before venturing forth. Danny had had a chance to get used to

49

the feel of it in lungs and bloodstream.

Jack O'Malley had not. He could endure the gas concentration for a while if he must, with no consequences afterward worse than a bad headache. But let him breathe the stuff too long and carbon dioxide acidosis would make him ill, nitrogen narcosis blur his brain, over-much oxygen begin slowly searing his tissues. Above his coverall, sealed at the neck, rose a glasite helmet with a reduction pump, an awkward water tube and chowlock for his nourishment, a heavy dessicator unit to prevent fogging from the sweat which already studded his face.

And yet he's spent his years on Rustum exploring the lowlands, Danny thought. *What could make a man waste that much life?*

'Okay, let's unload our stuff and saddle up.' O'Malley's voice boomed from a speaker, across the mutterings. 'At best, we won't get where we're bound before dark.'

'Won't we?' Danny asked, surprised. 'But you said it was about fifty kilometers, along a hard-packed game trail. And we must have, uh, twenty hours of daylight left. Even stopping to sleep, there shouldn't be any problem.'

O'Malley's smile flickered wistful. 'Not for you maybe. I'm not young anymore. Worse, I've got this thing on my head and torso. The pump's powered by my chest expansion when I breathe, you know. You'd be surprised how the work in that adds up, if you weren't so lucky you'll never need the gadget yourself.'

Lucky!

'However,' O'Malley continued, 'we can hike on after nightfall, and I guess we'll arrive with plenty of time for preliminary jobs before daybreak.'

Danny nodded. Sometimes he wondered if men wouldn't do best to adapt to the slow turning of Rustum. Whatever the medics said, he felt it should be possible to learn to stay active for forty hours, then sleep for twenty. Could it be that efficient electric lanterns were the single reason the effort had never been made?

'Come dawn, then, we can start constructing what we need to haul the salvage back here,' O'Malley said.

'If we can,' Danny mumbled.

He hadn't intended to be heard, but was. Blast the dense atmosphere! O'Malley frowned disapproval.

After a moment the man shrugged. 'Maybe we will have to

give up on the heaviest suff, like the engine,' he conceded. 'Maybe even on the biggest, bulkiest instruments, if my idea about the wagon doesn't work out. At a minimum, though, we are going to bring back those tapes – Huh? What's wrong?'

Danny hugged the metal of a pontoon to himself. 'N-n-nothing,' he pushed forth, around the shriek that still struggled to escape him. He couldn't halt the shudders of his body.

Above the meadow soared a spearfowl, not the big raptor of the highlands but its truly immense cousin, eight meters from wingtip to wingtip, with power to carry a little boy off and devour him.

Yet boughs overarched the trail. Nothing flew beneath that high, high ceiling of bronze, amber, and turquoise except multitudinous small volants like living rainbows. And when a flock of tarzans went by, leaping from branch to branch, chattering and posturing, Danny found himself joining O'Malley in laughter.

Astonishing, too, was the airiness of the forest. 'Jungle' was a false word. Roxana wasn't in the tropics, and no matter how much energy Rustum got from its nearby sun, the Ardashir coast was cooled by sea breezes. The weather was not so much hot as warm, actually: a dry warmth, at that. Brush grew riotously only where openings in the woods provided ample light. Elsewhere, between the boles were simply occasional shrubs. The ground was soft with humus; it smelled rich.

Nor was the forest gloomy. That appearance had merely been due to contrast. Pupils expanded, the human eye saw a kind of gentle brightness which brought out infinite tones and shadings of foliage, then faded away into mysterious cathedral distances.

Cathedral? Danny had seen pictures and read descriptions from Earth. He'd always thought of a big church as hushed. If so, that didn't qualify this wilderness, which hummed and sang and gurgled – breezes in the leaves, wings and paws, eager streams, a call, a carol. Where was the brooding cruelty he remembered?

Maybe the difference was that he wasn't lost; he had both a friend and a gun at his side. Or maybe his dread had not been so deep-rooted after all; maybe, even, what he had feared was not the thing in itself, but only memories and bad dreams which for some years had plagued a child who no longer existed.

The trail was easy, broad, beaten almost into a pavement. He scarcely felt the considerable load on his back. His feet moved themselves, they carried him afloat, until he must stop to let a panting O'Malley catch up.

Higher oxygen intake, of course. What an appetite he was building, and wouldn't dinner taste good? What separated him from his chief, besides age, was that for him this atmosphere was natural. Not that he was some kind of mutant: no such nonsense. If that had been the case, he couldn't have stood the highlands. But his genes did put him at the far end of a distribution curve with respect to certain biochemical details.

I don't have to like this country, he told himself. *It's just that, well, Mother used to say we should always listen to the other fellow twice.*

When they camped, he had no need to follow O'Malley into sleep immediately after eating. He lay in his bag, watched, listened, breathed. They had established themselves off the trail, though in sight of it. The man's decision proved right, because a herd of the pathmaking animals came by.

Danny grabbed for his rifle. The plan was to do pothunting, wild meat being abundant. Rustumite life didn't have all the nutrients that humans required, but supplemental pills weighed a lot less than even freeze-dried rations –

He let the weapon sink, unused. It wouldn't be possible to carry off more than a fraction of one of those bodies; and it would be a mortal sin to waste so towering-horned a splendor.

After a while he slept. He fell back into a tomb silence of trees and trees, where the spearfowl hovered on high. He woke strangling a scream. Although he soon mastered the terror, for the rest of his journey to the wreck he walked amidst ghastliness.

The last several kilometers went slowly. Not only did compass, metal detector, and blaze marks guide the travelers off the game path, while a starless night had fallen, but many patches were less thickly wooded than elsewhere, thus more heavily brush-covered. None were sufficiently big or clear for a safe landing. O'Malley showed Danny how to wield the machetes they carried, and the boy got a savage pleasure from it. *Take that, you devil! Take that!* When they reached the goal, he too could barely stay on his feet long enough to make camp, and this time his rest was not broken.

Later they studied the situation. The slender shape of the car lay crumpled and canted between massive trees. Flashbeams picked out a torn-off wing still caught among the limbs above. There went a deep, changeable pulsing through the odorous warmth. It came from the south, where the ground sloped evenly, almost like a ramp, four or five kilometers to the sea.

Danny had studied aerial photographs taken from the rescue car. In his troubled state, he had not until now given them much thought. Now he asked, 'Sir, uh, why'd you head inland, you and Mr Herskowitz? Why not just out onto the beach to get picked up?'

'Haven't got a beach here,' O'Malley explained. 'I know; went and looked. The bush continues right to the edge of a whacking great salt marsh, flooded at high tide and otherwise mucky. Wheels or pontoons would too damn likely stick fast in that gumbo. If you waited for flood, you'd find the water churned, mean and tricky, way out to the reefs at the bay mouth—nothing that a pilot would want to risk his car on, let alone his carcass.'

'I see.' Danny pondered a while. 'And with Mr Herskowitz injured, you couldn't swim out to where it'd be safe to meet you . . . But can't we raft this stuff to calm water, you and me?'

'Go see for yourself, come morning, and tell me.'

Danny had to force himself to do so. Alone again in the wilderness! But O'Malley still slept, and would want to start work immediately upon awakening. This might be Danny's one chance to scout a quicker way of getting the cursed job done. He set teeth and fists, and loped through the thin fog of sunrise.

At the coast he found what O'Malley had described. Of the two moons, Raksh alone raised significant tides; but those could rise to several times the deep-sea height of Earth's. (Earth, pictures, stories, legends, unattainable, one tiny star at night and otherwise never real.) Nor was the pull of the sun negligible.

From a treetop he squinted across a sheet of glistening mud. Beyond it, the incoming waters brawled gunmetal, white-streaked, furious. Rocks reared amidst spume and thunder. The low light picked out traces of cross-currents, rips, sinister eddies where sharpness lurked already submerged. Afar, the bay widened out in a chop of waves and finally reached a line of skerries whereon breakers exploded in steady rage. Past these, the Gulf of Ardashir glimmered more peaceful.

No doubt at slack water and ebb the passage would be less dangerous than now. But nothing would be guaranteed. Certainly two men couldn't row a sizeable, heavily laden raft or hull through such chaos. And who'd want to spend the fuel and cargo space to bring a motorboat here, or even an outboard motor? the potential gain in salvage wasn't worth the risk of losing still another of Rustum's scarce machines.

Nor was there any use reconnoitering elsewhere. The photographs had shown that eastward and westward, kilometer after kilometer, the coastline was worse yet: cliffs, bluffs, and banks where the savage erosive forces of this atmosphere had crumbled land away.

Above, the sky arched colorless, except where the sun made it brilliant or patches where the upper clouds had drifted apart for a while. Those showed so blue that homesickness grabbed Danny by the throat.

He made his way back. Since he'd gotten a proper rest, again the country did not seem out-and-out demonic. But Lord, how he wanted to leave!

O'Malley was up, had the teakettle on a fire and was climbing about the wreck making more detailed investigations. 'Satisfied?' he called. 'Okay, you can rustle us some breakfast. Did you enjoy the view?'

'Terrible,' Danny grumbled.

'Oh? I thought it was kind of impressive, even beautiful in its way. But frustrating, I admit. As frustrating as wanting to scratch my head in my helmet ... I'm afraid we'll accomplish less than I hoped.'

Danny's heart leaped to think they might simply make a few trips between here and the bus, backpacking data tapes and small instruments. The voice dashed him:

'It's bound to be such slow going at best, you see, especially when I'm as handicapped as I am. We won't finish our wagon in a hurry. Look how much work space we'll have to clear before we can start carpentering.' They had toted in lightweight wheels and brackets, as well as tools for building the rest of the vehicle from local timber and cannibalized metal. 'Then it'll be harder cutting a road back to our game trail than I guessed from what I remembered. And the uphill gradient is stiffer, too. We'll spend some days pushing and hauling our loot along.'

'Wh-what do you expect we'll be able to carry on the wagon?'

'Probably no more than the scientific stuff. Damn! I really did hope we could at least cut the jets and powerplant free, and block-and-tackle them onto the cart. They're in perfectly good shape.'

Danny felt puzzled. 'Why didn't we bring more men? Or a small tractor, or a team of mules?'

'The College couldn't afford that, especially now in planting season. Besides, a big enough bus would cost more to rent than the salvage is worth, there's such a shortage of that kind and such a demand elsewhere. What we have here is valuable, all right, but not that valuable.' O'Malley paused. 'Anyway, I doubt the owner of a really big vehicle would agree to risk it down here for any price.'

'It's only okay to risk us,' Danny muttered. *I'm not afraid,* he told himself. *I'm not! However ... all the reward I could win doesn't counterbalance the chance of my dying this young in hell.*

O'Malley heard and, unexpectedly, laughed. 'That's right. You and I are the most society can afford to gamble for these stakes. God never promised man a free ride.'

And Father always says, 'The laborer is worthy of his hire,' came to Danny. *In his mind, it meant the laborer* must *be.*

Day crept onward. The work was harsh – with machete, ax, cutting and welding torches, drill, wrench, hammer, saw, and tools less familiar to the boy. Nevertheless he found himself quite fascinated. O'Malley was a good instructor. More: the fact that they were moving ahead, that they were on their way to winning even a partial victory over the low country, was heart-lifting, healing.

Danny did object to being stuck with trail clearance while the other went off to bag them some meat. He kept quiet, but O'Malley read it on his face and said, 'Hunting hereabouts isn't like on High America. Different species; whole different ecology, in fact. You'd learn the basic tricks fast, I suppose. But we don't want to spend any extra time, do we?'

'No,' Danny replied, though it cost him an effort.

And yet the man was right. Wasn't he? The more efficiently they organized, the sooner they'd be home. It was just that – well, a hunt would have been more fun than this toil. *Anything* would be.

Slash, chop, hew, haul the cut brush aside and attack what stood beyond, in a rain and mist of sweat, till knees grew shaky and every muscle yelled forth its separate aches. It was hard to believe that this involved less total effort than simply clearing a landing space for the cargo bus. That was true, however. A field safe to descend on, in so thick a forest, would have been impossible to make without a lot of heavy equipment, from a bulldozer onward. A roadway need not be more than passable. It could snake about to avoid trees, logs, boulders, any important obstacle. When it meant a major saving of labor, Danny allowed himself to set off a small charge of fulgurite.

Returning, O'Malley was gratified at the progress. 'I couldn't have gotten this far,' he said. 'You couldn't yourself, up in thinner air.' He estimated that in two days and nights they would link their path to the game trail. Then remained the slogging, brutal forcing of the loaded wagon upward to the bus.

At midday dinner, O'Malley called his superiors in Anchor. The communicator in that distant cargo carrier had been set to amplify and relay signals from his little transceiver. Atmospherics were bad; you couldn't very well use FM across those reaches. But what words straggled through squeals, buzzes, and wines were like the touch of a friendly hand. *Wherever we go on Rustum*, Danny thought, *we'll belong*, and was wearily surprised that he should think this.

Rain fell shortly after he and his companion awoke at mid-afternoon, one of the cataracting lowland rains which left them no choice but to relax in their tent, listen to the roar outside, snack off cold rations, and talk. O'Malley had endless yarns to spin about his years of exploration, not simply deeds and escapes but comedies and sudden, startling loveliness. Danny realized for the first time how he had avoided, practially deliberately, learning more than he must about this planet which was his.

The downpour ended toward evening and they crawled out of the shelter. Danny drew a breath of amazement. It was likewise a breath of coolness, and an overwhelming fragrance of flowers abruptly come to bloom. Everywhere the forest glistened with raindrops, which chimed as they fell onto wet grass and eastward splintered the light into diamond shards. For heaven had opened, lay clear and dizzyingly high save where a few cloudbreaks like snowpeaks flung back the rays of the great

56

golden sun. Under that radiance, leaf colors were no longer sober, they flamed and glowed. In treetops a million creatures jubilated.

O'Malley regarded the boy, started to say something but decided on a prosaic: 'I'd better check the instruments.' They were still in the wreck and, though boxed, might have been soaked through rents in the fuselage.

He climbed up a sort of ladder he had made, a section of young treetrunk with lopped off branches leaned against a door which gaped among the lower boughs. Foliage hid just what happened. Danny thought later that besides making things slippery, the torrent had by sheer force loosened them in their places. He heard a yell, saw the ladder twist and topple, saw O'Malley crash to the ground under the full power of weight upon Rustum.

Night deepened. The upper clouds had not yet returned; stars and small hurtling Sohrab glimmered yonder, less sharply than on High America but all the more remote-looking and incomprehensible. The tent was hot, and O'Malley wanted breezes on his sweating skin. So he lay outside in his bag, half propped against a backpack. Light from a pair of lanterns glared upon him, picked out leaves, boles, glimmer of metal, and vanished down the throat of croaking darkness.

'Yes.' Though his voice came hoarse, it had regained a measure of strength. 'Let me rest till dawn, and I can hike to the bus.' He glanced down at his left arm, splinted, swathed, and slung. Fortune had guarded him. The facture was a clean one, and his only serious injury; the rest were bruises and shock. Danny had done well in the paramedical training which was part of every education on Rustum, and surgical supplies went in every traveling kit.

'Are you sure?' the boy fretted. 'If we called for help – a couple of stretcher-bearers –'

'No, I tell you! Their work is needed elsewhere. It was harder for Phil Herskowitz to walk with those ribs of his, than it'll be for me.' Pride as well as conscience stiffened O'Malley's tone. Bitterness followed: 'Bad enough that we've failed here.'

'Have we, sir? I can come back with somebody else and finish the job.'

'Sorry.' The man set his teeth against more than pain. 'I didn't mean you, son. *I've* failed.' He turned his face away.

57

'Lower me, will you? I'd like to try to sleep some more.'

'Sure.' Suddenly awkward, Danny hunkered down to help his chief. 'Uh, please, what should I do? I can push our roadway further.'

'If you want. Do what you like.' O'Malley closed his eyes.

Danny rose. For a long while he gazed down at the stubbled, pale, exhausted countenance. Before, O'Malley could take off his helmet temporarily to wash, shave, comb his hair. Danny hadn't dared allow that extra stress on the body. Dried perspiration made runnels across furrows which agony had plowed. It was terrible to see this big, genial, powerful man so beaten.

Was he asleep already, or hiding from his shame under a pretense of it?

What was disgraceful, anyway, about a run of bad luck?

Danny scuffed boot in dirt and groped after understanding. Jack O'Malley, admired surveyor-explorer, had finally miscalculated and crashed an aircar. He could make up for that – it could have happened to anybody, after all – by arranging to recover the most important things. But first it turned out that there was no way to haul back the motor, the heart of the vehicle. And then, maybe because he had actually continued to be a little careless, he fell and got disabled.... *All right. His pride, or vanity or whatever, is suffering. Why should it – this much? He's not a petty man. Think how patient and sympathetic he's been with me. What's wrong with another person completing his project? Certainly not a mere chunk of salvage money. He's well off.*

It must be pretty crucial to him, this. But why?

Danny looked around, to the stars which were relentlessly blinking out as vapors rose from sea and soil, to the shadowiness which hemmed him in. Trees stood half-seen like trolls. They mumbled in the slow, booming wind, and clawed the air. Across the years, his fear and aloneness rushed toward him.

But I can beat that! he cried, almost aloud. *I'm doing it!*

O'Malley groaned. His eyelids fluttered, then squeezed shut again. He threw hale arm across helmet as if to shield off the night.

Realization came like a blow: *He's been afraid too. It's that alien down here, that threatening. More than it ever can be to me ... He won his victory over himself, long ago. But a single bad defeat can undo it inside him.*

Jack O'Malley, alone and mortal as any small boy?

58

Danny shook his fist at the forest. *You won't beat him! I won't let you!*

A minute later he thought how melodramatic that had been. His ears smoldered. Yet blast, blast, blast, there had to be a way! The wagon was built. The few remaining kilometers of brush could be cleared in some hours. True, no one person could manhandle the thing, loaded, the whole way to the bus; and O'Malley lacked strength to help on that uphill drag . . .

'Do what you like,' the man had whispered in his crushed state, his breaking more of soul than bones.

Uphill?

Danny yelled.

O'Malley started, opened his eyes, fumbled after his pistol. 'What is it?'

'Nothing,' Danny chattered. 'Nothing, sir. Go back to sleep.' *Nothing – or everything!*

Roadmaking was a good deal easier between camp and sea than in the opposite direction. Besides the ground sloping downward, salt intrusions made it less fertile. Still, there was ample brush to lay on muddy spots where wheels might otherwise get stuck. By the brilliance of a lantern harnessed on his shoulders, Danny got the path done before he must likewise sleep.

'You're the busy bee, aren't you?' O'Malley said drowsily on one of his companion's returns to see to him. 'What're you up to?'

'Working, sir,' Danny answered, correctly if evasively. O'Malley didn't pursue the question. He soon dropped again into the slumber, half natural, half drugged, whereby his body was starting to heal itself.

Later Danny took the wagon to the shore. It went easily, aside from his occasional need for the brake. Unladen, it was light enough for him to bring back alone. But it would require more freeboard – he grinned – especially if it was to bear a heavier burden than planned. With power tools he quickly made ribs, to which he secured sheet metal torched out of the wreck. Rigging would be difficult. Well – tent and bags could be slashed for their fabric.

He labored on the far side of the site, beyond view of the hurt man. Toward morning, O'Malley regained the alertness to insist on knowing what was afoot. When Danny told him, he exclaimed, 'No! Have you gone kilters?'

'We can try, sir,' the boy pleaded. 'Look, I'll make several practice runs, empty, get the feel of it, learn the way, make what changes I feel we need before I stow her full. And you, you can pilot the bus one-handed, can't you? I mean, what can we lose?'

'Your fool life, if nothing else.'

'Sir, I'm an expert swimmer, and –'

Shamelessly, Danny used his vigor to wear O'Malley down.

Preparation took another pair of days. This included interruptions when Danny had to go hunting. He found O'Malley's advice about that easy to follow, game being plentiful and unafraid. Though he didn't acutally enjoy the shooting, it didn't weigh on his conscience; and the ranging around became relaxation and finally a joy.

Once a giant spearfowl passed within reach of his rifle. He got the creature in his sights and followed it till it was gone. Only then did he understand that he had not killed it because he no longer needed to. How majestic it was!

O'Malley managed camp, in spite of the clumsiness and the occasional need for pain-killer forced on him by his broken arm. With renewed cockiness, he refused to return to High America for medical attention, or even talk to a doctor on the radio. 'I'm coming along okay. You did a first-class job on me. If it turns out my flipper isn't set quite right, why, they can soon repair that at the hospital. Meanwhile, if I did call in, some officious idiot would be sure to come bustling out. If he didn't order us home, he'd cram his alleged help onto us, so he could claim a share in the salvage money – your money.'

'You really will go through with it, then, sir?'

'Yes. I'm doubtless as crazy as you are. No. Crazier, because at my age I should know better. But if the two of us can lick this country – Say, my name is Jack.'

Filled with aircraft motor and all, the wagon moved more sluggishly than on its trial trips ... at first. Then the downgrade steepened, the brake began to smoke, and for a time Danny was terrified that his load would run out of control and smash to ruin. But he tethered it safely above high-water mark. Thereafter he had to keep watch while O'Malley walked back to the bus carrying the data tapes which must not be risked. Danny could have done this faster, but the man said it was best if he spent the time studying the waters and how they behaved.

He also found chances to get to know the plants better, and the beasts, odors and winds and well-springs, the whole forest wonderland.

Wavelets lapped further and still further above the place to which he had let the wheels roll. He felt a rocking and knew they were upborne. Into the portable transceiver he said: 'I'm afloat.'

'Let's go, then.' O'Malley's was the voice drawn more taut.

Not that excitement didn't leap within Danny. He recalled a remark of his comrade's – 'You're too young to know you can fail, you can die' – but the words felt distant, unreal. Reality was raising the sail, securing the lift, taking sheet and tiller in hand, catching the breeze and standing out into the bay.

No matter how many modifications and rehearsals had gone in advance, the cart-turned-boat was cranky. It could not be otherwise. Danny knew sailing craft too well to imagine he would ever have taken something as jerry-built as this out upon Lake Olympus. The cat rig was an aerodynamic farce; the hull was fragile, ill-balanced, and overloaded; instead of a proper keel were merely leeboards and what lateral resistance the wheels provided.

Yet this was not High America. The set of mind which had decided, automatically, that here was water too hazardous for aircar or motorboat, had failed to see that a windjammer – built on the spot, involving no investment of machinery – possessed capabilities which would not exist in the uplands.

Here air masses thrust powerfully but slowly, too ponderous for high speed or sudden flaws, gusts, squalls. Here tide at its peak raised a hull above every rock and shoal except the highest-reaching; and, the period of Raksh being what it was, that tide would not change fast. An enormous steadiness surrounded the boat, enfolded it and bore it outward.

Not that there were no dangers! Regardless of how firm a control he had, it took a sailor who was better than good to work his way past reefs, fight clear of eddies and riptides, beat around regions against which the hovering man warned him.

Heaven was not leaden, it was silver. Lively little weather clouds caught the light of a half-hidden sun in flashes which gleamed off steel and violet hues beneath. The land that fell away aft was a many-colored lavishness of life; over the forest

61

passed uncountable wings and a wander-song to answer the drumbeat of breakers ahead. The air blew full of salt and strength, it lulled, it whistled, it frolicked and kissed. To sail was to dance with the world.

Now came the barrier. Surf spouted blinding white. Its roar shook the bones. 'Bear right!' O'Malley's voice screamed from the transceiver. 'You'll miss the channel – bear right!' *Starboard*, Danny grinned, and put his helm down. He could see the passage, clear and inviting ahead. It was good to have counsel from above, but not really needed, in this place that was his.

He passed through, out onto the Gulf of Ardashir, which gives on the Uranian Ocean and thence on a world. Waves ran easily. The boat swayed in the long swell of them. So did the airbus, after O'Malley settled it down on to its pontoons. Still, this could be the trickiest part of the whole business, laying alongside and transferring freight. Danny gave himself the challenge.

When both vessels were linked, the man leaned out of his open cargo hatch and cried in glory, 'We've done it!' After a moment, with no less joy: 'I'm sorry. You have.'

'We have, Jack,' Danny said. 'Now let me give you the instruments first. The motor's going to be the very devil to shift across. We could lose it.'

'I think not. Once the chains are made fast, this winch can snatch along three times that load. But sure, let's start with the lesser-weight items.'

Danny braced feet against the rolling and began to pass boxes over. O'Malley received them with some difficulty. Nevertheless, he received them. Once he remarked, through wind and wave-noise: 'What a shame we can't also take that remarkable boat back.'

Danny gazed at this work of his hands, then landward, and answered softly, 'That's all right. *We'll* be back – here.'

Chad Oliver

SHAKA!

Out of the deeps of space she came, a great metallic fish falling through the sky.

She was not built for primitive landings, that tremendous ship with the incongruous symbol of a laden camel on her gleaming bow; she was a creature of the vast night between the stars, and her normal port of call was the high sky. She was unused to winds and rain and the feel of grass and soil and rock against her taut hide. She carried landing shuttles, of course – graceful little spheroids that could drift down to a planet's surface and come to rest as lightly as a feather. But she was not using them this time.

She wanted to be seen. She wanted to make a commotion. She wanted to call attention to herself.

She came down through the sky roaring and hollering with fire spurting from her tail. Femalelike, she made herself a dramatic entrance.

She touched down gently for all her bulk, settling with a grinding hiss into the yielding ground. She hit her target area right on the button, within inches of the spot the computers had calculated months ago.

She did no damage, but she was observed clearly enough. A volcano does not fall from the heavens without causing a stir.

A strange sweet-smelling breeze soothed her skin. A swollen yellow-blue sun beamed down and took the long chill out of her bones. She was soundless now, at rest, relaxed.

She waited for what had to come.

The people had no name for their world, and no concept of what a planet was. Their land – their territory – was Ernake, and they were the Anake. They knew there were other lands, and other peoples; some of them, in other times, had journeyed for many days, and they knew the land went on forever.

The Anake gather around the silent towering ship. They were

filled with wonder, but they were not afraid. They had never seen anything like the ship before. They were aware that the thing had great power. Still, they were not stupid. They knew this place. This was where the round skyboats came. This was where they met the traders that flew out of the blazing sun. This was where they got good things. They made the connection.

The Anake were troubled. They did not fear the alien ship as long as it was quiet and motionless; in point of fact, they were not easily intimidated by anything. But they had enemies, the Kikusai, and the Kikusai were pressing them hard. It was difficult for the woodcarvers to find peace in which to work. It was dangerous to seek the firestones that the carvers blended with the dense, dark-grained woods.

They needed the carvings now, needed them more than in the olden days. They needed them to trade, and it was trade that made the Anake strong.

For many seasons, the traders had helped them. Useful things and new ideas had come to them from the skyboats. This time – although there had been no meeting arranged in advance, as was the custom – there might be a gift. Something big, something that was scaled to the size of this mighty visitor. Perhaps...

They could not know. They could not even try to guess.

They could only wait for the magic to happen. *If* it happened. The traders were funny sometimes. They had strange ways. They were not always like real people.

The Anake waited. All through the long afternoon of heat and stillness the ship did nothing. It was inert, but alive. It was aware, watching, but it took no action. The shadows lengthened and night winds whispered through the grasses. The great sun disappeared in a riot of color and there was only the little white sun that sometimes held back the darkness. The Anake built fires; the little sun burned with an uncertain heat.

They waited, not sleeping. In a lifeway that was not easy, the Anake had learned the value of patience.

The long silent hours passed and the stars moved and grew dim. The fires of the people died and the great fire in the sky returned, painting hot colors across the land.

There was ... change ... on the ship.

The Anake stared, expectantly.

The ship was ready.

*   *   *

A blurring on her smooth metal hide. Color: a perfect circle of heavy yellow. A thick pulsing beam, emerging from the circle and probing toward the ground.

Figures – dark, indistinct – floating down inside the beam.

Emerging.

The Anake stayed back, observing, giving them room.

One by one, men stepped out of the beam and stood in the brilliant sunlight. There were ten, then twenty. Thirty. Forty. Fifty. They looked like no traders the Anake had ever seen. Some of them were dressed like Anake, right down to the wooden crestcombs in their hair. Some of them were dressed like Kikusai.

All of them carried shields and long iron-pointed spears.

The men from the ship formed two facing lines in the clearing, those made up like Anake on one side and those arrayed like Kikusai on the other. The lines were about thirty-five yards apart.

They yelled abuse at each other and made threatening – and occasionally obscene – gestures.

They began to fight.

There was no plan of attack, no coordination. An Anake would rear back, run a step or two, and heave his long, heavy spear at the Kikusai. The Kikusai would deflect the incoming spear with his tough oblong hide and then throw *his* spear.

There was a lot of sweat, a lot of profanity, and very little damage.

The men played out their charade for nearly an hour, then called the whole thing off. They retired to the shade cast by the towering ship and flopped down to rest. Flasks and sandwiches came down the beam. The men ate and drank.

The Anake – the real ones – were dismayed. They had seen nothing of interest, nothing new. This was the way they had always fought. Was this some kind of trader joke? They were not amused. They were tired and hungry and thirsty. They muttered together and fingered their spears. They spoke critically of the poor throwing technique of the men from the ship. They were restless. Still, they waited. The traders were hard to figure sometimes. It was well to be patient.

In the early afternoon, when the winds were weak and the brown dust-haze hung in the warm air, the men from the ship went into action again.

This time it was different.

This time they acted as though they meant business.

The Kikusai arranged themselves as they had done before, forming a long single line with their shields up and their great spears poised for throwing.

The Anake came out in a totally different formation. First, they knelt and took their long spears apart. The spears were made in three sections. There was a fairly heavy tapered butt, a socketed center shaft, and a foreshaft that ended in a six-inch iron point. By elminating the center shaft and socketing the foreshaft directly into the butt, they created a different, shorter spead. You could not throw it accurately for any distance, but it had other uses.

While the Kikusai waited in their single line, the Anake turned their attention to their shields. Those shields, it was apparent, were not the simple devices they had seemed. By opening hidden latches, a portion of the shield was detached. The shield that remained was a new design: lighter, narrower, coming to a hooked point on the upper end, not quite as long as before.

With their equipment ready, the Anake moved into formation. They didn't really have the manpower for the job – they needed a regiment – but they sketched it in.

First, a rectangle of fighting men, three deep.

On either side, separated from the rectangle and a little behind it, curved hornlike columns of men, situated to form a pincers.

In the rear, a square of reserves.

It was very hot and still. Sweat glistened in the sun.

The Anake shouted and advanced. As they moved, they kept up the noise. They did not run. They simply walked forward at a steady pace.

Some of the Kikusai loosed their spears with random throws. The advancing Anake deflected them easily with their maneuverable shields. The Anake threw no spears.

They just kept coming.

As the Anake warriors closed the distance, the Kikusai line wavered but held.

The solid rectangle of fighting men hit the center of the Kikusai line. The long spears of the Kikusai were useless in close combat. The Anake warriors hooked the Kikusai shields with their slender pointed shields, forcing them to one side.

The Anake went in with their short jabbing spears. The

Kikusai had no defense. They were decimated.

The Kikusai who were still on their feet broke and fell back. The horns of the Anake formation closed around them, sealing them in.

The reserves came up.

Short, merciless spears thrust and ripped and tore. The brown dust was terrible. The heat hammered the clearing like a fist from hell.

When the dust finally lifted, the Kikusai lay in crumpled heaps where they had fallen. The tired, sweating Anake were bruised and exhausted and streaked with dirt, but they had not lost a man.

For a long moment suspended in time the tableau held. Then the Kikusai actors struggled to their feet, brushed themselves off, and mingled profanely with those who had played the victorious Anake.

The traders trooped wearily back to the pulsing yellow beam. They were ... absorbed ... into the ship. The beam vanished.

There was only the immense silent ship poised beneath a strange yellow-blue sun. There was only the cloudless vault of the sky and the first stirrings of wind.

And the real Anake, who had seen it all.

The real Anake, who could not leave.

The real Anake, who played no games but fought for survival against an enemy that was stronger than they knew.

The tremendous ship changed position. It did this almost without sound, almost without visible motion. It was rooted into the land and then it was free. There was space beneath it. There was a ... blurring ... around it.

There was no need now for fire and thunder and drama. There was no need and it would have been impossible. To start those engines would have seared the Anake to cinders.

The ship lifted. It was high in the sky before its thrusters flamed. Its roar was muted.

The ship was gone. Its task was finished.

Not a word had been spoken between the traders and the Anake. Nothing had been exchanged. Technically, there had been no instruction.

But communication can take many forms, and not all of them can be foreseen by distant laws.

The Anake had seen.

One in particular, a small tense man with bright and piercing eyes and a questing mind. He knew. He saw the possibilities.

While those around him babbled of food and drink and joked about small incidents of the mock battle, he stood alone.

He looked thoughtfully at the long spear he carried in his hand.

He stared at the deserted clearing, and he remembered.

The great lightship of Caravans, Unlimited, had left the system of Procyon far behind. Even in the coruscating gray abyss of not-space, it would take a long time before it could return. In any event, the ship had other ports of call to make; deep space travel was too complicated and too expensive to permit one-shot voyages. Like the laden camel that was its corporate symbol, the ship moved from oasis to oasis through a universe of desert. Like the caravans that once plied the Sahara sands of a long-ago Earth, it did what business it could along the way.

Alex Porvenir fiddled with his glass, not really wanting a drink. That wasn't like him; he was no lush, but he enjoyed his Scotch and it usually relaxed him. He took out his pipe, cleaned the foul thing with elaborate and pointless care, and stuffed it with tobacco. He fired up a long wooden match – he had no luck with lighters – and lit the pipe. It tasted like burned grease, which was normal. About one pipe in twenty turned out to be worth the effort.

'You don't have the look of a man consumed with joy,' Tucker Olton said, sipping *his* drink with gusto. 'What's the matter? I thought it all went off like a breeze.'

Alex Porvenir stared at his glass, watching the ice melt. He hated these moods of his, and they had been getting more frequent the last few years. When he had been Tucker Olton's age, he had the galaxy by the tail. Oh, he had known just about *everything*. It was surprising what a man unlearned as he grew older. Alex was only forty, and physically he was sound enough. He could take Tucker, for instance, and Tucker was ten years younger. Alex was a tall, lean man and he was hard. He worked at it; he was one of those men who needed physical outlets to keep his mind from going stale. He had a theory about that: man had been a hunting animal for a million years before he had been anything else, and that was the kind of animal he was. He wasn't designed to sit at a desk and push paper, not all the time. He needed a release, and the release came from the body rather than the brain. There was some gray in his hair, but his brown eyes were clear and sharp. Alex had a jaw on him; he could be stubborn.

Right now, he was troubled.

His thoughts were on Procyn V, and the Anake.

And the Kikusai.

'I'm worried, Tuck,' he said. 'I don't like the responsibility of playing God.'

Tucker Olton smiled. He knew Alex's moods; they had been together for six years now, and they had gotten beyond the master-student relationship. 'You're taking yourself a trifle seriously, aren't you? We're just doing our job.'

'I've heard that one before, I think.'

'But what's wrong? It was *your* plan, remember, and a damned good one. The boys acted out their little play perfectly. We *must* have communicated, unless the Anake have wood blocks between their ears. We broke no laws. The Caravans lawyers could go before the U.N. ET Council and win this one hands down.'

Alex puffed on his pipe. 'I'm not worried about the technical end of it; I know my business. It'll work. I'm not worried about the legal angle. That not my department. I regret using an old-fashioned word, but I'm worried about the *morality* of the thing.'

Tucker looked surprised. 'But there's no question there. We *had* to do it, no matter whose standards you apply.'

'I learned you better than that, old son.'

'Hell, this isn't a fog-brained seminar in Advanced Ethics. That's a real world we're dealing with, and real people. We couldn't just juggle our philosophies and do nothing. We did the best we could. The Anake are a good bunch, if you will excuse the value judgement. Forget about the profit motive if it makes you feel better. The Kikusai are bigger trouble than they know – those birds are on the verge of a conquest state that could take over a very big chunk of that planet, including the Anake. If we *don't* act, the Anake will be slaves. It's just that simple. It happens to be in our interest to preserve the Anake, but so what? That doesn't make it wrong.'

Alex shook his head. 'Right, wrong. I don't profess to know. But try this one on for size. Suppose our little plan not only works, but works *too* well? Try the argument you just made on that one.'

'I don't follow you.'

'Come on, Tuck. Dredge up a smattering of history, or reflect a bit on our distinguished predecessor, Dr. Frankenstein. What exactly did we do?'

Tucker Olton felt that his knowledge was being challenged, and he didn't like it. He spoke with cool precision, masking his annoyance. 'We need the Anake because they are producing for us. They were being threatened by the Kikusai to the point where it was interfering with their artisans. Tactically, as we both noticed, the situation was similar to the one in southern Africa about eighteen hundred. You had a series of tribally-organized peoples with economies based on mixed farming and herding. They raided back and forth, with no vast amount of harm done. The warriors just lined up and heaved their long spears at each other. But then the Kikusai began to get organized, and their population increased. They began to expand their territory –'

'Get back to Africa. You're on Procyon V. What happened in Africa?'

Tucker smiled. 'Shaka happened.'

Alex fiddled with his pipe. He couldn't resist digging at Tucker a trifle. 'Actually, Dingiswayo happened, then Shaka.'

'I know that, dammit. But the new formation and the new weapons were Shaka's. If it hadn't been for Shaka, the Zulus would have been just a minor historical footnote.'

'Maybe. But tell me about Shaka.'

Tucker sighed. Alex had a habit of asking questions when he already knew the answers. 'Shaka made himself an army. He drilled the old age-set regiments until they would march off a cliff at his command. He taught them his new encircling tactics and he trained them to fight to the death. He created a fighting machine that was good enough – later – to handle British regular troops. The other tribes didn't have a prayer. Shaka knocked some of them all the way to Lake Victoria, and that was a fair distance.'

'And what happened to Shaka?'

Tucker shrugged. 'He was a military genius. He was also a very peculiar gent. He became a dictator, in effect. He was something of a political mastermind; he destroyed the old tribal organization and converted it into a state system. When he wasn't performing cute little tricks like executing thousands of citizens so the people would remember his mother's funeral, he ruled fairly efficiently. He controlled over eighty thousand square miles before he was through. He terrorized southern Africa –'

'What happened to Shaka?' Alex repeated.

'I don't know,' Tucker admitted. 'Fire me.'

Alex poured himself another drink. 'Look it up sometime. You might need to know.'

'I'm beginning to get the drift.'

'Two cheers for our side. Maybe there's hope for you yet. Look, Tuck. We probably saved the Anake by sneaking in some new ideas – violating, of course, the spirit if not the letter of the law. And you're right – if we hadn't done it, the Anake would have gone under. But now what? Suppose a Shaka comes along among the Anake and puts it all together? Then the *Kikusai* are up the old creek. They are people too, remember. We have no right to exterminate them. That's the trouble with tinkering with cultural systems – you always get more problems than you started with. And if I may return briefly to the old profit motive – since Caravans doesn't pay me just to conduct social experiments and brood about them – how much carving do you think the Anake will do once they get caught up in the glories of military conquest?'

'They'll do plenty of carving. But they'll be carving Kikusai.'

Alex smiled. 'Still think it's simple?'

'It *could* be. We can't spend our time worrying about every conceivable development.'

'I figure that's one reason why we're here. Machines can calculate possibilities and probabilities. It takes a man to worry about the long shots.'

'Maybe there will be no Shaka.'

'Maybe not. But I'll tell you this, old son. You'd better bone up on what happened to our friend Shaka. If his counterpart *does* show up, the two of us will have to stop him. And that might take some doing.'

There was an uncomfortable silence between the two men.

The lightship flashed on through the grayness of not-space, and across a universe that was as uncaring as the sands of the desert.

His name was Nthenge. A small, nervous man. Energy radiated from him; he was tense even when he slept, which was seldom. His eyes were his most notable feature: deep eyes, direct, glowing, hypnotic. He was thin; he had no time to put meat on his bones. His voice was high but compelling. When Nthenge spoke, others listened.

There had been a time when Nthenge was nothing special. He was just one of the Anake. A good warrior, a man of experience, a man to consult in village crises – that was all. If he was unusual in any way, it was because he had never married.

His name was not widely known, then. Those Anake who knew him generally perferred his brother, Kioko. Kioko was a family man and had a gentler spirit. Kioko was a woodcarver, and his long, fine hands were skilled in making the dark-grained woods come alive.

That was before the great ship had landed.

That was before Nthenge had seen, and understood.

They knew the name of Nthenge now. The Anake knew him, and the Kikusai.

Nthenge!

He was a scourge, a destroyer, a flame across the land. The Kikusai feared and hated him. The Anake feared and needed him.

The Anake followed him.

Had he not shown them the way? Had he not taken the ideas of the traders and turned them into an army against which nothing could stand? Had he not saved them from their enemies?

Nthenge!

He was fearless in battle, but he was more than that. He was a thinker, a planner, a man who did not move until he was sure.

And he was – hard.

There were those who disagreed with Nthenge, at first. They were no longer among the living; they had a way of taking mortal wounds in battle. There were those who plotted against Nthenge. They had a way of disappearing.

Nthenge!

He gave his people power. It was a heady brew. It made people forget, for awhile.

Forget under the yellow-blue sun ...

Forget in the haze of brown dust that obscured a slaughter ...

Forget when the sweet nights winds rustled through the grasses ...

Forget what had been, and what might still be.

The people of the land of Ernake owed much to Nthenge.

He had shown them the way.

* * *

72

'Gentlemen,' said Carlos Coyanosa, 'we have a problem.'

Alex Porvenir smiled and stoked up his pipe, which was as rancid as ever. 'Which one did you have in mind?'

It was a familiar opening to a dialogue. Carlos Coyanosa, who was the senior Caravans representative aboard the lightship, always had a problem. It was his responsibility to oversee company policies – in some respects he outranked the captain – and that meant that problems were as much a part of him as his proverbial headache. Moreover, he had a habit of assuming that others knew precisely *which* problem he was dealing with at any given moment. In actuality, because of the mechanics of space travel and the nature of the enterprise, there were many situations unfolding concurrently. Just as a doctor has more than one patient – unless he is a very bad doctor indeed – a trading ship in space must interact with many clients on any given voyage. If cultural adjustments had to be made, that took time. A company could not afford to sit back and twiddle its corporate thumbs while waiting for a desired effect to take place. It was only on the tri-di that the traders dropped everything and concentrated on one situation to the exclusion of all others.

'It's Procyon V,' Carlos said, smoothing his long black hair with the palm of his hand. 'The Anake thing.'

'What about it?'

'Same old stuff, gentlemen. Our people filed the usual barebones report with the U.N. Trade Commission. They shot it over to the ET Council. The Nigerian representative smelled a rat. He went into a huddle with the man from Uganda, and they issued a formal protest. Our lawyers have tied the thing up, but they need more ammunition.'

Tucker Olton sighed. 'The protest being?'

'Their argument is that what we did is a clear case of cultural manipulation. They are raising the old bugaboo of colonialism in space. It's good politics back home, of course. They say that the Anake did not give their consent to a basic change in their way of life. They say that we are out for a fast buck. They say we have trampled on the rights of the people.'

Alex nodded. 'As an anthropologist, I agree with them. It *is* a clear case of cultural manipulation.'

'I didn't hear that,' Carlos said.

'Hear no evil, see no evil, evil go away. Right?'

'Wrong. Damn, you know as well as I do that Caravans'

policy expressly forbids any action detrimental to the welfare of the people we're dealing with –'

'Sure, but who decides?'

'*You* do, among others. Don't wear your holy hat with me, Alex. You bank your pay just like I do.'

'Let's not get into *that* again,' Tucker said.

Alex puffed on his pipe. 'I concur. We'll proceed on the assumption – mistaken, of course – that we're all rational men. At any rate, we're trying to do the best we can. I even happen to believe, for what it's worth, that Caravans does more good than harm. Hell, for that matter colonialism wasn't always the monster it was made out to be.'

'I didn't hear that, either.'

'Right. We must be fashionable. There were some rotten things about colonialism. One of them was paternalism, which is what we're guilty of right now. But there were a few small forgotten items – schools, roads, hospitals, political ideas, even some notion of human rights.'

'This isn't helping *me* at all,' Carlos observed.

'Okay, try this one on then. It doesn't matter whether we did or did not manipulate the Anake culture. We did, but that's another story. In any event, the Kikusai are the ones who are in trouble at the moment –'

'Please. Don't tangle it up more than it is already.'

'Check. We'll stay with the Anake; the ET Council is always worried about the wrong problem. Maybe there's a lesson in that somewhere. Never mind. Look, Carlos, what you've got is a *legal* problem – legal and political. I can't help you with public relations. The fact is that the exploration and utilization of interstellar space will be done by private outfits like Caravans or it won't be done at all. Governments can't risk tax revenues on space gambles; the sums involved are too immense, and the worthy citizens have enough troubles to cope with at home. Either we do it or Earth forgets it is part of a larger universe. If the PR boys can't sell that one they should chop up their shingles.'

'I'll pass on your accolades. And the legal aspects?'

'There I can help. From a strictly legal point of view, our hands are clean. We did not formally instruct the Anake in anything. We put on a little game to ease the tedium of life aboard ship. We made no threats, we offered no incentives. The change that occurred took place among the Anake –

hell, it was *entirely* their decision, with no prodding of any sort from us. We did not even speak to them. We pulled out right after our fun charade. As for the welfare of the people, they are in better shape now than they were then. Survival is a fairly basic right, you know. In terms of money, Caravans has not yet realized any added income from its action. In fact, the supply of carvings has diminished. Friend, even *I* could argue this case.'

'You may have to before we're through.' Carlos ventured a smile. 'But it does sound pretty good when you put it that way. Thanks, Alex.'

'Don't mention it. If the real problems were as easy as the fake problems, I'd turn in my ulcer.'

Carlos excused himself and returned to his office to work on his report.

'You're really worried, aren't you?' Tucker said. 'I thought you handled that nicely.'

Alex got some ice and poured himself a judiciously hefty portion of Scotch. He was tired and tense and needed to unwind. He flopped in a comfortable chair and took a long swallow of therapy.

'The legal situation doesn't alarm me, Tuck. We're clear on that one, and that's not my baby anyway. But you've seen the monitor reports. We've got to get back to the Procyon system before everything falls apart.'

'You mean Nthenge?'

'He's the key to it. The Kikusai are getting a very bloody nose, and that's our responsibility. The Anake are so wrapped up in playing soldier that the production of carvings is going down. Our moral problem is Nthenge. Our practical problem is to keep those carvings coming. You know, this is a very peculiar business we're in. Caravans has to show a profit. In order to do that, we need relatively small products to transport – small items that will bring high prices. The modern equivalents of salt and gold. Handicrafts are ideal, because they are no longer produced on Earth. Those Anake carvings are one of our gold mines. It took a long time to find them and a long time to set the thing up. We can't afford to lose them.'

And so?'

'And so we go back when we can work it in. We stop Nthenge.'

Tucker grinned. 'Nothing to it. We just introduce the Kikusai to some repeating rifles.'

'What would I do without you?'

'God knows. I vote we worry about it tomorrow. You need some sleep.'

'I'll see what I can do. Good night, Tuck.'

Tucker Olton waved and left.

Alex Porvenir collected the bottle of Scotch, two glasses, and a supply of ice. He walked through the silent corridor of the lightship and caught the tube to his room.

It was a pleasant chamber and spacious by crowded Earth standards. He had a bed big enough to accommodate his six-foot-plus frame with room to spare. He had three soft chairs and a battered foot-stool. There were two ancient priceless Navaho rugs on the floor. He had a computer terminal, a scanner, and some real books. He even had a genuine over-sized bathtub in the john.

'All the comforts of home,' he muttered. In fact, is *was* home. For fifteen years, Alex had spent more time in space and on other worlds than he had on Earth.

He stripped off his shirt and poured a drink. He had tried a great many concoctions from a variety of different worlds and he had yet to find anything better than Scotch.

He picked up the communicator and pressed a number.

'Helen? Were you asleep?'

'A little.' Her voice was drowsy, but the sound of it thrilled him as it always did.

'Can you spare an hour or two?'

'Do you need me?'

'Two guesses.'

'Then I'll try to fit you into my busy schedule, love.'

'My room or yours?'

'You've got a bigger bed.'

'Ten minutes?'

'Make it five.'

Alex disconnected and poured a second drink for Helen. As Tucker had said, Nthenge could wait until tomorrow.

Alex smiled and felt some of the tension leave him. He had tried a great many things on a variety of different worlds, and he had yet to find anything better than a good woman.

Both suns were still in the sky, but the great yellow-blue

fire had dipped close to the horizon. The air was hot and choked with brown dust kicked up by marching feet. Long shadows striped the village and brought no relief.

It was stifling inside the hut and the light was bad. Kioko had moved to his bench in the courtyard. One of his children played quietly in the dirt at his feet. Kioko frowned at the carving he held in his hands and tried to concentrate. The wood was dark and alive, flowing. But the firestone in the head of the ancestral figure was not right. It should glow softly with an inner radiance, shining through the eyes, as was the way with ancestral spirits. The firestone was clumsy, blatant. It had not become one with the wood. And there were so few firestones now, even for Kioko. He could not afford to make a mistake.

The noise from the soldiers bothered him. They were forever drilling and shouting commands. There was no peace, and today it was worse than usual. There was a sense of urgency and excitement in the square.

Reluctantly, Kioko replaced the carving on the bench. He picked up his stone-bladed knife and polished it absently. He sat back to watch.

Nthenge himself was there. Kioko studied his brother, remembering. Nthenge was the same and he was not the same. He had always been small and thin and consumed with a terrible restlessness. When they were children, Nthenge had twisted constantly in his sleep, and gotten up to think his long night thoughts. He had grown up hard and unyielding and without compassion. He had never danced with the girls, never laughed. He had always been strange, but now –

Kioko hardly knew him. Nthenge had power, and it had changed him. It had made him proud and arrogant and arbitrary. Kioko felt no kinship with his brother.

Nthenge faced his sweating troops and silenced them with a gesture of command. The painted wooden crest-comb in his hair was so big and elaborate that it almost dwarfed him. Kioko stifled a smile. It was dangerous to smile at Nthenge. He took himself very seriously indeed.

Nthenge harangued his men, his high voice piercing the still brown haze of the air. Kioko could not catch the words, but Nthenge sounded angry. That was standard these days.

Nthenge spoke for a long time, pacing up and down and shaking his fists at the sky. He was screaming before his speech ended, and then there was a sudden silence.

A soldier was brought before him. The man's hands were bound behind his back. He fell before Nthenge and groveled in the dirt.

Kioko started to his feet but thought better of it. He could do nothing, of course. These executions were becoming commonplace. Execution for cowardice in battle, for plotting against Nthenge, for appearing in Nthenge's dreams, for anything. Nthenge enjoyed them.

The bound soldier lay still, his face buried in the dust.

Nthenge kicked him in the head.

The man rolled and staggered to his feet.

Nthenge took one of the short spears from a trooper. He hefted it, took a grip on the foreshaft with both hands.

He swung it in a vicious arc and hit the man in the stomach with the heavy butt. The soldier doubled up in pain and sank to his knees.

Nthenge kicked him in the head again.

Nthenge backed off a step and gave a signal.

The man was picked up and thrown into the air. When his twisting body came down the soldiers caught it on the points of their spears.

The flopping, bloody body was hurled into the air again and again. A hundred hard metal points ripped its flesh.

When Nthenge gave the command to stop, the man was only a shredded chunk of bloody meat.

A disposal squad gathered up the remains in a blanket and carted the mess away for the scavengers.

Nthenge dismissed his troops.

It was growing dark now, and the night winds began to stir across the land. The dust settled and the breeze rustled through the thatch that hung down from the roofs of the Anake huts. A faint coolness crept down from the faraway mountains.

In the deserted square, Nthenge walked alone. His hands were clasped behind him in an unconscious parody of the soldier he had slain. He paced back and forth, back and forth, busy with the thoughts that never stopped.

Once, he looked in the direction of Kioko, hidden in the black shadows.

Kioko shivered. He reached out and touched the child playing at his feet. With his free hand, he stroked the polished stone blade of his carver's knife.

The firestone in the head of his unfinished ancestor-figure gleamed with an icy flame in the gathering darkness.

The bubble of the landing shuttle drifted down out of the night sky. She showed no lights and was invisible against the backdrop of the stars.

She touched down without a sound and Alex Porvenir stepped out.

He was alone and his best friend would not have recognized him. He was dressed in Anake clothing, complete with a wooden crest-comb in his hair. His features had been subtly blurred. There was a slight phosphorescent glow to his body and his eyes shone in the dark.

'Brother,' he muttered, 'if I run into the wrong guy in this get-up it could get interesting.'

He slipped through the night-damp grasses toward the Anake village, cursing the glow that radiated from him. He knew that Nthenge's security was not what it might be, but nonetheless he felt about as inconspicuous as an illuminated dinosaur.

'Wait until they hear about this one back at the U.N.,' he whispered to himself. 'They'll have me drawn and quartered.'

Of course, this trip was strictly off the record. They had better *not* hear about it.

The village was asleep, including the sentries. The Anake were not night fighters, and neither were the Kikusai. It was only civilized peoples who lacked enough sense to take time off to sleep.

Alex found Kioko's hut without difficulty. It was fortunate that Kioko was a relatively important man. That meant that he had a sleeping hut to himself, with his wives and children and the cooking quarters in a second hut.

Alex took a deep breath and walked through the open doorway of the hut.

He could see by his own glow. Kioko was alone, and asleep.

Alex stood over him and extended his arms. He did his level best to look like an ancestral spirit. He fought an insane urge to light his pipe that sat next to his ashtray aboard the ship. He could almost hear Helen laughing at him.

He composed himself.

'Kioko' he said in an urgent, level voice.

The sleeping figure stirred.

'Kioko!'

Kioko sat up. His eyes widened. Alex could smell the man's shocked surprise. It was one thing to believe in ancestral spirits. It was quite another to wake up and find one in the room with you.

'Kioko, I want you to listen carefully to what I say.'

Kioko fumbled under his bed and produced a bowl that had some food remnants in it. He offered it with shaking hands. 'Here is food, my father. I have no beer. Take it and go away.'

Alex could not understand him. He had memorized his speech and could not deviate from it. He did not speak the language of the Anake and of course translating equipment was not available. He did know that the people were constantly making small offerings of food to the ancestors; a tiny portion of each meal was set aside for them. He accepted the bowl and placed it on the floor. He extended his arms again.

'Kioko, I want you to listen carefully to what I say.'

Kioko listened. He had no choice.

'Kioko, the ancestors have been saddened. We have watched our people and we do not like what we see. Your ways are no longer our ways. We have come to you because you are the brother of Nthenge. Nthenge will not listen to us. You must listen. You must act. If you do not, the ancestors can no longer protect their people. The crops will fail. There will be sickness. The witches will destroy us all.'

Kioko tried to speak. Alex silenced him with a gesture and plunged on.

'One man has brought our people close to destruction. That man is your brother. One man can stop him. That man is you. You, Kioko. We will help you. We will protect you. Our people must be free again and you must lead them. Listen, Kioko. This is what you must do . . .'

Alex finished his prepared speech and gave Kioko no chance to reply. He stalked out of the hut in what he hoped was a majestic manner.

Once outside, he ran through the silent village. The glow from his body made him feel as though he were moving in the beam of a spotlight.

He did not feel good about what he had done. He did not

see what other choice had been open to him. He tried to put his misgivings out of his mind. He could live with his guilt. That was all.

He made it back to the landing shuttle undetected.

The spheroid lifted soundlessly toward the stars.

Within minutes, Alex Porvenir was back aboard the lightship.

Five days later – five anxious and expensive days while Caravans observers stayed glued to their monitors – Kioko acted.

He invited Nthenge to visit him in his home, stating that he had information that Nthenge should know. Normally, Nthenge would not have come. He was beyond that. If you wished to see Nthenge, you went to him. But Kioko was different. He was a brother of the same mother.

Nthenge came. As had been arranged, he came in the evening when the great sun went down but light still lingered between the shadows. He left his guard outside after they had inspected the hut. Nthenge did not lack courage, and he could not show fear before his own brother.

Nthenge entered the house.

Kioko said nothing. He embraced Nthenge in the traditional greeting between brothers.

Before Nthenge could speak, Kioko slipped his woodcarver's knife from his tunic. He plunged the polished stone blade into his brother's chest. Nthenge grunted with pain and surprise. Kioko yanked out the blade and cut his brother's throat.

There was a lot of blood. Kioko's hands were slippery.

In a daze, hardly comprehending what he had done, Kioko followed instructions. He picked Nthenge's body up in his arms. The weight was negligible; Nthenge had no meat on his bones. Kioko walked out the door carrying the body of Nthenge. It was still warm. It dripped a bright red trail.

Kioko carried the body to his workbench and put it down.

He stood up straight. 'I have done it,' he said in a loud, strong voice. 'I, Kioko, the brother of Nthenge. The Anake are free.'

There were many people crowded around the courtyard. They stood in total silence. There was no movement.

Then – motion.

Ancestral figures moved among the people. Their figures

were blurred. They glowed as they walked. They *touched* the people – soldiers, guards, old men, women, children. They whispered the ancient blessings.

The ancestors gathered around Kioko. One by one, they embraced him.

The strange silence held.

There were old, old stories that told of the ancestors visiting a village of the people, but no living man had seen such a thing with his own eyes. When the ancestors had appeared – magically, as though dropped from the sky – they had collected a crowd in a hurry.

It was a night that would be long remembered. In time, it too would become legend.

The ancestors formed a tight little group when they had finished indicating their approval of Kioko.

They withdrew, silently.

Their glow vanished into the night.

Still, the people did not speak. They waited to hear what Kioko would say.

Kioko stood with his dead brother sprawled on the bench behind him. He searched for the words that would lead the Anake back.

He faced his people and began.

Aboard the lightship, far now from the world of Procyon V, Alex Porvenir fired up one of his smelly pipes and blew an angry cloud of smoke in the general direction of Tucker Olton.

'It's easy for us,' he said. 'We commit a murder and then we just pull out. We're beyond the range of their concepts, to say nothing of their technology. We have achieved at least one age-old human goal: the perfect crime.'

'We didn't kill anybody,' Tucker said. 'You didn't kill anybody.'

'Sure,' Alex snorted. 'The ancestors did it. Don't play the fool, Tuck. I'm a big boy now. I made the decision. I'll take the responsibility.'

'Kioko killed him,' Tucker said doggedly.

'What choice did he have after I bamboozled him? Kioko was just the instrument I used. That's all.'

Tucker changed tactics. 'Nthenge was no loss, Alex.'

'No. I don't think so either. But he was a human being. We

are not gods. Who are we to sit in judgement?'

Tucker managed a grim smile. He understood the older man's moods; he knew he was being used. He respected Alex enough to put up with it. 'Two questions, Alex. If you see an evil – never mind its cause – and take no action, does that earn you a gold star in your hymn book? And how many lives did you *save* by the death of Nthenge?'

Alex poured himself a drink. 'Maybe. Maybe.'

'We've restored a balance in that situation. The Kikusai have learned a few tricks too, you know. Kioko is a decent man, and we've backed him up with our little ancestor squad. We can use the ancestors again if we have to. There will be a kind of a peace down there for generations.'

'And carvings. Don't forget our loot.'

'Yes, and carvings. Dammit, Alex, *they* don't hurt anybody. If you get really morbid on me, I'm yelling for the medics. We did the best we could.'

'Yes.' Alex downed his Scotch and felt a little better. 'We did the best we could. I'll give us that.'

Tucker nodded. 'I'm shoving off to get some sleep. Helen is waiting for you, in case you've forgotten.'

'I haven't forgotten.'

'I *do* have one question.'

'Shoot.'

'What in the hell *did* happen to the historical Shaka?'

Alex Porvenir grinned and poured himself another drink. 'Shaka had two brothers. They assassinated Shaka in 1828. Then one brother killed the other and took over. We simplified it a little on Procyon V.'

Tucker Olton shook his head and left the room.

The Caravans lightship plunged on through the desert of space. Against the stars, against the scale of the universe, the ship was nothing and less than nothing.

It carried a man and beside him a woman.

There was life, and purpose.

And there was a tiny thought, hurtled against the immensity of nothingness:

We try. We learn through our mistakes. We do the best we can.

Maybe we'll be remembered.

Thomas N. Scortia

THE ARMAGEDDON TAPES
TAPE I

...That the agency of its defeat should have come into being by the merest chance. The all-enveloping menace, the anti-life principle that was the Theos invested the nearest galaxy. It had destroyed race after race until the Angae fled from its implacable advance to the next galaxy. The hive personality of this race was completely alien to the humankind they encountered in the Sol system. Yet the elements of racial consciousness and personality immortality that was the basis of their survival were uniquely suited to the predatory instincts of humans. When the two were mated, the racial fusion presented the most formidable challenge that the Theos had encountered.

That mankind had been evolving to this group mind in its political institutions was obvious from the peculiar empathetic growth of the Holy State after the final Thermonuclear War. That this was a completely atheistic political structure did not detract from its essential mystical base. Indeed, the very nature of the so-called 'Holy State' depended on the almost fanatic religiosity that the humanism of the day invested in these institutions so that ...

Die Anelan de Galactea   Vol II, Ca 4300

I am dreaming now, a deep placid sleep in which all sensation is muted. It has been years since I slept in this fashion, years since the calm and the peace of a small death (as some poet once called sleep) is mine.

I have set out to change the world, to destroy the world if need be and now I am content.

(Are you asleep Martin?)

Yes, I am asleep but I'm conscious that you are talking with me ... to me ... about me ... and it really doesn't matter.

You think that in this fashion with your drugs and your flashing lights and your bright instruments, you have captured my psyche – my soul – but it isn't so. I am aware of you and at any moment I may shake this spell and be among you, giant and potent beyond belief.

(Odd! Paranoid. But we know that he is dangerous. What could have happened during the period when the creatures had him? There's a profound change in the biochemistry, of course. He takes in cellulose and excretes a complex mixture of purines and pentoses. Who ever heard of a human body manufacturing pentoses?)

I remember about pentoses. Yes, I heard you. I remember from long ago. We had a rhyme. Lyose, xylose, arabinose, ribose. Something, something, something.

(Martin, you are back with Them. Think back. Go back. You are back with Them and They are a part of your life, your being, your every concern.)

Cattle. I was cattle to Them, but They gave me something without knowing that They did, and for that They will eventually be destroyed. I love Them and I hate Them. I will give Them peace and I will give Them sleep and I will arise and give you peace – the peace of a world well ordered and unafraid.

(That's a recurrent theme. He wants to bring us some kind of peace. What peace, Martin?)

The peace of being, of unthinking. The peace that comes from a universe ordered in a manner that men could never order it.

(Another recurrent theme. Were it not for the fact that he has learned some remarkable things from Them, I would put it down to so much fantasy. He may well be able to implement the fantasy. Does the desire and the power to make a fantasy real make the concept any less a fantasy? A disturbing philosophical question.)

I will make it real. I have the vision and it is clear.

(Martin, listen to me. I am your friend.)

All men are my friends.

(Tell me, how did it happen? How did you come to be with Them?)

How did I come to be Their cow? How did They take me and the others like me and turn us, alien and yet brothers, into a herd for Their sustenance?

(How?)

How old am I?

(Thirty, twenty-five. It's hard to tell.)

Perhaps only five or six. I don't remember. I was only three or four when it happened. My mother and father – those are strange words for someone who has had a thousand mothers and fathers ... My mother and father were one of the last to die. They might have lived but they were too old and they could not accept the change. So They killed them. Not really. Actually They caused them to die because Mother and Father could not adapt. The children, many of them, could not adapt and they too died.

(What happened to the children?)

They died and they were eaten. Nothing is lost in the Group. They taught me that. Waste becomes a great sin. The waste of flesh and the waste of spirit are equally not to be tolerated.

(What happened in Marksville? Tell us.)

Marksville? That was home. The only home I had ever known. I wasn't born there but Mother and Father joined the colony when I was only a year old. They told me once ... I don't think I understood at the time ... but they told me that the world they grew up in had become too complicated, too restrictive with no privacy and a constant sense that someone was looking at you in your most intimate moments. There weren't many places left in the world where a man might have the privacy and the peace of mind that come with being his own person.

(That's treason, I think. Maybe we should erase this part of the tape. No? Well, God knows what will happen to him regardless.)

It was in the north, you know. Somewhere in Canada. I'm not sure exactly, but the winters were very cold so that the tractors and the automobiles had to be wrapped with electrical coils and hooked into the colony power supply at night. Otherwise the blocks would have frozen and they could have been permanently damaged. We lived in a communal hall and the heating plant would blast a surge of hot air across the common room one minute and then in the next minute the deadly cold would seep in until it seemed that it would penetrate to your very marrow.

It was a terribly isolated area. We had a helicopter that flew in supplies and mail. The mail came once a week and

86

there wasn't very much of that. After all, the old people had cut themselves off from the world and they didn't want most of their friends knowing where they were. There was a constant fear that someone would come after us and make us return to the old world and the old ways. Even at that age, I felt their fear of being returned to the cities and of the eyes that never stopped watching.

(God, what will happen when our auditor hears this tape? Do you think we dare show it? There's the doctrine of contamination and I sure as hell don't want to face an inquisitor.)

I can hear what you're saying and you have nothing to fear. Let me tell you how They came out of the sky. In one cold afternoon, Their ship came out of the sky. Completely without warning. They were the last of Their kind and They needed Kreels so that They would have food. It was a marvelously sophisticated technique They had for making Kreels and all They needed was a warm blooded organism that used glycogen or a similar starch.

They came out of the sky and at first the people thought that it was some remarkable new ship from the place They had left. The people were frightened but they did not expect to be mistreated, only captured and if need be – what was the word? – reindoctrinated.

The people didn't flee, at any rate, and when They came out of the ship, the horror was like a blanket. They were large, almost seven feet tall and Their chitinous exoskeletons gleamed golden in the cold north sun. My father thought They looked like something half way between ants and praying mantises.

They came out of the great ship (it turned out that it was only a subsidiary vehicle and the real ship was still orbiting the earth), and They spread a gas over the settlement and all the grown people fell down and lay as if they were dead.

They gathered them up. It was remarkable how gentle They were, these huge insectlike creatures. They were gentle and They carried the human into the ship and found for each of them a single crystal container with all the necessary attachments to support life.

You must understand that They were not predatory or evil. They think differently than we. They see the whole universe quite differently and that much I have learned from Them. They were the last of Their race and They had a right to survive.

We were all placed in our special containers and there were bright hoses that attached themselves to our veins and shining disks that rested against our bare chests and there were probes that insinuated themselves deep into our vitals.

Warm fluids washed our bodies and a deep sense of identity filled our minds until it seemed as if we had always been a part of the Group. We were Kreels, of course, but we were a part of the Group. I know that seems startling to humans. What human thinks of his cattle as being a part of human life? You feed them and milk them and slaughter them and eat their flesh. They are a part of your life stream but you never think of them in this manner. It was not that way with Them. The Kreel were a part of Them, to be nourished and cherished and brought into the totality of the Group and all the while ... harvested.

We were aware of the life of the ship and of the beings in the ship, of our fellows who had been brought into the ship and, as time went on, of the others who had been gathered from a hundred distant worlds. We were aware too of the flickering life force of those who could not adapt to these alien conditions and we mourned them as they slowly and quietly expired. I can remember the regret when I felt my father cease to be and soon after that my mother. It was that way with most of the adults and They silently resolved among themselves that They would not try again with adults of our species. We felt Their regret and at the time we forgave Them for it, we were so completely immersed in Their group thinking. Later our hate vied within us with the love we had learned in being close to Them.

The ship returned to space and held communion with the other ships and with the great craft that bore the major part of their race. In my crystal crysalis I could look out with my other senses and see Them moving through dimly lighted passages. I could feel the moist warmth that They needed to survive and smell the mustiness of Their nests and the acrid formaldehyde smell of Their bodies as They touched and talked and stroked each other in a peculiar mixture of communication and empathy.

More than this I and those that survived began to see through Their eyes. We began to understand the way the world and the universe was put together, see the discrete fine points of structure that human eyes and human minds can never comprehend. We watched the use They made of Their own internal energies to move the ships through space and we learned Their ways of manipulating matter and energy. All this while we were being groomed for Their cattle.

(That's sickening. Do you remember what the boarding party reported? The place stank like a sewer. I suppose our smell must be as repellant to Them but it must have been pretty horrible. If it had not been for Martin, They might have continued gathering Their Kreel and multiplied.)

No, that was not Their purpose. They were a static race waiting only for a chance to find an unoccupied home. They were no menace to us at the time. Only Their way of seeing the universe, Their ideas on community and the individual –

(I tell you, we'd better edit this tape. An Inquisitor will have our hides. No one dares think this way, not and come out with a whole mind ... What? ... Well, how do I know how to conceal the editing? I've never dared conceal anything in my life. I suppose we take our chances. God, how did I get this assignment?)

There came a time when my mind saw that I had changed and that the others about me had changed. It was a subtle physical change in which certain enzymes had been modified. I learned later from a mind I probed that the enclase in the citric acid cycle had been modified and that the muscle phosphorylase too had changed so that the energy source was not now dextrose from the muscle glycogen but a seven-member sugar, a glucoheptose. This was necessary so that the product of the digestive tract should include excreted pentoses. They needed five carbon sugars for sustenance of Their bodies and that was the purpose of the Kreel.

Long ago, native Kreel on Their home planet had provided these but most of the native Kreel had perished in the great disaster. It was a savage thing that destroyed Their world, a great and consuming menace beyond belief. They could not fight it. They could only flee. Fortunately They had learned enough of alien biochemistries during Their space colonization efforts in Their own system to modify warm-blooded creatures. They were assured forever of a source of Their needed food, just so long as They could find creatures with the proper muscle starches and the proper enzyme systems for modification.

They had observed the change Themselves. They came to the deep hold where we lay in our crystal containers and They roused us. They were gentle and considerate and when They discovered that some of us had not survived, I could sense Their regret. They seemed not at all disturbed at the sight of corruption in those who had died and They went about the simple business of disposing of the decaying bodies. The decay was too advanced in some of them to serve in food but in others the tissues were relatively fresh and they were returned to the food stores of the ship.

(Disgusting. Yet he seemed completely unaffected by such savagery. There's no question about his complete withdrawal from reality.)

Reality? What is reality? What do you know of reality? You presume that you cannot know the world except through your senses and you admit that your senses are limited. Even in the visible spectrum in which your eyes work, your perception is statistical rather than detailed. Your optic nerves do not even report their statistical data directly but operate as a somatic sensor on a part of your brain that generates random visual images. You can only perceive in terms of the impulses your own brain generates. Yet you fall into the trap of believing that you perceive reality.

(Nonsense, of course. A systematic delusion. I suppose extended contact with such alien minds would affect any human that way.)

You even assume that I am human.

(Again the pattern of systematic delusion. Can we trust any data we get from him? How do we separate fantasy and fact? We have to know. The other ships still exist and we have to know the degree of menace from them. God, to have these things descend upon the earth and turn it into Their feeding ground.)

It was not as horrible as all that. There was a kind of oneness in being a part of the Group, the sort of thing that humans have been seeking all of their lives. Your philosophers talk of individuality and the concept of man himself as the measure of all things. Yet you spend all of your lives trying to find an identity in a great group of men. Your whole present society is directed to that end. You preach freedom and submit to a monolithic state that leaves you in constant terror that you may deviate. Didn't I hear you speak fearfully earlier of an inquisitor? What are you afraid of? That you may stray from the narrow prescribed paths of thinking? Yet all of you have given your freedom of action and decision to this system. What are you afraid of? That you may find the kind of identity that I found?

(My God, now we're in for it. They'll monitor this examination room within the next twenty-four hours, perhaps sooner since they know we have him here. What will happen? They certainly can't allow him to live and contaminate others. They'll have to do something about us. Contamination of ideas, that's a sure ticket to the inquisitor.)

It was truly easy to fit into the life of the ship. They took me from the hold and we went through narrow passages that glowed with a soft ruby fire in their depths. Although They were very tall, They were extremely thin and the passages were narrow for my body. I had grown in the crysalis so that my shoulders and my chest filled the passage and in several turns I came close to being wedged tightly. Somehow I managed, for this was my clear duty – to follow Them and take my place in the vast masses of Kreel that fed in the depths of the ship and generated the sustenance for Them.

The quarters were extensive and complex like the branching alveoli of a mammalian lung. There were thousands of us, each filling his small compartment. We exercised daily so that our muscles would not atrophy, going through complex muscle-flexing motions in place as the Keepers directed us. The Keepers were a special part of Their social organization and They made sure of the health of the herds. We were fed a complex mixture high in partly-hydrolyzed cellulose and containing the nitrogen sources and the unsaturated sources we need for our health. We could manufacture all of the essential amino acids in our own body, a vast improvement over basic human biochemistry. Vitamins too we could manufacture and the only limitation was that we needed a source of unsaturated carbon chains. Our bodies could, only under limited circumstances, produce an unsaturated oil.

There were seven of us who survived the colony and we now became a part of the complex food chain of the group. We ate and we slept, and more than this, we thought. We extended our consciousness and we merged with Them. During certain regular period the Keepers came among us and tended to us. This was the most remarkable period of rapport. The Keepers were gentle and concerned and when they stroked us with their minds and touched us physically we gave up the exudate that sustained

91

them. There was no bulk to our diet other than the bulk of the excreted pentoses and certain subsidiary material developed by bacteria we harbored in our bodies. We became for them superior manufacturers of food – highly efficient. The only waste products in the cycle were those substances that went to sustain our own bodies and the carbon dioxide and water we expelled from our own metabolism.

(I think I'm going to be ill. Like ants milking aphids. Yet he seems pleased at the idea. Contented, even exalted at the concept.)

Exalted? Why not? You're struggling with an earlier concept. The substances your body discards are corrupt, useless – mere waste materials. Our bodies had become ordered to a different existence. Even the wastes of our bodies had a purpose. The water replenished the sores of the ship. The carbon-dioxide nourished the complex plants that provided the cellulose of our fodder. It was a true and lasting symbiosis.

The sybiosis of self, the emotional content of mind-to-mind contact was deeply satisfying. It was during this period that we seven discovered that there was, however, a difference. For Them the contact was one of emotional empathy; for us it was deeper wth a clearer semantic content. I suppose this was only natural when we consider why our parents took us from human society and brought us to the colony in the north.

(Now it comes out. The older records aren't clear. After all it was a hundred years ago that they left human society. Perhaps his alienness is not strictly the product of the creatures. Is it possible . . .?)

It's possible that this is why we left, that we differed so much in the function of our minds from our fellow humans. I remember that the contact and the emotional feeling I had for Mother and Father was one-sided. I could receive and send but they could only send. Still they knew that this was the way it should be and all the children that my father had gathered together knew that this was the way it should be. I suppose it was this special difference that allowed us to learn from Them and eventually to surpass Them.

This idyllic existence continued for what may have been months or even years. All the while Their ships marshalled outside the earth for the next great jump to another system. They knew that They could acquire more Kreels on earth but Their morality would not let Them subject an alien race to Their domination, benevolent as it might have been. That was a remarkable thing about Them: They respected the right of the separate races to work out their own destinies even though They might recruit individual members of the race. They had a concept of racial unity but no real understanding of individuality. Anymore than do you and the race of men as it has become.

(More treason. We'll never survive this session. They'll take us and remove the contamination and reintegrate us. You know what reintegration can mean?)

Among us evolved a new concept. It was my mind that first verbalized it but it was a product of our group thinking. We recognized that we had derived a special insight from Them that They Themselves were not aware of. They could see the universe on a pragmatic statistical level and more deeply They could see the fine structure of the universe, the detailed interactions that made up the statistical structure of Their senses. In a limited way this allowed Them to manipulate discrete sections of the universe in a manner that humans cannot. It's very much like the difference between humans who perceive the coming of the seasons and try to manipulate the phenomena with crude methods of cloud seeding and those humans who have learned to feed heat into the upper air streams and modify the climate of a whole subcontinent. It was that way with us. Through Them we saw the mechanism. We learned through our own differences to see and feel and move the factors that They saw. It came to me and the others that we were superior to Them.

It became a logical consequence of this that we could not share our existence further with Them. We would contaminate Them and destroy Their perfect society that had remained in dynamic stasis for eons. We had to leave.

Imagine cows taking over the farm? We became just that. In one period of ten hours we became the masters of the ship.

The effect was subtle. We could not invade and control Their minds. Indeed this would have been against our sensitivities. To sense, to participate in Their existence, to feel as They felt and see as They saw – this was permissible. To reach and control Them – this was as repugnant to us as it is natural to you. The difference is that our control would have been far more complete than your puny masters have ever achieved.

Rather we altered the operation of the ship. Here the inductance of an electrical circuit changed as we reached out and altered the conductivity of a coil or deepened the penetration of a magnetic field. There the mean-free-path of the electrons in a beam changed, enlarged as we interfered with the statistical randomness of the particals. Ion exchange rates in the depths of the chemical reservoirs speeded, in some cases even changed chemical order. The ship foundered, lost power and had to land.

It left the others and directed itself into the planetary atmosphere. It came down in a low sweeping approach while we perceived the radar beams scanning it and altered the information that they sent back. There must have been a great deal of panic since anything unknown in your culture is automatically a menace. You have lived so long in fear and the repression of the discipline that is supposed to meet that fear. Would you be surprised if I told you that there is no enemy? Unless Their survivors now see *us* as an enemy.

(Damn it. I'd sooner destroy the tape and take the punishment for that than face the Inquisitor after this. Kill him and destroy the tapes and take our chances. Surely you see that's the answer? ... What kind of nonsense is this – this thing a godsend? An answer to our problems? What problems? We have a perfect society, well ordered. We have no problems. Do we?)

The ship landed somewhere on the east coast of your continent. Amid mountains lightly frosted with the first snows of winter. They had once been beautiful if the memories of my father were correct but the pines and the soft scattering of underbrush had been stripped, leaving them bare and cold and the mountain streams diverted to concrete reservoirs. The only area that remained remotely like the natural condition of the land was that around the last stronghold of the aborigines. It was a place they called Cherokee and in the final battle with the intrusive conquerors they had somehow managed to stand fast and preserve the integrity of their land. Since you could not control them, you at least respected their treaty.

The ship landed in the smoky morning that crouched over the mountains and we waited for the reaction. Throughout the ship there was confusion as They realized that something had happened, that They no longer controlled the workings of Their machines. Then we left our chambers and moved painfully through the ship, passing Them as They stood. It was only just that we spare Them the horror of our going. We did certain things that freed unbound electrons in Their nervous systems and gave Them a pleasant passive sleep. Nothing was lost in the Group and though many weaker ones died in that physical existence, They continued to live in the broader consciousness of the Group, such is the unity of Their group mind. So you see it did not violate our morality or Theirs or even yours as you pretend it to be. It did not occur to me at the time that there was a simpler way.

(I'm getting a signal. Interrogation! Answer it, answer it before they check down here. The tape will be monitored soon enough. They report an inquiry. Our methods are the ones prescribed. A deviation? My sanity is as complete as any member of the staff. How can they say that it is not, how can my anointed superiors even think of sending me to the Fields? They'll come now. Perhaps we can complete the task and they'll be lenient. After all such complete devotion to duty to the sacrifice of self. Isn't that what they want? Activate the lock. Let them try to come in. We'll finish yet.)

It was only a matter of time before you found us. We knew that and we had decided that this was what we wanted. We spread among the community and we became a part of them, sharing in their consciousness and directing them in their total integration. It became obvious at that point that we had a mission and that it had certain evolutionary stages. This was the first and I admit that it was largely experimental. There was a special in-group empathy among them. After all, they had their tribal traditions and, through years of menace and social attack, they had integrated their group personality on a level that we could perceive and understand. This is the natural evolution of men and truly their one salvation in the total hostile universe.

(Of course, he would choose the village. We banished all of the Indians to that area long ago. What else could we do with them when their racial biochemistry prevents them from adjusting?)

(We should have destroyed them. Why should the Holy State allow them to exist unconditioned? They remain always a menace, just as long as their systems reject the Mettler serum that has brought peace and prosperity to our world.)

(But he and the other children did something to the villagers. We know that. It was like a mass schizophrenia, almost as if he had freed two personalities in every villager. What did they do

... and why?)

In the end we were one and we learned. The ship lay in the valley, canted where it had landed and They dreamed, at least the ones who had not died. We knew that They would not awake until we decided They would. It became apparent that we could not allow this, as much as we loved Them. We hated Them too but that was a different emotion, one derived from our memory of what They had done to our parents. That we learned to live with. The conflict was not as great as you might suppose.

Where They had changed us, we now changed ourselves. Where we now changed ourselves, we changed the people of the village. Again it was an experiment because we were still learning. There were failures, of course, and we were sorry for that. Still we learned in the weeks before you finally found us. We perfected our skills and when we perceived that you had located us and were coming in all the primitive vitality of your force, we were ready.

It was remarkable to see the primitive joy with which your people attacked Them. The ship could have defended itself, of course, but They were not aware that you were attacking. We did certain things to make it appear that They were in control. Your weapons blasted whole masses of the mountain down on Them. Your beams traced fiery lines through the rock that ran molten. It was a thrilling and primitive sight. Then when it appeared to you that the ship was inactivated, your teams blasted a hole in it and entered it and found Them and the Kreels. All of the Kreels were alien to your sight, and They filled you with loathing and disgust – poor creatures – and you killed Them.

We hated to see that but we had agreed by this time that certain sacrifices were necessary so that we might easily enter your society. Our hosts quite unconsciously helped us. When you came into the village you found us, apparently helpless and being cared for by the people. They seemed normal and concerned and they invoked the treaty so that you could not interrogate them. In the end you decided to take us away and care for us. Only we knew that you would do more, that you would try to find out about Them and how we had come to be with Them.

(*Open the door!*)

(No, we haven't finished yet. There's still much to learn.)

96

(This is the staff inquisitor. You are in open violation of the prime security directive. Open the door or suffer the consequences.)

Open the door. It makes no matter. At this point I will pass from the room and you will have no further need of me. You have learned all that I can give you at the moment.

(What do you mean? We have a great deal to learn yet, don't we?)

(Who's in there? Who are you talking to?)

(Shall we open the door? Of course, it's the only sensible thing.)

I'm sorry but this was the next step in learning. I had to learn from you while you learned from me. Out of that I can perceive the nature of my need.

(Need, what need?)

We all have a need and I have a need now that I am whole. I will go now and begin the work that you have shown me. Out of this will come something quite different. A natural part of human evolution when you stop and think about it.

(Open the door. I am the Inquisitor Jarvis. What are you doing with the subject, Citizen Interrogator? There at last. You were wise not to block the door further.)

(We were trying to carry out our assignment. We were interrogating the patient under deep narcohypnosis.)

It doesn't matter. We will all leave now and go about our task. Forgive me for deceiving you. I have left you with one gift. A unity with yourself, an ability to commune with that part of you that is forever submerged in human beings, the very gift we gave the villagers.

(There is no one here, citizen. What have you been up to?)

(We have been interrogating the patient, Inquisitor Jarvis.)

(We? We? What are you talking about? The door register shows only one occupancy. What are you trying to conceal from the Holy State? You are the only one here. You've been the only one here for the past three hours.)

(We're both here. Can't you see us. Please, can't you see us? Can't you see us? Can't you see us?)

Anne McCaffrey

PRELUDE TO A CRYSTAL SONG

Killashandra listened, the words like cold bombs dropping with leaden fatality into her frozen guts. She stared at the Maestro's famous profile as his lips opened and shut around the words that meant the death of all her hopes and ambitions, and rendered wasted ten years of hard work and study.

The Maestro finally turned to face her. The genuine regret in his expressive eyes made him look older as the heavy singer's muscles in his jaw relaxed sorrowfully into jowls.

One day Killashandra might remember those details. Now she was too crushed by this overwhelming defeat to be aware of more than her terrible personal failure.

'But ... but ... how *could* you?'

'How could I what?' the Maestro asked in surprise.

'How could you lead me on?'

'Lead you on? But, my dear girl, I didn't.'

'You did! You said ... you said all I needed was hard work and haven't I worked hard?'

'Of course you have worked hard.' Valdi was affronted. 'My students must apply themselves. It takes years of hard work to develop the voice, to learn a repertoire of even a segment of the outworld music that must be performed ...'

'I've the repertoire? I've worked hard and now ... *now* you tell me I've no voice?'

Maestro Valdi sighed heavily, a mannerism which had always irritated Killashandra and was insupportable in this instance. She opened her mouth to protest but he raised a restraining hand. The habit of four years made her pause.

'You haven't the voice to be a *top-rank* singer, my dear Killashandra, but that does not preclude any of the many other responsible and fulfilling ...'

'I won't be second-rank. I want ... I *wanted*' – and she had the satisfaction of seeing him wince at the bitterness in her voice – 'to be a top-rank concert singer. You said I had –'

He held up his hand again. 'You have the gift of perfect pitch, your musicality is faultless, your memory superb, your dramatic potential can't be criticized. But there is that burr in your voice which becomes intolerable in the higher register. While I *thought* it could be trained out, modified ...' he shrugged his helplessness. He eyed her sternly. 'Today's audition with completely impartial judges proved conclusively that the flaw is inherent in the voice. This moment is cruel for you and not particularly pleasant for me.' He gave her another quelling look for the rebellion in her manner. 'I make few errors in judgement as to voice. I honestly thought I could help you. I cannot and it would be doubly cruel of me to encourage you to go further as a soloist. No. You had best strengthen another facet of your potential.'

'And what, in your judgement,' demanded Killashandra in a voice so tight that her throat ached, 'would that be?'

He had the grace to blink at her caustic tone but he looked her squarely in the eye.

'You don't have the patience and temperament to teach, but you could do very well in one of the allied theater arts where your sympathy with the problems of a singer would stand you in good stead. No? You are a trained synthesizer? Hmmm. Too bad, your musical education would be a real asset there.' He paused, had a thought and dismissed it. 'Well then, I'd recommend you leave the theater arts entirely. With your sense of pitch you could be a crystal tuner, or an aircraft and shuttle dispatcher.'

'Thank you, Maestro,' she said, more from force of habit than any real gratitude. She gave him the half bow his rank required and withdrew. She did slam the panel shut behind her and stalked down the corridor, blinded by the tears she'd been too proud to shed. She half wanted and half feared to meet some other student who would question her tears, commiserate with her disaster, but was inordinately grateful when she reached the door of her study cubicle without encountering anyone. There she gave herself up to her misery, bawling into hysteria, past choking, until she was too spent to do more than breathe.

If her body protested the emotional excess, her mind reveled in it. For she'd been abused, misused, misguided, misdirected. And who knows how many of her peers had been secretly laughing at her for her dreams of glorious triumphs on the concert and opera stage. Killashandra had a generous portion of the conceit and ego required for her chosen profession, with no leavening dollop of humility: she'd felt her success and stellar-dom only a matter of time. Now she cringed against the panoramic memories of her self-assertiveness and arrogance, hugging her fractured, deflated self as she recalled the agony of that audition this morning. She had approached it with such confidence, so sure of receiving the necessary commendations to continue as a solo-aspirant. She remembered the faces of the examiners, so pleasantly composed – one man nodding absent-mindedly to the pulse of the test arias and lieder. She knew she'd been scrupulous in tempi – they'd marked her high on that. How could they have looked so – so impressed? So encouraging? She wanted to erase the morning's fiasco completely from her memory!

How could they record such verdicts against her? 'The voice is unsuited to the dynamics of opera; unpleasant burr too audible.' 'A good instrument for singing with orchestra and chorus where grating overtone will not be noticeable.' 'Strong choral leader quality: student should be positively dissuaded from solo work.'

The judgements burned in her mind, abrading the tortured strands of her ego and shattered aspirations.

Unfair! Unfair! How could she be allowed to come so far, be permitted to delude herself, only to be dashed down in the penultimate trial? And to be offered, as a sop, choral leadership? How degradingly ignominious!

Wiggling up out of her excruciating memories were the faces of brothers and sisters, taunting her for 'shrieking at the top of her lungs.' Teasing her for the hours she spent pounding out finger exercises and attempting to 'understand' some of the weird harmonics of off-world music. Her parents had surrendered to her choice of profession because it was, for starters, financed by the planetary educational system; secondly, it might accrue to their own standing in the community; and thirdly, she seemed to have the encouragement of her early voice teachers. Them! Was it to the ineptitude of one of those clods that she owed the flaw in her voice? A mishandling in the fragile early stages of training? Killashandra rolled in an agony of self-pitying memories.

Then she realized that it was self-pity and sat bolt upright in the chair, staring at herself in the mirror on the far wall, the mirror which had reflected all those long hours of study and self-perfection ... Self-deception.

What was it Valdi'd had the temerity to suggest? An allied art? A synthesizer? Bah! Spending her life catering to flawed minds in mental institutions because she had a flawed voice? Or mending flawed crystals to keep interplanetary travel or someone's power plant flowing smoothly?

All in an instant, Killashandra shook herself free of such wallowing self-indulgence. She looked around the study, a slice of a room with its musical scores neatly filed by the viewer, with the built-in keyboard and console that tapped the orchestral banks of the Music Center for any aria or song ever composed. She glanced over the repros of training performances – she'd always had a lead role – and she knew that she'd do best to forget the whole damned thing! If she couldn't be top rank, the hell with the theater arts! She'd be top in whatever she did or die in the attempt.

She stood up. There was nothing for her now in a room that three hours before had been the focal point of every waking minute and all her energies. Whatever personal items were in the drawer or shelves, the prize certificates on the wall, the signed repros of singers she'd hoped to emulate or excel, no longer concerned nor belonged to her.

She reached for her coat, ripped off the student badge and threw the cloak across her shoulders. She remembered, hand on panel, that she'd better take her credit plate with her. As she fumbled in the slip drawer for it, she saw the notation on her engagement pad.

'Party at Rory's to celebrate!'

She snorted. They'd all know. Let them chortle over her downfall. She'd not play the bravely-smiling-courageous-under-adversity role tonight. Or ever.

Exit Killashandra, quietly, stage center, she said to herself as she ran down the long shallow flight of steps to the Mall in front of the Culture Center. Again she experienced both satisfaction and regret that no one witnessed her departure.

Actually she couldn't have asked for a more dramatic exit. They'd wonder this evening what had happened. Maybe someone would know ... someone always did know even the most confidential things about fellow students. She knew that Valdi would never talk ... not about his failures, or anyone else's. They'd not know from him. And the verdict of the examiners

101

would be classified in the computer; but someone would 'know' that Killashandra Ree had failed her vocal finals, and what the grounds for the failure were. In the meantime, she would have effectively disappeared and they could speculate. They'd remember, when she rose to prominence in another field. Then they'd marvel that nothing could suppress the excellence in her.

These reflections consoled Killashandra all the way to her lodgings. Students rated supported dwellings: no more the terrible bohemian semi-filth and overcrowding of old, but her room was hardly palatial. After she had failed to re-register at the Music Center, her landlady would be notified and the room locked to her. Subsistence living was abhorrent to Killashandra: it suggested an inability to achieve. But she'd take the initiative on that too. Therefore leave the room now. And all the memories it held.

Also, it would spoil her mysterious disappearance if she were to be 'discovered moping in her digs.' So, with a brief nod to the landlady who always checked comings and goings, Killashandra ascended to her floor, keyed open her room and looked around it. Really nothing here to take but clothing. Despite that decision, Killashandra packed the lute which she had handcrafted to satisfy that requirement of her profession. She couldn't bear to play it but she also couldn't abandon it. Clothes in carisak, lute in case, she left the key in the lock. She nodded to the landlady just as she always did and exited.

Having fulfilled the dramatic requirement of her assumed role, she now didn't have an earthly idea what to do with herself. She skipped onto the fast belt of the pedestrian way, heading into the center of the city. She ought to register with a work bureau, she ought to apply for subsistence. She ought to do many things but suddenly Killashandra discovered that 'ought to' no longer ruled her. No more tedious commitments to schedule, to rehearsals, to lessons, to study, to any of her so-called friends and associates. She was free, utterly and completely free, with a lifetime ahead of her that ought to be filled. Ought to? With what?

The walkway was whipping her rapidly into the busier commercial stations of the city. Pedestrian directions flashed at cross-points: mercantile purple crossed with social services' orange: green manufactory and dormitory blue-hatching; medical green-red stripes and then airport red and spaceport star-spangled blue.

Killashandra was enmeshed by indecision. And while she toyed with the variety of things she ought to do, she was carried past the crosspoints that would take her where she ought to go.

Ought to, again, she thought. And stayed on the speed-way. Half of Killashandra was amused that she, once so certain of her goal, could be so irresolute. It did not, at that moment, occur to her that she was suffering an intense, traumatic shock. Nor that she was reacting to that shock, first in a somewhat immature fashion with her abrupt withdrawal from the abortive sphere of interest; secondly in a mature one, as she divorced herself from the indulgence of self-pity and began a positive search for an alternative life.

She couldn't know that Esmond Valdi was concerned about her, realizing that the girl would be reacting in some fashion to the death of her ambition. She might have thought more kindly of him had she known, though he hadn't pursued her further than her study or do more than call to the Personnel Section to report his concern for her. He'd taken the comfortable conclusion that she was in some other student's room, having a good cry. Knowing her dedication to music, he'd come to the equally incorrect assumption that she'd undoubtedly continue in music, accepting a choral leadership in due time. That's where he wanted her. It simply didn't occur to him that Killashandra would be able to discard ten years of intensive training in one split second. He would not have done so, faced with her decision. He'd have been shocked if he'd known how completely she was to reject all references to those ten years.

Killashandra was halfway to the spaceport before she came to the decision that that was where she ought to go. 'Ought,' this time not in an obligatory but in an investigative sense.

This planet held nothing but distressing memories for her. She'd leave it and erase all vestiges of its painful associations, domestic and career. Good thing she had the lute. She had sufficient training credentials to go along as a casual entertainer on some liner at the best, or as a crystal tuner at the worst. She might as well travel about a bit to see what else she 'ought' to do with her life *now*.

The 'now' both exacerbated and amused her until the speed-way slowed to run into the spaceport terminal. For the first time since he'd left Maestro Valdi's studio, Killashandra was aware of externals – people and things.

Come to think of it, she'd never actually been to the starburst-design spaceport. She'd never been on any of the welcoming committees for off-planet Stellars. A shuttle took off from its bay, its powerful plasma engines making the port buildings rumble. There was, however, a very disconcerting whine that she was subsonically aware of, feeling it down the mastoid bone right to her heel. She shook her head. The whine intensified – it must have to do with the shuttle – until she had to clamp her hands over her ears to cut the irritation. The sonics abated and she forgot the incident, wandering around the immense, bubble-domed reception hall of the port facility. Consoles were ranked across the inner wall, each one labeled with the name of the freight or passenger service, each with its screen plate. *Faraway places with strange sounding names:* an ancient fragment of song obtruded and was suppressed. No more music.

She paused at a portal to watch a shuttle off-loading cargo, the dockmen working with aircushions to remove odd-sized packages which had traveled by drone from who-knew-where in the galaxy. A supercargo was scurrying about, checking numbers against the arm-computer he wore, juggling weigh-units and arguing with the dockees. He was a bustling portentous man, utterly involved in his lot of life. Killashandra snorted. She'd have more than such trivia to occupy her energies. In the process of inhaling, she caught the whiff of appetising odors not entirely cleansed from the air.

She was hungry! Hungry? When her whole life had been shattered? How banal! But the odors made her salivate. Well, her credit plate ought to be good for a meal. She'd better check the balance lest she be embarrassed if the plate was spewed back out in the restaurant check-desk.

She slapped the credit plate into one of the many public outlets in the reception hall and was agreeably surprised to see that there'd been a credit that very day. A student credit she was forced to notice. Her last one. The fact that the total represented a bonus did not please her. A bonus to signalize the fact that she could never be a soloist?

She walked quickly to the nearest restaurant, noticing that it was not an economy establishment. The old, dutiful Killashandra would have backed out hastily. The new Killashandra entered imperiously.

At this hour the place was uncrowded so she took a booth

on the upper level by the viewplate so she could watch the flow of shuttle and small space craft. She'd never realized how much traffic passed through the space port of her not very important planet. She had heard it was a change-over point. She ate, with relish and appetite, of some piscine casserole purportedly composed of off-world fish. Exotic but not too highly spiced for a student's untutored palate. An off-world wine included in the selection pleased her so much that she ordered a second carafe just as dusk closed in on the planet.

She thought at first it was the unfamiliar wine that made her nerves jangle so. But the discomfort increased so rapidly that it couldn't be the effect of the alcohol. She looked around for the source of irritation, rubbing her neck and frowning. She shook her head and then, with the appearance of a descending shuttle's retro-blasts, realized that it must be a sonic disturbance – though how it could penetrate the shielded restaurant she didn't know. She had to cover her ears, pressing as hard as she could against her skull, but there seemed to be no escape from that piercing ache. When she thought she couldn't bear the agony a second longer, it ceased.

'I tell you, that shuttle drive's about to explode,' a man's baritone voice cried in the ensuing quiet.

Killasandra looked round, startled.

'How do I know? I know!' A tall man was arguing with the human attendant of the restaurant and trying to get to the comunit which the attendant was covering with his body. 'Let me speak to the control tower. Is everyone deaf up there? Let me at the unit, man. Do you want a shuttle explosion? Are you deaf that you can't hear it?'

'I heard it,' Killashandra said, rushing over to the pair. Any action might relieve the itch which had replaced the agony in her skull.

'You heard it, miss?' The attendant was genuinely surprised.

'I certainly did. All but cracked my skull wide open. What was it?' she asked the tall man. He had an air of command about him, frustrated at the moment by the officiousness of the stupid attendant. He carried his overlean body with a haughty arrogance that went with the fine fabric of his clothes, obviously of an off-world design and texture.

'She heard it, too. Now get that control tower, man.'

'Really, sir. We have the most explicit orders –'

'Don't be a complete sub,' Killashandra said insultingly and gestured with operatic imperiousness at the console. 'He obviously knows what he's talking about!'

The fact that she was obviously a Fuertan like himself did more to persuade him than the insult but he was still reluctant until the man, ripping off an off-world oath as colorful as it was descriptive of bureaucratic stupidities, flipped open his card case. Whatever identification he showed made the attendant's eyes bug out and his fingers dash out a call code on the comunit.

'I'm sorry, sir. I didn't know, sir. Here you are, sir.' There was awe and a certain amount of fear in his manner.

The off-worlder ignored his reaction. 'Control? That shuttle which just landed? It can't be permitted to take off. Crystal drive's gone sour. Must be recut or you'll have an – No, this is not a drunk and this is not a threat. It's a fact. Why that shuttle pilot didn't insist on a hold, I can't guess, but he must be deaf! Of course I know what I'm talking about! For the sake of whatever gods this mudball worships, don't send that shuttle off again! What do you want, a drive check or a blasted port facility? Is this shuttlestop of a world too poor to employ a crystal tuner?'

The console muttered something back to him but, like all public facilities, the audio was shielded from anyone not in its direct line.

'Well, now that's a more reasonable attitude,' the man said. 'As to my credentials, I'm Carrik of the Heptite Guild. Yes, that's what I said. And I could hear the crystal whine right through the walls so I know farging well how bad the drive is.' Another pause. 'Thanks, but I've paid my bill already. No, that's all right. Yes ...' and Killashandra could see that the gratitude irritated Carrik. 'Oh, as you will.' He stepped back, jerking his head for the attendant to take his place at the unit.

'And make that for two,' Carrik said over his shoulder at the man, as he cupped his hands under Killashandra's elbow and led her to a secluded booth.

'I've a bottle of wine over there,' she said, half-protesting, half-laughing at his peremptory escort.

'You'll have better shortly. I'm Carrik and you're ...'

'Killashandra Ree.'

He smiled, gray eyes lighting briefly with surprise. 'That's a lovely name.'

'Oh, come now. Surely you can do better than that?'

106

He laughed, absently blotting the sweat on his forehead and upper lip as he slid into his place.

'I could and I will but it still is a lovely name. A musical one. What did I say wrong?'

'Nothing. Nothing.'

He gave her a skeptical look for that insincere disclaimer just as the attendant came bustling up with a chilled bottle, bowing as he offered it.

Carrik peered at the label. 'I'd prefer the '72 and ... some Forellan biscuits, if you have them? Good, and Aldebaran paste? Hmmm. Well, I'll revise my opinion of Fuerte.'

'Really, I only just finished ...' Killashandra began.

'On the contrary, my dear Killashandra Ree, you've only just started.'

'Oh?' Any one of Killashandra's former associates would have modified his attitude at that tone in her voice.

'Yes,' Carrik continued blithely, a sparkling challenge in his eyes, 'for this is a night for feasting and frolicking – on the management, as it were. Having just saved the facility from being leveled, my wish – and yours – is their command. They'll be more grateful,' he continued in a droller tone, 'when they take that drive down and see the cracks in the crystals. Off the true by a hundred vibes at least.'

Her half-formed intention of making a dignified exit died and she stared at Carrik. It took a highly trained ear to have caught that variation in pitch.

'Off a hundred vibes ...? What do you mean? Are you a musician?'

Carrik stared at her as if she ought to know who, or what, he was. He looked to see where the attendant was and then, leaning indolently back in the seat, smiled at her in an enigmatic fashion.

'Yes, I think you'd say I was a musician. Are you?'

'Not anymore,' Killashandra replied in a caustic tone. Her desire to leave returned with irresistible intensity. She'd been able for a very short time to forget why she was at a spaceport. He'd reminded her and she wanted no more such reminders.

His hand, fingers gripping hard into the flesh of her arm, held her in her seat. The attendant came bursting back with another chilled bottle which Carrik accepted and gestured him to pour. Carrik smiled at Killashandra, half daring her to contest his restraint in front of the attendant. Despite herself,

Killashandra discovered she couldn't start a scene and she'd no real grounds – yet – for a personal-liberty-infringements charge. He grinned at her, knowing her dilemma, and had the audacity to give her a semi-insolent toast as he took the traditional sample sip of the wine.

'Yes, an excellent vintage. How long must we wait for the paste and biscuits?'

'A few moments, sir. We're warming the biscuits. They take the paste so much better then.'

'At least they know how to serve it properly,' Carrik told Killashandra in a patronizingly blasé tone.

The attendant who would have screamed insult at any other time bowed and smiled at Carrik and scurried away for the delicacies.

'How do you get away with that?' Killashandra asked Carrik.

He smiled. 'Try the wine, Killashandra.' And his smile suggested that this was going to be a long evening and the prelude to an intimate association.

In protest Killashandra stood up, but she sat down again immediately, very hard, an action imposed on her by Carrik whose eyes glittered with anger and amusement.

'Who are you?' she demanded, angry now.

'I'm Carrik of the Heptite Guild,' he repeated cryptically.

'And that gives you the right to infringe on my personal freedom?'

'It does if you heard that crystal whine.'

'How do you construe that?'

'Try the wine first, Killashandra Ree. Surely your throat must be dry and I imagine you've got a skull ache from that subsonic torture. That would account for your shrewish temper.'

Actually she did have a pain in her head. The sudden re-seating had made that obvious. He was right about her dry throat ... and about her shrewish temper. But he'd modified that criticism by stroking her hand caressingly.

'I must apologize for my bad manners,' he said without genuine remorse but with a charming smile. 'That crystal whine is so unnerving. It brings out the worst in us.'

She nodded as she sipped the wine. It was fantastic. She looked at him with delight and pleasure. He patted her arm again and gestured her to drink more.

'Who are you, Carrik of the Heptite Guild, that port authorities listen and control towers order exorbitant delicacies in gratitude?'

'You don't really know?'

'I wouldn't ask if I did know,' she said with a show of her characteristic acerbity.

'Where have you been all your life that you've never heard of the Heptite Guild?'

'I've been studying music in Fuerte,' she said, spitting out the words.

'You wouldn't, by any chance, have *perfect* pitch?' The question, both unexpected and too casually said, caught her halfway into a foul temper.

'Yes, I do but I don't –'

His face which was not unattractive in its most supercilious expressions became almost radiant with unfeigned elation.

'What fantastic luck! I shall have to tip the agent who ticketed me here! Why this is unbelievable luck ...'

'Luck? If you knew why I was here –'

'I don't care *why*. You are and I am.' He took both her hands and seemed to devour her face with his eyes, grinning with such intense joy she found herself embarrassingly smiling back.

'Oh, luck indeed, my dear girl. Fate, destiny, Karma, Lequol, Fidalkoram, whatever you care to call this coincidence of our life lines, I ought to order bottles of this wine for that lousy shuttle pilot for letting his crystals sour.'

'I don't know what you're ranting about, Carrik of Heptite,' Killashandra said, but she was not impervious to the compliments or the charm he exuded. She knew that she tended to put men off by her self-assurance and here was a well-traveled off-worlder, a man of obvious rank and position, genuinely taken with her, however inexplicably.

'You don't?' He teased her for the banality of her protest and she closed her mouth on the rest of her customary rebuff. 'Seriously,' he went on, stroking the palms of her hands with his fingers as if to soothe the anger from her, 'have you never heard of crystal singers?'

'Crystal singers? Crystal tuners, yes.'

He dismissed tuners with a contemptuous flick of his fingers. 'Imagine singing a note, a pure clear C, and hearing it answered across an entire mountain range?'

She stared at him.

'Go up a third, or down, it makes no difference. Sing out and hear the harmony come back at you. A whole mountainside pitched to C, and another sheer wall of pink quartz echoing back in a dominant. Night brings out the minors, like an ache in your breast, the most beautiful pain in the world because the music of the crystal is in your bones, in your blood ...'

'You're mad!' Killashandra dug her fingers into his hands to shut off those words. They conjured too many painful associations. She simply had to forget all that. 'I hate music. I hate anything to do with music.'

He regarded her with disbelief for a moment and then, with an unexpected tenderness and concern reflected in his eyes, he put an arm around her shoulders and drew himself against her despite her resistance.

'My dear girl, what happened to you today?'

A moment before she would have swallowed glass shards rather than confide in anyone but the warmth in his voice, his solicitude, were so timely and unexpected that the whole of her personal disaster came tumbling out. He listened to every word, occasionally squeezing her hand with sympathetic understanding. But at the end of the recital, she was amazed to see the fullness in his eyes as tears threatened to embarrass her.

'My dear Killashandra, what can I say? There's no possible consolation for such a personal catastrophe as that! And there you were,' and his eyes were brilliant with what Killashandra chose to interpret as admiration, 'having a bottle of wine as coolly as a queen. Or,' and he leaned over her, grinning maliciously, 'were you just gathering enough courage to step under a shuttle?' He kept hold of her when she tried to free herself at his outrageous suggestion. 'No, I can see that suicide was furthest from *your* mind.' She subsided at that implicit compliment. 'Although,' and his expression altered thoughtfully, 'you might have inadvertently succeeded if that shuttle'd been allowed to take off again. If I hadn't been here to stop it ...' He flashed her that charmingly reprehensible smile of his.

'You're full of yourself, aren't you?' But her accusation was said in jest for she found his autocratic manner an irresistible contrast to anyone of her previous acquaintance.

He grinned unrepentantly and nodded towards the remains of their exotic snack, which the attendant had obsequiously deposited on the table at some point during Killashandra's tale.

'Not without justification, dear girl. But look, you're free of

110

any commitments right now, aren't you?' he asked, eagerly. When she hesitantly nodded, 'Or is there a friend you've been seeing?' He asked that almost savagely, as if he'd eliminate any rival immediately.

Later Killashandra might remember how adroitly Carrik had handled her, preying on her unsettled state of mind, on her essential femininity, but that tinge of jealousy was highly complimentary and the eagerness in his eyes, in his hands, was not feigned.

'No one to matter or miss me.'

Carrik looked so skeptical that she reminded him that she'd devoted all her energies to singing.

'Surely not all?' He mocked her for such dedication.

'No one to matter,' she repeated firmly.

'Then I will make an honest invitation to you. I'm off-world on holiday. I don't have to be back to the Guild till ... well,' and he gave a nonchalant shrug, 'when I wish. I've all the credits I need ... Help me spend them. It'll purge the music school from your system.'

She looked at him squarely, for their acquaintanceship was of so brief and hectic a duration she simply hadn't thought of him as a possible companion. She didn't quite trust him. She was both attracted and repelled by his domineering, high-handed ways and yet he presented a challenge to her. He was certainly the diametric opposite of the young men she'd encountered on Fuerte.

'We don't have to stay on this mudball either.'

'Why did you come?'

He laughed. 'I'm told I haven't been on Fuerte before. I can't say it lives up to it's name – or maybe you'll live up to the name for it? Oh come now, Killashandra,' he said when she bridled. 'Surely you've been jollied before? Or have music students changed so much since my day?'

'You studied music?'

An odd shadow flickered through his eyes. 'Probably. I don't rightly remember. Another time, another life perhaps.' Then his charming smile deepened, and a warmth came into his expression that she found rather unsettling. 'Tell me, what's on this planet that's fun to do?'

Killashandra considered for a moment and then blinked. 'You know, I haven't an earthly.'

'Then we'll find out together!'

111

What with the wine, his cajoling importunities, her own recklessness, Killashandra could not withstand his invitation. She ought to do so many things, she knew, but 'ought' got suspended someplace during the third bottle of that classic vintage. After spending the rest of the night in his arms in the most expensive accommodation of the spaceport hostelry, Killashandra decided that she'd suspend duty for a few days and be kind to the charming visitor.

The travel console popped out dozens of cards on the resort possibilities of Fuerte, more than she'd ever suspected the planet boasted. But then her means had been limited and so had her time. She'd never water-skiied so Carrik decided they'd both try that. He ordered a private skimmer to be ready within the hour. As he sang cheerily at the top of a dammed good bass voice, floundering in the elegant sunken bathtub of the suite, Killashandra recalled some vestige of self-preserving shrewdness and tapped out a few discreet inquiries on the console.

' "Crystal singer" – colloquial/universal euphemism for the members of the Heptite Guild, planet-based Ballybran, Regulus System, A-S-F/128/4. Ballybran crystals, vital to the production of coherent light, and as modules in tachyon drive components, are limited to the quartz mountains of Ballybran.' She skimmed the intricate geological assay. 'The cutting of Ballybran crystal is a highly skilled art and requires the inherent ability of perfect pitch. Crystal cutters are perforce members of the Heptite Guild which trains and maintains its applicants, exacting ten percent tithe from all working members. The current membership of the Guild is 425 but fluctuates considerably. Aspirants are advised that this profession is rated "highly dangerous" and the Heptite Guild is required to give full particulars of the dangers involved before contracting new members.'

Four hundred and twenty-five was an absurdly small membership for a universal Guild supplying an element essential to galactic intercourse, Killashandra thought. Most guilds ran to four hundred million on a universal basis. But that explained why Carrik had been insistent to know if she'd perfect pitch. 'Full particulars of the dangers involved' didn't dissuade Killashandra one iota. Danger was relative.

There was more to the print out, mainly about the type of crystal cut, the types of subsonic cutters especially developed to slice the living quartz from the mountains, technical information which was beyond Killashandra's musically oriented edu-

112

cation. She aborted the rest of that tape and asked for a check on Heptite Guildman Carrik. Anyone could pose as a member of a Guild – chancers often produced exquisitely forged documentation but a computer check could not be forged. She got the affirmation that Carrik was a member in good standing of the Heptite Guild, currently on leave of absence, and a repro of Carrik rolled out of the console, dated a scant five days before. Well, he was who he said he was, and doing what he said he was doing. His being a bona fide Guild member was a safeguard for her so she could relax in his offer of an honest invitation to share his holiday. He'd not leave her to pay the charges if he decided to skip off-world unexpectedly. She smiled to herself, stretching sensuously. Carrik thought himself lucky, did he? Well, so did she. The last vestige of 'ought' was the fleeting thought that she 'ought to' register herself with the Fuertan Central Computer as a transient but, as she was by no means obligated to do so as long as she didn't require subsistence, she did nothing.

At that moment several of her classmates began to experience some twinges of anxiety for her. Everyone knew Killashandra must have been terribly upset by the examiners' verdict. While it served her right, in some opinions, for being such an overbearing conceited grind, the kinder of heart felt oddly disquieted about her disappearance. So did Maestro Esmond Valdi.

They propably wouldn't have recognized Killashandra sluicing about on waterskis on the southern waters of the western continent, or swathed in elegant clothes, escorted by a tall distinguished man to whom the most supercilious hoteliers deferred.

It was a glorious feeling for Killashandra to have unlimited funds. Carrik encouraged her to spend and practice permitted her to suspend what few scruples remained to her from years of barely getting by on student credits. She did have the grace to protest his extravagance at the outset.

'Not to worry, pet, I've got it to spend,' Carrik reassured her. 'I made a killing in dominant thirds in the Blue Range about the time some idiot revolutionists blew half a planet's reactors out of existence.' He paused, his eyes narrowed as he recalled something not quite pleasant. 'I was lucky on shape, too. It's not enough, you see, to catch the resonances when you're cutting. You've got to chance what shape to cut and that's where you're made or broken as a crystal singer. You've *got* to remember political scenes. Like that revolution on Hardesty.' He pounded the table in emphasis, obtusely pleased with that memory. 'I did remember that all right when it mattered.'

'I don't understand.'

He gave her a quick look. 'Not to worry, pet.' His standard evasive phrase. 'Come give me a kiss and get the crystal out of my blood.'

There was nothing crystalline about his love-making nor the enjoyment he got out of her body, so Killashandra elected to forget how often he avoided answering her questions about crystal singing. At first she felt that, well, the man was on holiday and wouldn't want to talk about his work. Then she had the feeling that he resented her questions as if they were distasteful to him and that he wanted, above all other things, to forget crystal singing. That didn't forward her ends but Carrik was not a malleable adolescent, imploring her grace and favor. So she helped him forget crystal singing.

Which, in the pursuit of the pleasure of herself and Fuerte, he was patently able to do until the night he awakened her with his groans and writhings.

'Carrik, what's the matter? Those shell fish from dinner? Shall I get the medic?'

'No, no!' He twisted about frantically and caught her hand from the comunit. 'Don't leave me. It'll pass.'

She held him in her arms as he cried out, clenching his teeth against an internal agony. Sweat oozed from his pores and yet he steadfastly refused to let her get competent help. The spasms racked him for almost an hour before they passed, leaving him spent and weak in her arms. Somehow, in that hour, she realized how much he had come to mean to her, how much fun he was to be with, how much she had missed by denying herself any such intimate relationships before.

After he'd slept, she ventured to ask what had possessed him.

'Crystal, my girl, crystal.' His manner, terse to sullen, and the haggard expression on his face – he suddenly looked very old – made her drop the subject.

He was himself ... almost ... by the afternoon. But some of his spontaneity of spirit was missing. He seemed to go through the motions of enjoying himself, of egging her on to more daring exercises on the waterskis while he only splashed in the shallows.

They were finishing a leisurely meal at their favorite seaside restaurant when he broke the news that he must return to work.

'I can't say "so soon?" ' Killashandra said with a light laugh. 'But isn't the decision sudden?'

He gave her an odd smile. 'Yes, but most of my decisions are, aren't they? Like showing you another side of fusty fogey Fuerte.'

'And now our idyll is over?' She tried to sound nonchalant but an edge crept into her voice.

'I must return to Ballybran. Ha, that sounds like one of those fisherfolk songs, doesn't it?' He hummed a banal tune, the melody so predictable she could join in firm harmony.

'We do make beautiful music together,' he said, his eyes mocking her. 'I suppose you'll go back to music now.'

'Doing what?' she asked. 'Lead soprano for the chorus of some annotated, orchestrated grunts and groans by Fififididi-pidi of the planet Grnch?'

'You could tune crystals. They obviously need a competent one at your spaceport.'

She made a rude noise in her throat and looked at him expectantly.

He smiled back, turning his head politely awaiting her verbal answer.

'Or,' she said in a drawl, watching him obliquely, 'I could apply to the Heptite Guild as a crystal singer.'

His expression went blank. 'You don't want to be a crystal singer.'

'How do you know what I want?' She flared up in spite of herself, in spite of a gnawing uncertainty about his feelings for her. She might be fine to loll about on a sandy beach, but as a constant companion in a dangerous profession?

He smiled sadly. 'You don't want to be a crystal singer.'

'Oh, fardles with that nonsense in the print out!'

'They mean what they say.'

'Then if I've perfect pitch, I can apply.'

'You don't know what you're getting in for.' He said that in a flat, toneless voice, his expression at once wary and forbidding. 'Singing crystal is a terrible, lonely life. You can't always

115

find someone to sing with you, the tones don't always strike the right vibes for the crystals. You do make terrific cuts singing duo.' He seemed to vacillate.

'How do you find out?'

He gave an unamused snort. 'The hard way, of course. But you don't want to be a crystal singer.'

There was an almost frightening sadness in his voice. 'Once you sing crystal, you don't stop. That's why I urge you not to consider it.'

'So you've urged me not to consider it.'

He caught her hand. 'You've never been in a mach storm in the Milekeys,' he said, his voice rough with remembered anxiety. 'They blow up out of nowhere,' he gestured vigorously, 'and crash down on you like all hell let loose.' She felt the tremor through his body into her hand. 'That's what that phrase means, "the Guild maintains its own." A mach storm can reduce a man to a vegetable in one sonic crescendo.'

'There are other – albeit less violent – ways of reducing a man to a vegetable,' she said, thinking of the attendant in the restaurant, of the bustling supercargo worrying over drone-pod weights, of teachers apathetically reviewing the scales of novice students. 'Surely there are instruments that warn you of approaching storms, even mach ones in a crystal range.'

He nodded. 'But you get to cutting crystal, and you're halfway through, you know the pitches will be changed once the storm has passed and you're cutting your safety margin fine but that last crystal might mean you get off-world ...'

'You don't get off-world with every trip to the ranges?'

He shook his head. 'You don't always clear the costs of the trip, particularly if you cut the wrong shape or tone.'

'As you said, you have to pay attention to the news and outguess what'll be needed.' She was serenely confident that she could master that facet of the new profession.

'You have to *remember* the news,' he said, oddly emphasizing the change of verb.

Killashandra was contemptuous of such a lapse. Memory was only a matter of habit, of training, of handy mnemonic phrases which easily triggered vital information.

'You wouldn't by any chance let me go back to Ballybran with you to see if I can join that chorus?'

His hand on hers, his body, even his breath, seemed to halt for a moment. 'You asked. Remember that!'

'Well, if my company is so –'

'Kiss me and don't say anything you'll regret,' he said, abruptly pulling her with rough urgency into his arms and kissing her so thoroughly she couldn't speak.

The second convulsion caught him so soon after the climax of their love-making that she thought, guiltily, that overstimulation was the cause. The spasms were even more severe and he dropped into an exhausted sleep when they finally eased.

He looked old and drawn when he woke some fourteen hours later. And he moved like an advanced geriatric case.

'I've got to get back to Ballybran, Killa.'

'For treatment?'

He hesitated and then nodded. 'Get the spaceport on the comunit and book us.'

'Us?'

'You may come with me,' he said, nodding, though she was piqued at the phrasing and the invitation was more plea than permission. 'I don't care how often we have to reroute. Get us there as fast as possible.'

She got the spaceport and routing, and, after what seemed an age and considerable ineptitude on the part of the ticketing clerk, they were confirmed passengers on a shuttle flight leaving Fuerte in four hours, with a four hour satellite wait before the first liner due to relay in their direction.

There were a good deal of oddments to pack and Killashandra was for just walking out and leaving everything.

'You don't get such goods on Ballybran, Killa,' Carrik told her, and began, slowly, to fold the bright gaudy shirts of a pounded tree fibre. The stimulus of confirmed passage had given him a surge of energy. But Killashandra had been rather unnerved by the transformation of a charming, vital, if domineering man, into a frail shadow. 'Sometimes, something as flimsy as a shirt helps you remember so much.'

She was touched by the sentiment, and vowed to be kinder to him.

'There are hazards to every profession. And the hazards to crystal singing –'

'It depends on what you're willing to consider a hazard,' Killashandra replied, soothingly. She was glad to take along the filmy wraparounds in luminous dyes. They were a far cry from coarse durable student issue. Any hazard seemed a fair price for these bouts of high living. And only four hundred

117

twenty-five in the Guild.

'Do you really understand what you'd be giving up, Killashandra?' His voice had a guilty edge.

She looked at his lined, aging face and did experience a twinge of honest apprehension. Anyone would look appalling after the convulsions which had racked him. She didn't much care for Carrik in a philosophical vein and hoped he wasn't so dreary all the time back on Ballybran. Was that what he meant? A man on holiday was often a different personality to a man at work?

'What have I to look forward to on Fuerte?' She asked with a shrug of her shoulders. She wouldn't necessarily have to team up with Carrik once she got to Ballybran. 'I'd rather take a chance no matter what it entails in preference to dragging about on Fuerte!'

He stroked her palm with his thumb and, for the first time, the caress didn't send thrills up her spine but then, he was scarcely in a condition to make love and the gesture reflected that.

'You've only seen the glamorous side of crystal singing ...'

'You've told me of the dangers, Carrik, as you're supposed to. The decision is mine. And I'm holding you to it.'

He gripped her hand tightly and there was a sort of gladness in his eyes that reassured her more thoroughly than any glib phrase.

'It's also one of the smallest Guilds in the world,' she went on, freeing her hand to finish packing the last bits. 'I prefer those odds.'

He raised his eyebrows, giving her a sardonic look more like the old Carrik. 'A two-cell in a one-cell pond?'

'If you please. I won't be second-rate anything.'

'A dead hero in preference to a live coward?' He taunted her.

'If you prefer. There! That's all our clothes. We'd better skim back to the spaceport. I've got to check with planetary regulations if I'm going off-world. I might even have some credit left.'

She did the flying back as Carrik dozed in the passenger seat. The rest did him some good, or he was mindful of his public image. Either way, Killashandra's doubts about him as a partner faded as he began ordering the port officials about imperiously, badgering the routing agent to be certain the man hadn't overlooked a more direct flight, or a more advantageous connection.

Killashandra left him to it and began to clear her own records with Fuerte Central. The moment she placed her credit card in the plate, the console began to chatter wildly. She was startled. She'd programmed a credit check and the information that she was going off-world and wanted to know what immunization shots would comply with the worlds they'd touch. But the supervisor came leaping down the ramp from his desk, all boredom erased from his flushed face, and two port officials converged on her. The exits of the reception hall flashed warning red as holdlocks were applied to the consternation of people trying to enter and leave. Killashandra was too stunned to move and stared at the men who charged up to her.

'Killashandra Ree?' asked the supervisor, panting.

'Yes?'

'You are to be detained.'

'Why?' Now she was angry. She could conceive of no crime she'd committed, no infringement on anyone's liberties. Non-registration was no offense so long as she didn't use planetary resources without credit.

'Please come with us,' the port officials said in chorus.

'Why?'

'Ah, hmm,' muttered the supervisor as both officials turned to him. 'There's hold out for you.'

'I've done nothing wrong.'

'Here, what's going on?' Carrik was indeed his old self as he pushed through to place a protesting arm around Killashandra. 'This young lady is under my protection.'

At which the supervisor and the officials looked suddenly stern and determined.

'The young lady is under the protection of her planet of origin,' said the supervisor in a stuffy tone. 'There is some doubt as to her mental health.'

'What? Because she accepted an honest invitation from a visitor? Do you know who I am?'

The man flushed. 'Indeed I do, sir,' and he was considerably more respectful suddenly.

'Well then, take my assurances that Miss Ree is in excellent mental health.'

The supervisor was adamant. 'Please come this way.'

There was nothing for it but to comply, although Carrik reminded their escorts that they'd booked a shuttle flight due to lift off in one hour and he had every intention of keeping that schedule – and with Killashandra Ree. She got the distinct impression that this ambition might be thwarted and rather than give rise to any speculation about her mental health, she remained uncharacteristically quiet.

'I know,' she said *sotto voce* to Carrik as they waited in the small office. 'The Music School may've thought me suicidal.' She giggled and suppressed it behind her hand when the supervisor glanced up at her nervously. 'I did just walk out of the Center and my digs, and I saw no one on my way here. So they did miss me! Well, that's gratifying.' She was inordinately pleased but Carrik wasn't. She'd only to reassure the authorities and she was certain she could. 'I think it's rather complimentary, actually. I'm going to leave Fuerte dramatically after all.'

Carrik snorted but the wait plainly irritated him.

Killashandra half expected to see her father though she couldn't have imagined him bestirring himself on her behalf. She didn't expect Maestro Esmond Valdi to enter, acting the outraged parent. Nor was she prepared for the attack he immediately launched on Carrik.

'You! You! I know what you are! A silicate spider paralyzing its prey, a crystal cuckoo taking the promising fledglings from their maternal nest.'

As stunned as everyone else was at the almost physical attack on the Heptite Guildman, Killashandra stared at the usually dignified and imperturbable Maestro and wondered what operatic role he was playing. He had to be. His dialogue was so ... so extravagant. 'Silicate spider.' 'Crystal cuckoo.' And he had the analogy wrong anyhow.

'Play on the emotions of a young, innocent girl. Shower her with unaccustomed luxuries and pervert her until she's spoiled as a decent contributing citizen. Until she's so besotted she has to go to that den of addled brains and sonic-soured nerves!'

Carrik made no attempt to divert the flow of vituperation or counter the accusations. He stood, head up, smiling tolerantly down at the stalky figure of Valdi.

'What lies has he been feeding you about crystal singing? What extravagant tales has he used to lure you there?' Valdi whirled to Killashandra.

'I asked to go.'

120

Valdi's wild expression hardened into disbelief at her calm reply.

'You *asked* to go?'

'Yes. He didn't ask me.' Killashandra saw Carrik smile with relief.

'You heard her, Valdi,' Carrik said and glanced at the officials taking in that admission.

The Maestro's shoulders sagged. 'He's done his recruiting work well,' he said in a defeated tone, even managing an effective slight break in his voice.

'I don't think so,' Killashandra said.

Maestro Valdi took a breath, obviously going to make one last final attempt to dissuade the poor misguided girl. 'Did he tell you about the mach storms?'

She nodded.

'That scramble your brains and reduce you to a vegetable?'

She nodded dutifully.

'Did he fill your mind with a lot of garbage about mountains giving back symphonies of sound? Crystalline choruses? Valleys that echo arpeggios?'

'No,' she replied in an acid tone, bored with the scene. 'And he also didn't feed me pap that all I needed was hard work and time.'

Esmond Valdi drew himself up, more than ever an exaggeration of a classical operatic pose.

'Did he tell you that once you start cutting crystal you can never stop? And too long away from Ballybran produces convulsions?'

'I know that.'

'That something in the water, the soil, the crystals affects your mind? You don't remember anything?'

'That could be an advantage,' Killashandra replied, staring at the little man until he had to drop his glance.

She felt it first of the three, an itch behind her ears in the mastoid bone, an itch that rapidly became a wrenching nauseating pain. She grabbed Carrik by the arm just as the subsonic noise touched him. As Esmond Valdi lifted protecting hands to his ears.

'The fools!' cried Carrik, panic in his face and voice. He threw aside the door panel, running as fast as he could toward the control tower, Killashandra behind him. Anything to shut off that agonizing pain in her skull.

Carrik vaulted the decorative barrier into the restricted area, to be stopped by the force curtain.

'Stop it! Stop it!' he screamed, rocking in anguish.

The pain was no less supportable for Killashandra but she'd presence enough of mind left to bang on the nearest comunit, to strike the fire buttons, press the emergency signals.

'The shuttle coming in ... the crystals are defective ... it's going to blow,' she yelled at the top of operatically trained lungs. She was barely conscious of the panic in the vast reception hall resulting from her all too audible warning.

But the wild stampede of an hysterical mob was evident to the control tower personnel and automatically someone slapped on the abort signal to all incoming and outgoing shuttles and craft. Moments later, while the comunit was demanding an explanation from Killashandra, from anyone who could make themselves heard over the bedlam in the reception area, a fireball blossomed in the sky, raining hot molten fragments on the spaceport below. The exploding shuttle spewed bits and pieces over a radius of several kilometers, several larger hunks burned craters in the heavy plastic dome of the port facility. Had the shuttle exploded any closer, the damage would have been disastrous.

Apart from bumps, bruises, lacerations and a broken arm sustained in the crush to leave the hall, there were only two serious casualties. The shuttle pilot was dead and Carrik would have been better off so. The final sonic blast knocked him out and he never did recover his senses with consciousness. After consultation with the Heptite Guild medics it was decided to return him to Ballybran for treatment and care.

'He won't recover,' the medic told Killashandra and Maestro Valdi who instantly assumed the role of her comforter. His manner provided Killashandra with a fine counter-irritant to her shock over Carrik's state.

She chose to disbelieve the medic for surely they could restore Carrik to mental health on Ballybran. It was just that he'd been away from crystal too long: that he was weakened by the seizures. There'd been no mach storm to scramble his mind. She'd escort him back to Ballybran. She owed him that in any reckoning for teaching her how to live, fully, not vicariously as she'd been doing rehearsing opera roles of by-gone griefs and antedated conflicts.

She took a good long look at the posturing Valdi and

thanked her luck that Carrick had removed the scales from her eyes. How could she have believed such an artificial life as the theatre was suitable? Just look at Valdi! Present him with a situation, hand him a cue and he was on in the appropriate role. None existed for these circumstances but Valdi was struggling to find one to suit.

'What will you do now, Killashandra?' he asked in sepulchral tones, obviously settling for Dignified Elder Gentleman Consoling the Innocent Bereaved.

'I'll take him to Ballybran, of course.'

Valdi nodded solemnly. 'I mean, when you return from Ballybran.'

'I don't intend to return.'

Valdi stared, dropping out of character, and then gestured theatrically as the aircushion stretcher on which Carrick was strapped drifted past them to the shuttle gate.

'After that?' Valdi cried, full of dramatic plight.

'That won't happen to me,' she said confidently.

'But it could! And you, too, could be reduced to a thing with no mind, no memories, unalterably scrambled brains.'

'I think,' Killashandra said slowly, regarding the mannered little man with thinly veiled contempt, 'that everyone's brains get scrambled some way or other.'

'You'll rue this day –' began Valdi, raising his left arm in a classical rejection gesture, fingers gracefully spread.

'That is, if I *remember* it!' she said and her mocking laugh cut him off mid-scene.

Still laughing, Killashandra made her exit, stage center, through the passenger shuttle door.

Gene Wolfe

THE DARK OF THE JUNE

Untouched by any change of the last twenty-five years, the
Nailer living room continued to reflect (like a lost photograph
unexpectedly found between the pages of a book) the tastes
of Henry's late wife, May Nailer. These tastes had been simple
but not good, and save for Henry's old trophies and some tat-
tered physics books, it was just such a room as May might have
seen in a newspaper the day she ordered the furniture. To this
unpromising setting Henry had added little over the years –
though he had collaborated with May, the year after the room
was set up, to produce their daughter June. Except for June
and her clothing the nineteen-nineties were not so much ex-
cluded as denied.

On this spring evening, June wore a soft gown without visible
hem or seam, a gown that fell to her ankles and left her right
breast bare. On her right wrist was a bracelet of glo-lite bangles
and in her right ear a dangling glo-lite earring. The nails of her
left hand were red, and those of her right black; her dramatic
lashes were her own now, surgically implanted and gracefully
long; she was a beautiful girl, Henry thought, although somewhat too slender to look her best in the current fashions.
'They're here,' she said, and he nodded, pretending he had not
been looking at her.

'They really are here,' his daughter continued as though he
had denied it. 'A translucent thing like a scarf came out of the
bedroom and went into the kitchen a moment ago.'

'I didn't notice,' he said.

'We're living in a haunted world, Daddy, and it ought to
bother you – I know you, and you're a thoroughgoing materi-
alist whose whole cast of mind was formed before any of this
started – but you hardly seem to care.'

'They're not dead,' her father said. He was a broad-
shouldered, placid man who wore a black patch over the socket
of an eye lost years before in a motorcycle accident; his curly,

almost-full beard was going gray. 'They're just people.' He went back to his book.

At midnight the lights flickered, a sign that the rates had doubled; Henry waved a hand at Bellini's *Portrait of the Doge Loredano* above the fireplace; they went out leaving only the night-light gleam of the bank nearest the stair. He used an old leather bookmark imprinted with an unconvincing dragon to record the fact that he had abandoned *An Incident at Krechetovka Station* before it had had time to make steam, and went up to bed. There was a note on his pillow, and he called the police.

'She's over eighteen?'

Henry nodded.

'Then there's nothing we can do.'

'You could stop her,' Henry said. 'You could book her, if that were necessary, on some minor charge, give me time to talk to her, give her time to think.'

'I could give the city manager a jaywalking ticket too,' the computer-generated police surrogate said. Henry's old 3V made him sallow and a trifle unreal, even projecting into the darkened room. 'But I'm not going to.'

A nothing went past, a luminous wisp that might have been steam from a coffee pot if steam were faintly blue. 'Look at that,' Henry said, 'that might have been her.' He felt as if he were about to weep, but no tears came, only a greater and greater ache in his chest.

'I didn't see it,' the police surrogate said, 'but anyway it couldn't have been that quick. How old did you say she was?'

'Twenty-three. Junie's twenty-three, I think.'

'Then it couldn't be anywhere near that quick; the older they are the longer it takes, and they flash in and out and fade – that's why they won't accept anybody over thirty. Did you call the center?'

Henry looked at him blankly.

'Didn't you call the center yet? Call them.'

'I didn't think they'd cooperate – they want people to come, don't they?'

'They got to tell you for legal purposes – everybody leaves an estate, you know what I mean? I mean she can't take it with her. Even if it's just clothes. Turn on your recorder and tell them it's an official request – they'll tell you.'

125

Henry said, 'It's not as though they're dead.'

'Not to them it ain't.' The police surrogate switched off.

Henry coded the center; the girl who answered said, 'Who is it?'

'My name is Henry Boyce Nailer –'

'I mean who're you looking for? Man or woman?'

'A woman.' Henry cleared his throat. 'Her name is June Nailer, and she's my daughter.'

The girl flipped through a register on her desk. 'Recent?'

'Tonight.'

'She hasn't been here. Now don't you come down trying to make trouble; we won't even let you in the building.'

Outside the air was soft with the feeling of new growth, the crickets were singing in the grass. He took off the suitcoat he had put on from force of habit and carried it over his shoulder as he strode toward the station; twice black things passed over the broad face of the moon as he walked: one was a whippoorwill; the other a nin – one of them. The nin was like a flying flag, Henry thought, a fluttering banner, this last bit of someone who would soon – in a few months or years – be totally *not in nature*, the dark flag of a vessel putting out for all the wonders of the night sky. He paid his tokens to the gate and stepped onto the starter belt, then across it to the speedup belt, and then onto the fast belt. Even there at a steady speed of forty kilometers an hour the wind was not cold, but his coat whipped behind him; he was afraid his checkbook would fall out and put the coat on. There were boxes ahead of him, and the boxman came back to ask if he wanted to rent one.

'I guess you're surprised I'm still open this late, right, pal? I mean when it ain't raining or nothing. Well, when I said did you wanna rent a box that was just what I meant – I got a girl in one, you get me? A nice girl. Young. Young. You looking for a girl, bud?'

'Yes' Henry said, 'but not your kind of girl.' He discovered that he was happy to have someone to talk to, even the boxman.

'I'd show her to you,' the boxman said, 'but she's taking a little nappy-poo in there between tricks. Listen, if you got any interest I'll wake her up and show her to you anyhow.' Henry told him to let his girl sleep and got off in the downtown mall three kilometers down the belt. He had felt an irrational desire, though he would hardly admit it to himself, to see the trans-tart – to order her led yawning out of her box (they were officially called rental-mobile weather shelters, and the boxman paid an annual fee for the privilege of putting each aboard the belts), her makeup smeared with sleep, and the inevitable pink-tinted three mil Saran gown fluttering in the wind. He imagined himself escorting a much younger woman into a restaurant – they would be father and daughter until the other diners saw their hands clasped beneath the table.

The building was not that, only a two-floor complex. Amateurish posters in its windows: THE BUTCHERS KILL FOR YOU, and DO YOU WANT TO BE A PART OF ALL MANKIND HAS DONE, and LIVE WITHOUT MEAT – IN YOU OR ON YOU – DIS-INCARNATE, and RESIGNATION IS THE ONLY WAY OUT – SO I'M RESIGNING. Henry went inside; there was an athletic young man at a desk in the first room, and a softball bat leaning in the corner behind the young man. He said, 'What do you want?'

'I want to know if my daughter's here.'

'You can't come farther than this,' the young man said. 'There's a phone on the wall in back of you – call them up inside.'

'I did,' Henry told him. 'Now I'm going to see for myself.'

The young man reached behind him for the softball bat and laid it across his desk. 'There's a switch in the seat of this chair, and every time I stand up without shutting it off it rings an alarm in police headquarters. They like for people to go away – they think it reduces the crime rate. They don't like people who try to stop it; sometimes they shoot them.'

'Why don't you go?'

'I am going,' the young man said, 'in November. Some-one else I know is going to be ready to go too by then, and we're going to do it together. Meantime I want to do some-thing right here. We're going to go, and we're never going to die.'

'Something else happens to them,' Henry said.

'But not death; they never die. That's what they say.'

Someone came in behind Henry, a narrow-shouldered young man of about nineteen. He said, 'This is the place, isn't it?' He had an air of desperate triumph, as though he had won through to some frightful goal.

127

'This is the place,' the young man with the ball bat said, and as he did Henry bolted for the inner door, slamming it and locking it behind him.

A man and two women sat talking in a room filled with ashtrays and stale coffee cups; neither of the women was June. As they stared at Henry one flickered out of sight, then, as he found the next door, returned. She might have been traced in neon, and the bright room a dark street.

He burst into a third room, and a young woman (the same young woman, he realized a moment afterward, that he had talked to earlier) said, 'You're Mr Nailer?'

He nodded.

'Good. She's still on.' The young woman pressed a switch on the desk before her, and Junie was in the room. 'Daddy,' she said.

'Where are you, honey?' He recognized the chair in which she sat, the rug around her feet, even as he spoke.

'Daddy, I'm home. I want to see you before I go.'

He said, 'Are you going so soon, honey?' and as he spoke she was flicked away. The 3V was still on; the old wing-backed chair that had been May's still stood on the patternless blue carpet, but June was no longer there. He waited, watching it, realizing that the young woman at the desk was watching too.

'She may return in a few seconds,' the young woman said, 'but she may not. If you want to see her in person I'd go back home if I were you.'

Henry nodded and turned to step back into the room of stale coffee cups. A plainclothesman hit him in the mouth as he came through the door; he fell to his knees from the shock, and was jerked to his feet again. He hit the plainclothesman in the stomach, kneed him, then grabbed his lapels and smashed his nose with his forehead. Somehow the plainclothesman's gun was no longer attached to him and went skittering across the floor. A uniformed patrolman was coming through the door Henry had to go out of; he made the mistake of diving for the gun, and Henry hit him in the back of the neck.

When he stepped off the belt he was still panting. He reflected on how difficult it was for a man his age to keep in condition; they could discover who he was easily enough – though perhaps they wouldn't make too much trouble about it – it shouldn't be pleasant for them to confess they had been beaten by a middle-aged scholar. Or perhaps they would; with Junie gone he really didn't care.

She met him at the gate. 'It's past your bedtime, Dad. You shouldn't have gone into the city at this time of night.'

He said: 'The sun'll be up in two, three more hours. I think I'll just stay up now.'

'To be with me as long as you can – isn't that it?'

He nodded.

'What do you want to do?'

'Let's just walk in the garden. For a minute.' Her left hand was in his, and he could see the faint glow of her bracelet when she raised her right hand to touch her hair, the shine of her earring when she turned to look at him. 'When you were a little girl I used to think about your dying,' he told her. 'You do, you know, with children; you were so fragile. And your mother had just died. Now I'll never see you dead, and I'm glad; I want you to know that.'

'I'll never see you dead either, Dad. That was part of it.'

'What was the rest of it?'

'All you expected of me, a little. And ...'

She was gone, her hand no longer in his. 'June!' he yelled. 'June!' He ran past the stone birdbath and saw the twinkle of her bracelet and earring under the willow; then the little lights winked out one by one.

Edgar Pangborn

THE CHILDREN'S CRUSADE

Malachi never shunted off the children and their questions, nor did he madden them by promising they'd understand when they were older. He even asked them questions in return. If they giggled or squirmed or ran away it was not, he thought, in rejection, but because there was crisis in his inquiries: – *What do YOU think is on the other side of the hill? – Where does the music go when the sound stops? – Was there really a world before you were born?* They lacked the language to deal with this sort of thing, except Jesse Lodson, the six-toed boy, who read books and had a mind of his own and was old enough to be allowed to sit on the steps of The Store and listen to men's talk. Maybe the other kids hoped to find words by running off to search for them in green pastures; but Malachi would still be ahead of them, ready with new questions when they came running back.

Who does have patience for long labor over anything so slippery and ungentle as a question? Malachi's, and he knew it, often raised thunder out of a past that hung like a midnight shadow over himself and his people. We may scold the most appalling future into quiet by proving it doesn't exist, but the past did, once. The challenges of doubt or denial reverberate, though the cheeks that flushed and lips that curled in the passions of argument are with the leaf mold.

Born among the flailing ideologies of what we call the late 20th Century, Malachi Peters never admitted that children should be spared the peril of using their brains.

The red plague followed the twenty-minute war; the Children's Crusade happened some thirty years after that. Malachi's people were calling it the Year 30; one might as well go along with their chronology, for they weren't stupid, and many could remember the 20th Century.

Most of them also recalled the existence of a religion named Christianity. Hardly any two could have agreed about its doctrines and practice, but in this time when a technological culture was so recently self-slain, religion had come to seem important again. Among the children fantastic sparrow-arguments broke out from time to time about God and the Devil, heaven and hell and all that bit. And you could hear endless adult exegesis, logomachy, and heart-burning on the front porch of The Store, or around the stove in winter. How do you ever define 'religion' itself in terms that will meet the dry thorny jabs of the rebel five percent – or three percent, or whatever the minority amounts to? Up on the northeastern shore of the Hudson Sea, that minority presents an irreducible factor of serene cussedness: they're Vermonters.

(Even three percent may be too big. It doesn't imply that the remaining ninety-seven percent are too dumb or too bland to enjoy the thrills of theoretical squabblings; but they are apt to devote their energies to timely, *important* problems, such as the distinction between *Homoiousian* and *Homoousian*, or im-morality among the heathen, or the Only Decent Way to Make Clam Chowder.)

Malachi Peters of Melton Village sometimes laid it out openly for his cronies along about these lines: Say a village of one hundred heavenbound sons of bitches like you supports a population of one sound atheist like Mr Goudy over there; then you'll find about four who'll venture to agree with him out loud in a half-ass kind of way, in some place where no-body happens to be listening; makes a good five percent rebellion, don't it? Of course, even if you add in us agnostics the rebellion still can't so much as elect a town clerk, but we make noise. By the way, did you know it was T. H. Huxley himself who invented the word 'agnostic' for crackpots like me who'd rather be truthful than sanctified?

And sometimes he went Socratic, though with caution:

What is God? Well – oh, a Supreme Being.

What is the nature of Being? Supreme over what? Why, hell, everybody knows what being is.

All but me. I'm ignorant. Supreme means infinite? Sure.

Jesus Christ was the son of God? Ayah, don't the Book say so?

God is infinite? Well, sure.

Therefore Christ was the son of Infinity? Ayah.

How does Infinity beget a son? It's got balls? You trying to make a man look stupid?

131

(Hearing it reach this point, old Mr Goudy chuckles, scratches his desiccated crotch, and spits a bollop over the porch rail. Fifty-five, oldest man in town; has a patch of Connecticut tobacco and does some business in the fall blending marijuana with the chaws, packing the mixture on his back through the neighbouring towns. Malachi often addressed him as Messenger of Light, which caused Mr Goudy to cackle like one of Jud Hobart's guinea hens; Jesse Lodson wasn't quite old enough to figure that one out.)

I'm just trying to find out the sex of Infinity. Man your age could get his mind off sex, seems like.

Why? ...

Melton Village was typical of those shrunken communities on the northeastern coast of what people were beginning to call the Hudson Sea. The villages maintained a tenuous, suspicious communication with each other along the mountain trails and the disintegrating grandeur of Old-Time roads. The people did cherish a faith in a few things, but not in the dollar anymore, with no central government to create one, and not in the ancient air-castle fantasy of squeezing an income out of the goddamn summer people. Weren't any.

At fifty Malachi Peters was typical of himself. So increasingly, was his friend Jesse Lodson at fourteen, who had the run of Malachi's library and who loved him.

Melton Village sprawls in the foothills of a green range looking down, yes, on the Hudson Sea, that long arm of ocean extending now from the Lorenta Sea all the long way to a confused tangle of islets and inlets several hundred miles south, where the Black Rocks mark the site of New York City. That tragic place was stricken by the peripheral blast of a fusion toy that annihilated the western end of Long Island, including Brooklyn and a tree that is said to have grown there. Then New York's ruins were engulfed in the rising waters, the noisy history done. West of Melton Village, the opposite shore is occasionally visible on those days of clear atmosphere that seem to be coming more frequently. Out there under windy water and skittish tides lies the bed of what was Lake Champlain. The lake was beautiful, history says, until the Age of Progress shat in it and made it, like so many others, a desolation and a stink. The waters climbed; years of earthquake, cloudburst, landslide crumbled the narrow watersheds. The ocean, itself a

132

universe in torment, perhaps renews itself in long labor, healing the worst afflictions of the human visitation.

Malachi Peters was in the habit of sprawling on his own elderly front porch, when he wasn't tending his garden and chickens or doing his fastidious bachelor housekeeping, or mending a kite for the kids, or describing the universe to Jesse who had (Malachi thought) a rather too dewy-eyed view of it even for fourteen. Or arguing, of course, down at the venerable shanty that retained the name of The Store.

Trading was negligible: all the nearby communities were in the same fix as Melton Village. There was in theory a sort of state government still at Montpelier but you never heard from it – sometimes an excellent thing in governments. The overland trails into Massachusetts or New Hampshire got more snarled up each year as the rise in mean temperature transformed temperate zone forest into subtropical – a few degrees are enough. A visit to New York meant a sea voyage through tough waters by a people who had scant taste for recovering the art of sailing ships. Bud Maxon maintained The Store as a public service; he couldn't support himself and his family with it, but managed like everyone else with a knee-scrabble garden, chickens and goats and pigs, and hunting. He owned the town bull; his brother ran a bit of a dairy. Bud learned archery, but kept his old rifle oiled just as if he thought there'd be cartridges for it again some day. The Store's front steps and porch in summer, its stove in the softening winters, drew the lonely in their hunger for talk, that limping substitute for love.

Malachi could also watch the sea from his own front porch. To older generations of his family Lake Champlain had gleamed more distantly, where the Lamoille River ran into it. In that time a group of islands stood out there. Mr Goudy remembered hunting and camping on Grand Isle when he was a boy. Watching the ocean, Malachi could let his thoughts ride free, as he might have if a world had not ended.

Fifty now, he had been twenty, with two years experience of Harvard, when civilization encountered the Bang, and presently the red plague that made the 14th Century Black Death look like a cold in the head. Destroying civilization, always a task for fools, was relatively easy with the tools constructed for the purpose in the 20th Century. To recreate one you need something stronger than divine guidance.

In the Year 30 the residents of Melton Village numbered about a hundred adults (the red plague having wiped out the old as you wipe chalk squiggles off a slate) and eighteen teen-agers and children. The population before the war and the plague had been three thousand.

Malachi Peters numbered precisely one. Six-feet-two, weighed 160 pounds. Standing erect he resembled a weedy figure One, with wind-wavering hair already ice-white.

Of the children, thirteen were physically normal except perhaps in their genes. The village had no statistical information on the incidence of radiation-induced birth deformities, fetal deaths, and stillbirths. Many good souls were inclined to blame the trouble on the infinite wisdom of God (after all, it's been blamed for everything else ever since we invented it). The village did try to cherish the children. Some of the mues, as they began to be called about that time, were hard to cherish, especially the brain-mues who could only sit where they were put, smile and drool when they were fed, cry when they were cleaned. Others, like Jesse who had no physical oddity except his six-toed feet, were not yet regarded with superstitious terror. As for Jesse's peculiarity, as Malachi told him more than once, such things weren't too uncommon long before techno-logy started monkeying with the sunfire – except that his extra toes were functional. They gave a special buoyancy to his walking and running. Jesse was slim like a marsh reed, dark-haired and faun-eyed. At fourteen he could outrun anyone in the village and not even be winded.

Most of the adults could read, but books were few – some volumes that had been in the tiny public library in the Year Zero, as many more privately owned in houses that survived flood, fire, night-raiders, and abandonment in the worst of the bad years, and Malachi's library of maybe three thousand at the Old Peters Place where he had lived most of his years alone since the crash. Except for Malachi's lot, a high proportion of the surviving books were less than useful to a society that might have liked to recreate civilization, or anyhow Vermont, if it had known how. But to understand that one shall see no more *new* books, ever, is a horror even to some of the illiterate, like smashing blind into a stone wall.

A little school limped along under good Miss Seton, whose resources were near to nothing. The greatest difference the old lady noted after the death of American culture was that in the new age she was treated with some respect even by the children. Especially by the children.

Malachi knew (but seldom said to his neighbors except for Tad Doremus the blacksmith) that the rise of waters was engulfing the dry land because of the determined blundering of expert technological man in the recent past. What else but man-made fumes, particularly those of humanity's dearest buzztoy, had heated the atmospheric greenhouse the critical few degrees that hastened the melting of polar ice? And choking on atmospheric garbage meant Progress: so choke. All toward what conclusion – who tried to know? Not the engineers – it wasn't their job. They were earnest and righteous about that: it was never their job to forsee anything beyond the immediate achievement and immediate profit. They could only build and grow – one says that of cancer. 'We climbed Mount Everest because it was there!' – that was the Golden Cliché of the 20th Century, mock-modest bombast quite as banal and unthinking as any 19th Century godsaking, and like most popular swashbuckling it went unchallenged.

It was an exhausted world – beaten, raped, robbed, mutilated by industrial greed and political stupidity, and left for dead. Malachi himself knew exhaustion, hours when his head could hold little except despair at human folly. He looked then on Jesse, the boy's uncalculating goodness, simplicity, power to love and to wonder, and could only think: *This is the world they left you. The rain itself as it falls on your head is poisoned.* Sometimes instead of *they* he said *we*; but Malachi was not given to wallowing in unearned guilt. A yeasty college student at the age of twenty, there wasn't much he could have done to prevent the idiot from pushing the button. If burning himself with gasoline in front of the White House would have had that effect, he was the sort of ardent youth who might have done it; plain reason told him it wouldn't: the Juggernaut is mindless. The danger would remain simply because those in power had not the intelligence nor the good will to remove it, and what had been representative government had given way to the corporate state. To say these things in the 20th Century usually seemed like hooting down a rain-barrel. In the pig-scramble to be good consumers for the blessed state, honor and virtue and reason could not be heard; it was natural to assume that they had died.

In the Year 30 it seemed to Malachi that not enough

survivors existed to renew the species. Within a generation or two there would be a lights-out, somewhere a last man perishing. Hadn't a critical moment arrived when the dinosaurs became dry bones without issue? He could see his contemporaries as like insects crowded to the high end of a piece of driftwood and going out on the flood. He would have been happy, if only for Jesse, to invent God and a heaven, but he couldn't do it. For a mind once honestly wedded to reason there is no divorce.

And yet, mercilessly comparing grown-ups, the children said of Malachi: 'Tshee, he never acts *bored!*'

Jesse's father had been a veterinary who somehow retained the conscience of a specialized profession through years when the complex drugs, antiseptics, antibiotics, all that, were no longer obtainable. No immunology, no anesthetics, nothing that depended on the vanished 20th Century laboratories and the huge complex of supporting industries. Lost or broken instruments could not be replaced. No more scientific journals – no more science. For the blunder, the incomparable brass-bound goof, is one thing that *homo quasi-sapiens* can carry off magnificently: out goes the baby with the bath-water, and what's left (if anything is left) is an astonished and very naked primate.

Dr Lodson did what he could, with herbs, observation, common sense, memory, and that mixture of hunch and sympathy which is justly called 'a feeling for animals,' through years when probably no one understood his difficulties except Dr Stern, who was in the same fix with his human patients, and Malachi Peters who liked to play chess with Dr Lodson and who was inclined to take all Melton Village troubles as his own – for no good reason except that this was Malachi's way. It was not meddlesome, nor particularly aristocratic, this concern of Malachi's for his own people. The village had an exasperated, partly loving name for it. They called it Malachi's Thing.

In the Year 24, when his son Jesse was eight years old (this was the same year Dr Stern died of intestinal cancer with none to succeed him), Dr Lodson got momentarily careless while treating Bud Maxon's priceless Jersey bull for a leg ulcer. With the lightning-flash of an act of God, the brute wheeled and gored him to death.

136

In that year Jesse began to see that love and mercy, like hate, are man-made. He had adored his cheerful, unexacting father. He was there when it happened, though Bud got him out quickly. The death was a hurricane smashing a door inward – maybe the house can't take it. He learned later that the world is also beautiful – *'sounds, and sweet airs, that give delight and hurt not,'* as two-faced Caliban murmured to him in the peace of Malachi's library – but on your life, expect no conscious mercy except from merciful people! The bull can turn.

God's will, said Jesse's meek mother. Jesse wished at eight – and at nine, and ten – that he could discover what she meant. Couldn't God have stopped the bull? At eight he was only beginning to learn he could ask questions of Malachi, and this one was too difficult. By the time he was ten Jesse had acquired a stepfather, and Malachi's library was not only a haven but a necessity.

The stepfather, a hardworking religious man who took over Dr Lodson's haphazard little farm and improved it, didn't like to have Jesse go barefoot. Knowing a little about leatherwork, he cobbled a pair of shoes that fitted Jesse's broad feet, more or less. He said it looked tacky for the boy to go barefoot, as if his family was no better than the heathen mountain folk. Even Jesse's mother could hardly look at his feet without her eyes brimming. Jesse wore the painful shoes except when he visited the Old Peters Place. There he slipped them off at the door, and walked with his friend.

His earliest memory of Malachi dated back to a time when he had been small enough for Malachi to take him up in his lap. He remember a long hand curving over his bare feet, and some remark – he did not retain the words – that made it seem a potent distinction to possess twelve working toes.

Love is a wordless thing in childhood and maybe ought to be. Grown-ups forget this at their peril.

Mr Goudy brought the first word of Preacher Abraham to Melton Village, a casual profane mention of one more end-of-the-world preacher spouting hellfire and resurrection – only this guy, he said, is appealing to the *kids* for God's sake. Stuff about a pilgrimage to found the New Jerusalem. Them golden streets, said Mr Goudy, spitting over the rail. All our troubles over, or some shit like that.

Abraham was a great tall man with flame-colored hair and a voice of thunder, said a traveling tinker who hadn't seen him – heard about him, though, from an old woman at Pittsfield Ruins who told fortunes. Abraham was come, she says, to prophesy the Messiar just like John the Baptist. The tinker hemself didn't buy it, much.

Later came another man through Melton Village, a burly gentleman leading a caravan – three wagons which once had been half-ton pickups and pulled easy on the rims if you knew how to get the work out of the mules. This gentleman, Homer Hobson, and his henchmen were heading for the open country north of the St Lawrence – might start a colony, he thought. They were foreigners from the south – New Haven. That's in Connecticut. There he had seen Preacher Abraham, talked to him and shaken him by the hand.

No, he said, the fella wasn't nine feet tall, just average or a mite under. Big voice though, that part was true, and you could say his beard was reddish like. No Goddamn hippie, talked like a gentleman. Peaceful-looking, said Hobson, thinking back over it – peaceful till you stared him straight in the eye, and then you felt maybe a wildness. Blue eyes, and Hobson admitted he generally couldn't remember the color of a person's eyes. Bright blue – stuck in his mind, sort of.

'What does he *say*, about the New Jerusalem?'

That was Jesse Lodson, talking out of turn and annoying his stepfather, but Hobson gazed down on him without reproach, knitting his brows and trying to remember. 'Well, boy, he says the New Jerusalem will be – be a place where the earth is so cherished that God will return and live among men.' Then Hobson seemed surprised, and added: 'Why – don't sound so bad, you say it right out like that.'

At the time Hobson saw Abraham the Crusade must have been barely started. Hobson saw no large crowd with him, only a couple of dozen children between ten and fifteen – yes, quite a few mues among them – who might have merely gathered there in the New Haven street out of curiosity to hear the red-bearded man talk.

Time passed, and word came that Preacher Abraham was healing the sick with prayer and laying on of hands. Word came that in New Providence he raised from the dead a poor man who had perished of smallpox and lain two days without life. Elsewhere the Preacher blessed a woman afflicted by an evil spirit, and the devil passed out of her.

Word came that a thousand children followed Preacher Abraham, foraging, taking care of their prophet with certain miracles.

These tales lit fires. Until even Jesse Lodson, fourteen and never foolish, began to wonder: *Can God after all exist? Mother believes in him. Not all-benevolent, or the bull – but Mother says we aren't wise enough to understand ... Should I place so much faith in my own power of reason? Can there be miracles? Then what becomes of the natural order? A New Jerusalem, 'where the earth is so cherished' – but the books, the books! Or have I (and Malachi) been mistaken all this time? I pray, and it's all silence.*

He hungered to believe in the marvelous. (Who doesn't?) For most of existence in Melton Village had a flatness, a sourness partly generated by adult despair, and he was lonely in spite of Malachi. The other children had little to do with him, put off by the strangeness of an original mind that is not willing to hide itself or has not learned how. He was aching and changing with the needs of puberty. There was a coolness in Malachi, a steadiness that Jesse Lodson sometimes felt as a chill because he could not yet share it.

His mother and stepfather of course distrusted the love of an old man. Still, they did not forbid him those many hours with Malachi. Miss Seton herself said there was nothing more she was capable of teaching him, and Malachi was, in a way, important to Melton Village, like a monument or a natural force.

On his side, perhaps Malachi expected too much. He needed the freshness of youth with the companionship of maturity.

And word came that when Preacher Abraham entered a village and preached and asked who would help him found the New Jerusalem, the mue-children were first to forget their afflictions and follow him.

He was coming from the north. People talked now not only of Preacher Abraham but of 'Abraham's Army.' Or 'the Crusaders.'

They had gone north, rumor said, through the Maine and New Hampshire wilderness. Most of this had already returned to the rude health of nature, but it was still possible to follow the roads of the old industrial culture, the skeletal remains that demonstrate the articulation of the original monster, and its indifference to the welfare and beauty of the planet that endured it for so long a century. The Crusaders had taken one of the highways into Canada, and soon headed south again, but instead of coming by the Connecticut River they marched north of Lake Memphremagog to the Hudson Sea. They were at Richford. They were at St Albans.

A thousand were coming, said rumor – uprooted, exalted, dangerous. Whatever was not freely given, these children took, rumor said. Melton Village stood next in their line of march.

On the porch of The Store – it was summer and robins were nesting in their wonderfully increasing numbers – Bud Maxon grumbled: 'By God, them Crusaders better not come this-away! We got to feed 'em when we a'n't got a pot to piss in ourself?'

Malachi asked: 'You about to stop 'em, Bud?'

Maxon looked old and frightened, a 20th Century man hating every other way of life. Big Tad Doremus, who made out as a blacksmith in what had once been his father's filling station near the Old Peters Place, sat on the top step whittling applewood. He was always at some bit of art work that would have a woman's buttocks in it, though he might not be up to sculpting the rest of her. Mr Goudy spat over the rail. Jesse Lodson sat on the bottom step and kept his young mouth shut and his young ears open.

'Eating up the Goddamn country!' said Maxon. 'Grasshoppers!'

'Hippies is what they be,' said Lucas Hackstraw. His face was like a worm-chewed windfall, and he was married to the saddest woman in town. 'Boys and girls jumbled up together.'

'How else would they travel?' Tad Doremus asked.

'And some of 'em pretty well growed,' said Mr Goudy, who liked to keep Hackstraw mentally goosed. 'Exceedingly well growed and also sprightly, I'm told. Lively times in the hay-pile.'

'They got no moral sense,' said Hackstraw.

'I've always taken a great personal interest in the moral sense,' said Malachi. 'By the way, does anybody know what it is, to relieve my ignorance? Would you define the moral sense, Brother Maxon?'

'Up yours too, Malachi,' said Bud, but his heart wasn't in it.

Tad said to his sculpture: 'Anyway we got Malachi going.'

140

'I don't suppose I'm going anywhere, Tad,' said Malachi. 'Doubt Preacher Abraham is either.' Jesse looked up at him, unhappy, both remembering a recent conversation. 'He's just traveling.'

'Malachi,' said Bud Maxon, 'sometimes you don't make sense.'

Tad said to his wooden woman's rump: 'He's making sense.'

Jesse heard, before the others, a high murmuring as though a thousand starlings had settled up the road on the far side of Maxon's woodlot. He thought at first it might be that, a gathering of little birds. But Malachi said: 'Ready or not, gentlemen, here they come!'

Jesse watched the road. Yesterday in Malachi's library the talk had turned to Preacher Abraham, and Malachi had dropped some casual sarcasm. Driven by swift unexpected impulse, Jesse had stumbled into an awkward defense of the preacher as startling to himself as to Malachi. Maybe in making his remark Malachi had taken the boy's agreement too much for granted. Unused to anything resembling antagonism in their relation, both had been wary, puzzled and hurt. 'You know evangelists have promised to save the world before, Jesse. All they do is drum up faith in magic. This one's no different.'

Supported by nothing much but his own unease, Jesse had demanded with too much passion: 'How do you *know* he isn't?'

'Ah – 'scuse it, I suppose I don't. I went off half-cocked. We wait until he shows up and see who's right, okay?'

Now from afternoon shadow Malachi watched Jesse's intently listening face. Some airy voices up there beyond the woodlot were singing, and with sweetness. Malachi had felt no such fear since a long-ago morning when he discovered ten-year-old Jesse walking cheerfully along the ridgepole of this house, arms out, six-toed feet proudly sure of themselves, miserable death or injury waiting on either side, and Malachi had not even dared to yell. *Who will deliver him from evil?*

The holy man came around the turn of the road with one of his disciples on either side of him. These were scarcely older than Jesse but almost as tall as the Preacher. Both were grace-ful, slim, yellow-haired, gray-eyed. They were twins, Jesse would learn later – Lucia and John. The Crusaders rejected last names, to signify they had given up home, family, every-thing, to follow the Lord.

141

Preacher Abraham advanced slowly, a smallish man with shoulderlength sandy hair, straggle of reddish beard, lowered head of thoughtfulness. Like his followers, he wore grass sandals and a shapeless knee-length white smock; his bony legs were muscular, toughened with journeying. Malachi saw in him the simplicity of a man prepared to walk through a stone wall in the trust that the Lord would turn it to vapor and let him through. By such singlehearted fantastics are the legends made; the Red Sea divides at Moses' command. *How am I to contend with this for the life of a boy?*

The Crusaders marched four abreast. They had ceased singing. The watchers could study the symbol they wore on the fronts of the shapeless, sexless white smocks, done big in crude red paint on the unbleached linen – a spoked wheel crossed out with two zigzag lines. Rumor had explained this symbol – the wheel stood for industry, mechanism, the things of the marketplace, all the Crusaders conceived the old civilization to have been; and God had crossed it out, utterly abolished it. Henceforth God's people were to live by the labor of their hands without machines, without enslaving animals or hunting: no meat, no money, no trade. Greed and cruelty would end forever in the kingdom of heaven; God and the angels would return.

The children matched the slow pace of Preacher Abraham, even the little ones and the lame keeping orderly in the ranks. When the Preacher was in speaking distance of The Store, the last ones had marched into sight. Malachi estimated there were not more than two hundred of them: the rumors of a thousand were like most rumors. He noticed a few considerably older men and women in their twenties – a dozen of them perhaps. There was no one older than the Preacher, who looked about thirty-five.

And Malachi brooded on Melton Village, a lonely society from which all the old had vanished, in which many of the children were stillborn, sickly, deformed. There had been serious talk of stockading the village; Malachi favored it – maybe it ought to become a part of Malachi's Thing. A few years ago the people had suffered brutal raids by the mountain people on their shaggy ponies. These had ceased after a party of young men, skilled at archery and equipped with swords contrived by Tad Doremus, had pursued a band of marauders and wiped them out – an unpredictable fury that might not have happened if Malachi had gone along. They had strung up the bodies on the trees and come home not quite the same youths they had been, having tasted the style of a world that was bound to come. For this reason Malachi had not condemned their action too severely: in a world going back to violence perhaps the village could not survive without violent responses. Turn back the clock and run the bloody course again! – if there's no help for it. The mountain people might forget the lesson. And other creatures prowled the encroaching forest that had not been known there in the old time – black wolves, giant bear. A great tawny cat had been glimpsed twice, with faint tiger markings of dark yellow, no puma certainly, maybe something escaped from an old-time zoo, or the descendant of such an escape. Melton Village was beset with strangeness within and without, full of trouble, and tired, and excited, and afraid.

Preacher Abraham stopped in the sunny warmth of the road with his two beautiful disciples. He said: 'God keep all here. We're come to promise you the founding of the New Jerusalem.'

Malachi unfolded his spidery legs and went down the porch steps, squeezing Jesse's shoulder in passing. He stepped forward alone to greet the Preacher. 'We can't do much except wish you well.'

'Why, that's a great deal,' said Preacher Abraham. It was a great voice to come from such a common-seeming, middle-sized man. 'Your good will, something to feed the children, opportunity to give you our good news – that's all we ask. We'll be gone tomorrow.'

'There's been a scarcity of good news lately,' said Malachi, and Jesse sat in amazement: *Malachi* the one to give the Preacher friendly greeting, while the rest including himself sat mute like lunkheads? 'Little news of any kind. We did learn that a civilization died.'

The Preacher's gaze was level – searching for his soul, Malachi supposed. 'Are you the mayor, sir?'

'Why,' said Malachi, 'we haven't rightly got one of those, unless it'd be Bud Maxon over there. How about that, Bud?' He tried with a backward glance to pry Bud off his butt and fetch him down to share the chores; Bud wasn't moving. Jesse's face was inaccessible; the Preacher had possession of Jesse's troubled eyes. 'About all we have in that line is a Board of Selectmen, and they don't meet too regular. I'm just Malachi

Peters, been around since the flood. We're a sort of Sleepy Hollow, Preacher, a wide place in the road.'

'It doesn't matter. My children can camp here, I suppose? And I hope they may go about among your houses to ask bread, flour, a few vegetables, whatever can be spared.'

'This man is a scoffer,' said the girl, the beautiful disciple.

'Why, I don't think I am, my dear,' said Malachi. 'History has done the scoffing. If you need a camp site, Preacher, you can use the field below my house. Over there – you can see my roof from here. There's a stream, a pool where the children could bathe.'

'Lucia,' said the Preacher kindly, 'maybe you are too quick to judge.' The girl flushed and looked away. 'I thank you, Mr Peters, in the name of all of us. We are happy to accept.'

Hackstraw rasped: 'Them kids got anything on under them smocks?'

'Why, yes,' said the Preacher, 'they have.' One of the shining young who had gathered close pulled up his smock, showing a trim loin-cloth. The flirt of the cloth and jerk of the boy's hips amounted to more than an answer to the question; he even tossed a wink toward Jesse. 'No need of that, Simon,' the Preacher said.

'Well, it didn't look like they had,' said Hackstraw, but he was routed, and subsided into dithering and grumbling.

Mr Goudy sighed, saying to the air: 'Malachi's Thing.'

'I'll show you the path, Preacher,' Malachi said. 'It's been getting overgrown with the munificence of nature since the old lady foreclosed the mortgage on her most heedless borrower.'

'You have an odd way of expressing yourself,' said Preacher Abraham, 'but I understand you. You say nature when you mean God.'

'Or you may be saying God when you mean nature. If we don't understand each other now we might arrive at it. This way, please.'

And Jesse went along.

So did Tad Doremus, who hadn't spoken. He tucked his sculpture in his hip pocket and slouched down the single file path behind Jesse, followed by the multitude; he could hear them breathing, and the brush of young feet in the grass. It occurred to Tad that the back of Jesse's neck looked thin and lonesome. Tad too was a friend of Malachi Peters, and wondered whether the old man was slipping from grace, if it's possible for an agnostic to do that.

Jesse stepped to one side when the path entered the meadow. He usually came this way when going to Malachi; his home was in the village on the dull Main Street and it made a short cut; his feet had done more than any others to keep the path trodden. Countless times he had entered the meadow and seen Malachi, white hair and raggedy gray-brown clothes on the porch two hundred yards away, and waved, and made a game of his progress across the field where now and then a dip of the surface would hide him. In such a hollow he'd pause, for the obscure thrill of teasing the old man, and then when amusement reached bursting point, bounce over the crest and run like a whirlwind, arriving flushed, queer-in-the-head, wondering what to say.

Paths move in time. This was not the old one, now that these strangers were filing past on it curious-eyed. He stood apart, letting them fill the meadow. The wave of them was murmuring, breaking up into separate faces, bodies, voices curiously soft. It dazed Jesse to remember that they came from everywhere – Connecticut, New Hampshire, Massachusetts, even Maine. Maybe they didn't all speak English. In a thirty-second daydream he taught one of the girls English, and how she loved him!

Malachi looked back, finding him for a long gaze, then walking on, matching his stride to the Preacher's as a taller man should.

The countries of love and terror border each other here and there. Jesse became a small boy alone in a crowd.

Most of these people were older, taller. They were following a pattern familiar to themselves. Every third Crusader carried a rolled strip of heavy cloth; these were being joined in pairs and pegged into long pup tents, big enough to hold three at each end with some snuggling. Within ten minutes the meadow had blossomed into a camp. Some of the Crusaders brought water from the pond, others searched under the bordering trees for fallen wood; a young woman with flint and steel went about lighting small campfires. Never a whine or argument or quarrelsome voice. Jesse shuffled off those shoes, tying them together at his neck. He worked his feet in the grass, swallowing something bitter, not panic exactly. Not merely loneliness.

He was the only one not bound for the New Jerusalem. The only one wearing brown instead of white. Shirt and loin-cloth, no tunic.

He walked up the meadow toward Malachi's house in a dark passion of aloneness – *touch me not, touch me not, take heed of loving me!* – silently passing these friendly souls, some of whom would have spoken to him but for that blind, unhearing look. He was thinking: *I could outrun every single one of you.* Then one of them did speak, a girl with a warm voice, a mouth like a geranium. 'Hello – aren't you the son of the man who's letting us have this field?'

Jesse fell in love. 'No, I'm not his son.' He was lost for more to say. She did not press for more, just waited, smiling without mockery. 'I'm his friend.'

'Oh,' she said, interested in him, not in Malachi. 'I'm Philippa.'

'My name's Jesse Lodson.'

'If you come with us you'll be just Jesse. We give up family, and home, and all things, for to follow our Preacher to the New Jerusalem.' And she was so happy about it – that afternoon anyway, in that place and time, the sun choosing gold lights in her brown hair and blessing the freckles on her honestly chubby cheeks – that her speech was a singing and her innocence like fresh cream.

If you come with us – but of course! They expected it, took it for granted; that was supposed to be the purpose of their pilgrimage. And Jesse longed to say: 'I'll go with you.' He could not, quite.

The town hall bell rang five o'clock. Almost time to go home for heaven's sake, lend a hand with the chores, wash up for supper. To be home not later than half past five was the understood price of being allowed to tag around after Malachi.

Malachi had found that bell three years ago in the ruins of a back-country church. Its village had been emptied – a raid by mountain people, or pestilence, or both; forest was reclaiming everything; bones were whitened, scattered, gnawed by wolves. As Malachi had told the story to Jesse, the bronze bell lay there among charred timbers and rubbish, gleaming like a great open mouth of suffering. Malachi and Tad Doremus had brought the bell home and installed it in the town hall. Then Malachi had persuaded the Board of Selectmen – there really was one, Malachi was sometimes president of it, and it did

146

provide about as much local government as well-behaved people ought to need – to employ half-witted Jem Thorpe to ring that bell every hour through the days. In return for this and a bit of easy janitor work, Jem got enough to eat, a place to sleep, and something to worship. He adored the bell, and the wonderful clock which he had been taught to wind and which told him when to pull the rope. He would have happily died to protect the bell, or the ritual, or Malachi. Just another part of that complex of the unpredictable that followed Malachi Peters like a leitmotif through the orchestration of these years of sadness and perplexity. Malachi's Thing.

'I have to go home.'

Philippa nodded sweetly. 'But the only real home is the New Jerusalem, Jesse.'

He knew her words came from Preacher Abraham, yet her sincerity made them hers too. She had a warm strange smell; her breasts were big enough to push out against the formless smock, and she carried them with no slouch. Jesse realized he was staring, and flushed. But she put her hands on his shoulders and kissed his cheek, bumping against his dangling shoes. 'We want you with us,' she said. He knew she had glanced down at his bare feet. 'Our Preacher says, Let all who are strange and lonely come with us, for we go to build a place where none shall be lonely or strange.'

Part of Jesse's mind protested that without loneliness and strangeness this world would not be this world at all and maybe not worth having; but it was a formless protest: he knew he would have grass sandals and a white tunic, and go with Philippa to the New Jerusalem.

Malachi felt silence around him as he climbed the slope to his house. The children's voices had fallen behind them. The Preacher had sent off those attending him on various errands, all but two young men in their early twenties whom he called Andrew and Jude. Andrew seemed cheerful – thoughtful too, plainfaced and kind. Jude's young face was already cut with worry lines and the start of a chronic frown.

Tad Doremus kept quiet – a natural occupation, almost a life-work.

Malachi asked: 'Where will you found the New Jerusalem?'

'I think I shall know the place when I see it,' said Preacher Abraham. 'We turned south in Canada because Andrew here brought me word of a place called Nuber on the west shore of the Hudson Sea. I must go there – it may be the place.'

'Nuber? There was a town, Newburgh,' said Malachi. 'I drove through it the summer I was eighteen. But that area of the Hudson Valley was destroyed, you know, in the floods and earthquakes.'

'This place is on higher ground, ten or fifteen miles inland.'

'You're a New Yorker, sir?'

'I was born in Maryland. I have almost no memory of the old time. Barely five, the year of the war, and I spent my youth in witless sin and folly until I was given light. Andrew is my right hand,' he said, and smiled at the young man as they climbed the steps of Malachi's porch. 'We separated a few months ago so that he could explore western New York while we went through New England. Then he rejoined us in the north. Tell Mr Peters about Nuber, Andrew.'

They settled on the porch, for the Preacher wanted to watch the preparation of the camp site in the meadow. Andrew spoke almost bookishly. 'What they call Nuber is an area fifteen miles by twenty – say three hundred square miles – where there were wealthy estates in the old time, and some arable land too, not spoiled by commercial agriculture. Long before the last build-up of political tensions in 1993 the rich people of that region were running a private oligarchy, nominally within the American political framework. They had a little bit of foresight, enough intelligence to see that the commercial-technological rat race couldn't keep up much longer – raw materials were running out for one thing – and they may have been wise enough to fear the end result of political insanity in a world with atomic power. At any rate they were much concerned with survival – their own, that is. According to their cult, so far as they had any beliefs, altruism was a bad word, and they had always considered their society as not much more than a source of loot and personal power. They dug in against the storm. They built underground refuges, hoarded enormous quantities of food, fuel, arms, ammunition. They couldn't make new guns, but even now, I understand, there's a miniature subterranean factory in Nuber that turns out gunpowder, and usable cartridges for the old weapons.'

'Nice people,' said Malachi.

'It is after all,' said Andrew sententiously, 'a primary pre-occupation of any dictatorial state.'

'Yes,' said Malachi. The Preacher watched the meadow.

'They shall be humbled,' said Jude, his voice sudden and harsh. His white hands knotted in front of him. 'It is in Ezekiel: *Moreover the word of the Lord came unto me, saying, Son of man, when the house of Israel dwelt in their own land, they defiled it by their own way and by their doings: their way was before me as the uncleanness of a removed woman. Wherefore I poured my fury upon them for the blood that they had shed upon the land, and their idols wherewith they had polluted it.*'

'Amen,' said Andrew mildly. He might even have a sense of humor, Malachi thought, but his devotion was complete and obvious. Intelligence and literacy he possessed, both wholly at the service of Preacher Abraham. He continued: 'They hired a lot of laborers, technicians, and a police force. Also a great many more personal servants than was usual among the rich at that time, paying high for them. Mostly they seem to have been following the advice of a man named Bridgeman, one of history's little Hitlers. Before the world blew up the police were called security guards – I suppose nobody asked, security for what? Then the world did blow up, they did survive, the police force was an army, some of the technicians were a palace elite, Bridgeman was king in everything but name, and the blue-collar people and servants were slaves. Specifically, Mr Peters. Nuber today makes no secret of being a slave-holding state. Bridgeman had a mint, turning out pretty gold and silver and copper money: trust him to think of that and grab control of it, among people who had thought all their lives that money was a paper fairy-tale told by themselves.'

'He must have known a little history.'

'Yes, Mr Peters, but not enough to do him any good. His official title, by the way, assumed right after the twenty-minute war, was –' Andrew smiled, his young face pleasantly professorial. 'Guess.'

'Couldn't.'

'Secretary,' said Andrew. 'Secretary of the Nuber Historical Society. Well, in a year or so he began hankering after something more like imperial purple, the name as well as the game, and somebody eager for his job stuck a ten-inch knife in his back, taking the job *and* the name of king. Bridgeman should have expected it: it was the kind of political operation Nuber was built to understand.'

Malachi asked: 'Preacher Abraham, do you propose to advance on a vicious military state, with a horde of defenseless children? How? How and why?'

'I will first explain the why,' said Preacher Abraham. 'Because it does seem impossible. Mr Peters, the world cannot be saved unless we show God's power in us by doing the seemingly impossible.'

'Oh,' said Malachi. 'The world is sickened of attempts to save it. The world is saving itself now in the only way it has or ever can – by small, brave individual efforts at recovery now that the storm's over. It will take centuries. Institutions have never done it and never will. Well, I see you don't agree, you're not hearing me.'

'To God nothing is impossible,' said the Preacher, as if he truly had not heard. 'As to the how, Mr Peters, we go there under God's guidance. As I have been assured by his very voice.' His face was glowing. 'Do not tell me this is a subjective experience – those wise little words! I know, Mr Peters, I *know!* If we fail, then the failure itself is God's will: we can only die in the Lord a little sooner than the natural time.'

'Have the children asked to die young?'

'You seem angry. The children understand, as perhaps you do not yet, the meaning of eternal life.' The Preacher rose. 'Thank you for the meadow, Mr Peters, and for this little time of rest.'

But Malachi had risen too and grasped his arm. The Preacher gazed back unmoving. 'Preacher Abraham, will you allow me to come with you? Will you give me your light, as you see it, and perhaps – perhaps –'

'No one who wishes to follow me is refused,' said Preacher Abraham.

'I think he has no faith,' said Jude.

'If some follow me for the wrong reasons,' said Preacher Abraham mildly, 'perhaps right reason will come later. We shall break camp early in the morning. Come to me then if you will.'

'Will you – stop in now and have something to eat?'

'Thank you, sir, but I see you keep goats and chickens. We must no longer exploit the captivity of living things. But thank you for the offer, which was kindly meant.'

Malachi sagged, watching the Preacher depart with Andrew and Jude. Tad sighed harshly. 'I don't think you sold him,

150

Malachi.'

'Come inside, Tad. The elderberry's near-about the best I've got. I distilled her some, see, and exploited her captivity in a bottle, sort of. Maybe she ain't a living thing, though.'

'Seemed like one, time I sampled her last.' Tad reached for the glass, drank, and nibbled his lips. 'She's living.' Malachi dropped in his big armchair by the hearth, the armchair where Jesse discovered Shakespeare and Mark Twain and Melville. 'You look a mite bushed, Malachi.'

'Am.'

'I a'n't exactly making you out.'

'Could you look after this place a while, Tad? Feed the stock – and help yourself naturally. Keep an eye out the public doesn't go off with the books for luck charms?'

'Could of course, Malachi.'

'Place'd be yours, come to that, I'm not back in a reasonable time. I'll write that in the form of a will, tonight.'

'Jesus, Malachi, I don't see you in one of them fucking nightgowns.'

'Maybe I'll be let to keep my pants.' Malachi refilled his glass. 'Jesse,' he said. 'I believe Jesse is hooked on the New Jerusalem.'

Tad reached down a blacksmith's hand to Malachi's bowed scrawny shoulder. 'Ayah. Uhha.'

'Why do we love?'

'I don't know,' said Tad. 'I'll mind the house. No trouble.'

'*Jesse*,' said Malachi, and drank his glass empty, and flung it against the fireplace stones.

There are many new islands. Wherever the land was low to the west of the Green Mountains the climbing water intervened, carving them into new solitude. Little islands, maybe good for a family and a farm if anyone chose to come; larger islands, where deer could breed, and bear, and the new-come coyotes, and wildcat. The toiling waters were fresh in the first few years except for flood rubbish and other pollution, then brackish as the vastly expanding Sea of St Lawrence (but it was becoming easier to speak of the Lawrent Sea, or sometimes just the Lorenta) swallowed the Richelieu River, and the earthquake that destroyed St Jean, Rouses Point, Plattsburg, a hundred other towns, brought southward the taste of ocean. In a few years another earthquake, another adjustment to the fearful stresses of the new weight of water on the land, flung together Lake George, Sacandaga, the upper tributaries of the Hudson, in a muddy boiling confusion. The Ontario Sea breaks through along the country that once knew Lake Oneida and the Mohawk River; some now call that passage Moha Water. Where the Lorenta and Hudson and Ontario Seas come together at the southeastern corner of the great Adirondack Island, outrageous complex tides tear about in a crazy Sabbat of the elements, and scour an unknown bottom. In the Year 9, they say, steam hung for six months over four hundred square miles of that tidal country; there was no one to go in under it and search for the cause. No volcano – none known, that is, not yet; but today there are hot springs along the southeastern coast of Adirondack that certainly did not exist in the old days.

At a place called Ticonderoga small sailing vessels can often make fair passage to and from Adirondack Island, passing out of sight of land for hardly more than an hour if the wind is right. Where the sea is narrower up in the north there's too much jungle and, they say, malaria or something like it; the Ticonderoga crossing is the best. Then, if you must go south, there are several places – Herkimer, Fonda, Amsterdam – where Moha Water can be crossed with not much danger except from pirates. Amsterdam, to be sure, is a little too near the tidal country and its frequent mists, which the pirates are apt to understand better than the ferry captains do. The devils come nipping out from the heavily wooded shores in their canoe fleets – true savages, reversions to the Stone Age, many of whose grandfathers must have sold insurance, real estate, and advertising just like anybody.

As for crossing the Hudson Sea in the far south, that's for professional heroes. Those tidal waves are treacherous and frightful. The pirates there have all the advantages, and they can do things with a lateen rig and a shallow craft that no decent sailor would think of doing unless he'd sold his soul to Shaitan. There, in fact, modern piracy may have developed; the canoe operators up north are imitators, amateurs. That corner of the world south of the Catskills needs more earthquakes. 'The Crusaders will have rough travel, if they mean to go as far as Nuber.'

'Yes,' said Jesse, who had come to Malachi dragging his feet after Tad Doremus went home. Malachi was back on his porch; bats were darting in the cool air; at the far end of

152

the meadow some of the children were singing. 'But Andrew came north by way of Fonda, and he didn't have any trouble. Malachi . . .'

'Get it off your mind.' Malachi patted the step beside him, and Jesse sat there. Malachi could feel his warmth. Wisdom, or fear, or that dismal blend of the two called caution prevented Malachi from putting an arm over the boy's shoulder as he would have done an evening or two earlier.

'What does it mean when – when all of a sudden everything changes, like upside down – I mean, you start believing one or two things different, or even just try to think how it would be if you *did* believe those things, and then a hundred other things change, and – and –'

'Your syntax is slipping.'

'I know. I got excited.'

'Like turning the kaleidoscope?'

'Man, yes – it *is* like that, sort of.'

'I guess,' said Malachi presently, 'it means you have to look at the new pattern . . . Do your folks know you're thinking of leaving with the Preacher?'

'I haven't been home,' said Jesse almost sullenly. 'Gah, you always know everything. If I told 'em they'd lock me up till he's gone, you know they would . . . Are you going to tell them?'

Malachi brooded. 'If I intended to, I would tell you first. I don't think of you as a child these days, Jesse.'

And Jesse thought in panic and misery: *But I'm not ready – not ready to be anything else. Oh, it's easy for YOU to be wise, Malachi!* 'Malachi, I – oh, I wish to *God* my old man – the bull –'

Jesse was lost in a sudden agony of weeping such as Malachi had never seen. It was easy then to take hold of him and cherish him as if he were still a child. 'I know,' said Malachi, rocking him lightly. 'I loved him too, your father. We used to play chess. He was a wonderful man, Jesse. Everybody knew it.'

'So how can you believe he's dead? There *has* to be a – a – the Preacher – yes, I talked to the Preacher for a minute, and he blessed me. Don't say anything, Malachi, just don't say anything for a while.' He gasped and blew his nose. 'I'm not going back to the house tonight. I'm to sleep in John's tent. They're going to have sandals for me.' He took the leather shoes from his neck, and set them inside the porch rail, his hands saying: *So much for my stepfather.* 'Can I leave them there, Malachi?'

'Yes.'

'I guess you're pretty disappointed with me.'

'No ... Jesse, I am considering going with Preacher Abraham myself, for my own sake. I even spoke to him about it.'

Jesse started and turned his wet face to Malachi in the dusk. '*You!* Why?'

'Oh, let us say that sometimes I too find Melton Village to be a kind of dead end. I have worked for the town, and you might say loved it – an ugly duckling – ai-yah, Malachi's Thing. But I need to learn what's happening in a bigger world. I've got in a rut. Why, man, for more than your lifetime I've had no news of the world except what's trickled in as gossip from the occasional traveler or tramp, most of it worthless, I expect. It's shameful. I needed something to fetch me loose. Besides, Preacher Abraham interests me, and he said that no one who elected to follow him was refused. He has his own kind of wisdom. It's not my kind, Jesse – I won't pretend. But perhaps I can be of some use to him, who knows?'

Jesse's stare would not let him go. 'You've got other reasons. You're not quite leveling with me, Malachi.'

'Maybe not. Not crooked either. Some things I find hard to explain, even to you. Suppose we just let it work out.'

Jesse relaxed. 'All right.' One of the natural surges of affection that made him what he was brought him back to Malachi, warm and close. He sat still with his head resting over Malachi's heart, and said at last: 'Well, I'm glad you're coming along.' Then he was gone, walking down the meadow to the little camp-fires.

Malachi carried the shoes indoors and put them away in an old trunk already loaded with history – the ancient kaleidoscope for instance, given to Malachi by his grandmother long before the Year Zero and still miraculously unbroken for Jesse's brief pleasure and amusement; and his father's diary that ended in the old year 1972, when the extinction of the Republic was obvious; and a photograph of a girl who had died with so many others in 1993.

The company of two hundred started in the early morning, marched east two or three miles to reach the old mountain road, and followed it south. They camped for the night where they could look toward distant Burlington Ruins, an old wound of flood and earthquake never healed. Malachi slept alone that night under the big dark. He had brought on his back a rolled blanket and change of clothing. He contributed a sack of potatoes to the general supply and whatever else he could find that seemed innocent in the Crusaders' terms. He also wore at his belt his old hunting knife, which Preacher Abraham deplored. 'I cut my food with it,' said Malachi, 'and sometimes I whittle. And no, sir, I'll decline the tunic for the present and just wear these.' They studied each other, antagonists not too unfriendly; Malachi perhaps had an advantage in knowing where the true conflict lay. 'Now if you can persuade me of the existence of God, Preacher, I will wear the tunic and throw away my knife. But don't rush it, sir. I'm inclined to make up my mind on my own time. Meanwhile let me be the oddity among you. I wash and I don't eat little girls.' The Preacher brooded and then smiled, and surprisingly patted Malachi's arm before he turned away to more important matters.

At home Malachi had often slept outdoors, in his back yard or out in the meadow. He knew the Pleiades, and the wandering of the planets and the stars. He had found his strength more than equal to the day's march, and was healthily tired. The camp-fires burned low; Malachi noticed Jude and one or two others taking up sentry duty out at the fringes of the light. Then someone – Malachi could not see him in the dark – sounded on a bugle the ancient army music of Taps. How did it happen the Preacher had resurrected that, and did he have any idea of the far-off associations of ideas? After the music died slowly – no one can hear it unmoved – there was a rhythmic murmuring all through the camp; it ended all in the same moment, and Malachi understood it was the sound of the children praying. Somewhere among them, Jesse, snug in a tent with the disciple John and three or four others. It would take Jesse no time to learn the words and rituals: he was always a quick study. Malachi sighed, and after less pain than he had feared, he slept.

In hilly country Preacher Abraham did not demand of his children more than twelve to fifteen miles of marching in a day. A majority of them, Malachi guessed as the march resumed in the morning, would have been delighted to exceed that. But an army, and sometimes a civilization, must proceed at the pace

155

of its weakest marcher. Some were very young. The mue-girl Dinah, twelve years old, slight and small with the patient look of sainthood, had a defect in her knee-structure that made her stiff-legged and slow. Whenever she tired Jude carried her. These were the only times when his haggard face lost its frown and became tender; but with that frail burden he could make no speed himself.

On the second and third days Malachi stayed most of the time in the rear, knowing that to all of them, even to the Preacher and Jesse, he must seem monstrously old. But the rear was a good vantage point. He could see whatever happened. He could watch Jesse's dark head, and know at least who his new friends were, and read whatever was told by the set of the boy's shoulders. And sometimes Jesse dropped back to walk with him; though in a too exalted, precarious way, Jesse did seem happy, and full of a natural interest in the new country.

Reading history, Malachi had noted that throughout most of the past the counsel of the old had been valued, even sought for; it was not until the 20th Century that old people were declared obsolete and swept under the rug; and the 20th Century itself was now merely one more lump in the record.

On the third night out the company reached the settlement of Shorum, where the ferry sails for Ticonderoga now and then if the captain considers it worth his while. He has been known to stir his stumps for one old woman with her cat in a basket who wanted to get over to Chilson Landing and see a new grandchild; and once he made the mayor of Shorum wait a week on account of a few cross words. About transporting two hundred kids from here to nowhere to found the New Jerusalem, he was not pleased, pointing out that it would take four trips, two days' work considering the tides, and even with four trips the crowding would be somewhat much. 'We are patient,' said Preacher Abraham, 'and used to material difficulties.'

'It'll cost you a dime a head,' said Captain Gibbleson.

'Dependence on money is the death of the spirit. What can you buy with it?' asked the Preacher. 'The old system's gone, Captain.'

'State gov'ment says the old coinage is still money. Naturally I wouldn't take no paper.'

'I've hardly been aware you had a state government.'

Very much the wrong thing to say. Malachi intervened deprecatingly: 'We sort of invoke it, Preacher. Some claim to've seen it.' But his wink at the Captain did not restore the peace.

'Got no money,' said Captain Gibbleson, 'you can swim.'

Andrew took over. 'Captain, I see you have quite a miscellaneous log pile, there along the bank.'

'Ayah, driftwood, some of it.' Captain chewed on his plug and eyed him unhopefully; the plug smelled as if it had been sold him by Mr Goudy. 'You wouldn't believe what high water fetches in sometimes. Got a whole cabin one day, with a dead man in it. Blowed up like a punkin he was, you should've seen.'

'I offer you two alternatives,' said Andrew. 'We will stack that wood for you, and split any that's worth splitting, in return for our passage. Or, overriding your wishes as it were, we will simply take whatever wood we need to build a raft.' Behind Andrew's back the disciple Simon explained further by sticking out his tongue.

'Why, you'd drown,' said Captain Gibbleson, chewing. 'Like bugs. I can't have that on my conscience. Stack the Goddamn wood and it's a deal.' Later, hunkered on the pier and watching Andrew oversee the labor, he confided to Malachi: 'Sometimes I almost half-way like a man that don't mind being a damn fool.' His back turned to the Crusaders, Malachi slipped him five bucks in 1984 quarters.

The gray-blue reach of the Hudson Sea proved not unkind. Preacher Abraham and Andrew went with the first group on the ferry, a flat-bottomed barge with a crude square sail. Her name was *Pug*, after Gibbleson's third wife, and he claimed she was too squat and wide to turn over – in a hurricane she might go straight up or straight down, but she wouldn't tip. Jude was in charge of the group that would go on the fourth sailing; Jesse lingered for the transparent reason that this group included Philippa. Malachi observed that he won no profit from it beyond a staring and a few choked attempts at conversation. Philippa, Malachi thought, was managing Jesse's compulsive adoration rather well. Malachi had also seen the look that Philippa had for Andrew only: an ancient story, one who loves and one who is loved; maybe a constant in the human pattern, the exceptions shining only for a most fortunate few. But it seemed to Malachi that Philippa might be not without the rudiments of compassion. Before Shorum, Jesse had brought her to Malachi, saying with glazed casualness: 'This is

157

Philippa.'

'How do you do?' said Malachi. The freckles were appealing.

'We are sure to do well in the Lord's grace,' said Philippa.

Now Malachi, loafing in the stern with Captain Gibbleson (almost a friend), watched the clumsiness and grace of youth. The scow crept torpidly across a placid sea toward a gray excrescence of rock on a hillside; there's water all around it now, a few people and goats inhabit the island, and it is still overlooked by that mountain which General Burgoyne's artillery found so convenient once upon a time. Malachi heard Jesse offering some news, up forward: 'They restored the old fort in 1909 –' *What's he done, memorized the Britannica?* – 'but it probably isn't true that Ethan Allen demanded its surrender in the name of the Great Jehovah and the continental Congress.' Except for a passing uneasiness Philippa looked quite blank.

Then up on the wharf and goodbye to Gibbleson, and on into the perilous world of Adirondack Island. There would be nearly a hundred miles of it as the trail winds from Ticonderoga to Fonda, following the roads of the old time whenever they seem practical. Nature is trying not unsuccessfully to heal those scars. The busy vine spreads across with sucker rootlets, the innocent seed reaches down through any crack in the dreary concrete or asphalt and is sustained.

Already at many places the easiest route will be a new earthen road with no decaying metal hulks or broken slabs of rubbish. (But the automobile corpses that held their shape so persistently, when overgrown with cool Virginia creeper are of benefit to rabbits, weasels, ground-birds, and such folk, who know how to make honest use of them.) In this Adirondack Island country you are better off with a guide, if you find one you can trust.

There is for instance the matter of bandits and large wild animals. If one of the outlaw or savage groups does come after you on those burr-shaggy mountain ponies, bent on loot or women or violence for its own sake, the guide isn't much help, and whatever happens will be soon over; but the guide is expected to know the latest rumors about those devils, and find you the safest routes. Guiding is an honorable profession, at least in theory. A guide must know the animals too, and steer you right if you need to hunt. Some of them of course are no damn good.

A long day's march from Fort Ti brought the Crusaders to Brant Lake, and they camped beside it. Here in the morning a guide offered his services, a small brown smiling man in the skimpy G-string of a savage. (We already begin to hear something of the Cayugas in the central part of what used to be New York; they are a difficult people, with old grievances rooted deep.) He wore a more civilized belt above his hips to hold a steel hunting knife, and he carried at his shoulder a quiver of brass-tipped arrows and a short bow unpleasing to Preacher Abraham. Andrew tried the man with sign-language and grunts, transmitting the message that he apparently wanted no money in return for showing them a safe way southward, but just their company as far as Moha Water and a roll of the linsey cloth their tunics were cut from.

'The knife and bow will be his living, Preacher,' said Malachi. 'No one has taught him any better.'

Preacher Abraham sighed and said: 'I know. Grace does not come unsought, nor overnight unless the Lord wills.' Then he looked deep in the guide's squirrely brown eyes and inquired in simple English whether he believed in God. The guide nodded with solemn reverence.

A few hours later, when the brown man had led them down a wood-road that became a pleasant sun-speckled green trail, Malachi ranged ahead to walk beside him. Jesse came too, evidently wanting just then to reestablish closeness. Speaking too softly for those behind to hear, Malachi asked the guide whether he believed in Satan and the ideological solidarity of the capitalist class. The little man nodded again several times, delightedly.

Jesse smiled too, but the smile wiped itself out. 'Malachi,' he said, 'why do people always make such a tremendous thing about words?'

Malachi worried over it for him, and presently said: 'They are clumsy, and often unnecessary. But I think they may be the best means we have for probing certain kinds of darkness. As for communication, Jesse, we might survive for a while without it, but I'm not sure the survival would be worth having. Words weren't invented *only* to conceal thoughts as the old wheeze has it. They create thoughts, give thoughts, and are thoughts. People live by honest words and die by the other kind.'

Frowning and still bothered, Jesse said after a while: 'Yes, I guess that makes sense.'

There was no denying the guide's usefulness. When they camped beside the Sacandaga River he found early mushrooms for them and showed them edible marsh plants, so that the grim diet of cornmeal mush and potatoes and soggy wheat cakes could be a little varied. It puzzled Malachi that he should have apparently known the Crusader's vegetarian principles without being told, but no one commented on it. At the music of Taps the little guide bowed his face to the ground.

All the following day he led his charges along firm earth through a region of brackish swamp where the Sacandaga once comfortably paralleled a 20th Century road. Dark country here, too close to that outrageous great tidal pocket of the Hudson Sea. Mists float unexpected through the more open reaches of the woods. It is quiet. No snowmobiles nor snarling chain saws nor bulldozer flatbeds shuddering uphill. Wind sometimes or the other sounds of storm, or of a deer dying to feed panther or wolf or brown tiger. You may hear a coyote desolately howling, or a loon in the marsh. No transistors.

On the morning of the ninth day after leaving Melton Village, an inquiry from Andrew about Fonda drew from the guide the gestured response that the place was two sleeps away, meaning perhaps anywhere from twenty-five to forty miles. The black flies that day were a torment. The Crusaders marched four abreast, a cloud of needling misery all about them. It was one of the old highways, in fair condition. Forest stood oppressively deep on either side; imagination provided glimpses of motion in the heavy green, hints of pathways not to be followed. But the march was bringing them into open country, and shortly after the second rest of the morning – scant rest it was with the tiny black demons whining and settling, nothing to do but slap and suffer – they came out into it.

The deep woods lay a few hundred yards behind them when Malachi saw another road up ahead, a simple line of reddish dirt emerging from thick tree cover and snaking down a long slope to meet their highway. The guide flung up his hand. The company halted as Andrew dutifully repeated the motion, and stood raggedly, slapping at the flies, two hundred children wondering, murmuring. Preacher Abraham called out: 'What is it? What's the matter?' Andrew shook his head don't-know.

The guide was running forward bent over as one might do to evade a stone or arrow from behind; in his stooping haste Malachi saw a thing turned suddenly feral and vicious. At the end of his long rush he flung up his arms and sent to that wooden summit a sharp yell, the word *'Here!'* His mission achieved, he crouched then, smiling and ugly, holding an arrow leveled toward Andrew as the horsemen plunged out from under the trees.

Andrew shouted: 'Scatter! Back to the woods!' Malachi shouted it too, and he saw Andrew crumple and fall, the guide's arrow in his chest. Jude had already snatched up Dinah in his arms and was running with her. John too shrilled at the company: 'To the woods! *Hide!'*

Too many of the children were slow to grasp it, and stood in a sick daze until the Preacher added his urgent voice. Then they began to go, stragglingly and late, staring over their shoulders, maybe not quite believing any of it until they saw Lucia snatched up and flung across a pony's back, and John leaping at the rider's leg, falling back with blood spurting from his throat.

The riders were not more than a dozen, and strangely silent except for a gurgle of excited laughter. Naked but for loin-rags and moccasins, they rode bareback as if they had spent half their lives that way, and they were men of any breed, all breeds. They did not trouble to draw their small bows, seeing (or knowing in advance) that the victims were unarmed – their servant might do as he pleased. They wanted women, but young girls would do very well. They rode their fiery little horses in and out among the fleeing, now terrified children, and picked them off as they chose, each man as soon as he had secured his captive riding back up the long hill. It was over in minutes. Europe's 5th Century would have been proud of them.

Malachi looked at the knife in his hand. He could have used it, if there had been time, and anything in reach. Maybe the sight of it was what had made the riders circle clear of him and Jesse. Philippa had been with them when the storm went by; now she had run to where Andrew was lying and flung herself down. Malachi saw the last rider disappear up the hill and into the woods, and behind him scampered the busy small figure of their smiling guide.

The Preacher was saying: *'Resist not evil.* This was the word of Christ: *Love your enemies, bless them that curse you.'* Was

161

the Preacher counseling himself? The disciple John was dead, Lucia and eleven others gone; Andrew whom he had called his right hand could no longer serve or hear him, though Philippa with her clutching hands and crying voice was trying to make him live.

'For he maketh his sun to rise on the evil and the good, and sendeth the rain on the just and the unjust.'

'Philippa.' Malachi knelt by her. 'You must come away.'

'Come away,' said Jesse. 'Come away, Philippa.'

'Be ye therefore perfect even as your Father which is in Heaven is perfect.'

Philippa rose and brushed past them. She stood before Preacher Abraham and said: 'You did this.'

'Forgive me then,' said the Preacher.

Philippa stared at Andrew's blood on her hands. 'We were going to marry, in the New Jerusalem.' She turned her face to the woods, and Malachi felt Jesse tense with readiness to run after her, bring her back from that suicide. She took a few sleepwalking steps that way and halted, looking about her, saying: 'But I have no place to go.'

'Philippa,' said the Preacher, 'there *is* the New Jerusalem.'

She did not answer.

They carried the bodies of Andrew and John down the road, and made a burial place in the open country; that wooded hilltop stood vague in the north. The day was still, no sounds but those of peace, and the Preacher spoke to them. 'I will go to Nuber,' he said, 'and preach there the founding of the New Jerusalem as I am commanded to do by my Father which is in Heaven. I will wear on my breast this image of the conquered wheel, and I will testify.'

Malachi wondered: *Does he know who he is, in his own mind at least and in the minds of many of us? Would he have us know?*

'But I am weak in the vessel of the flesh, and do not always see my way clearly, and at times I may have been deceived and unwise.'

Well, Christ would not have said that.

'It may be, my children, that it is not for us to build that city, in Nuber or anywhere, by the labor or our hands, though I still hope it will be so. Therefore I do release from the vows any of you who for any reason no longer hear the call of God

162

to follow me. There are other ways you may serve his purpose, many honorable ways. From our beloved disciple Andrew, I learned more about the sorry kingdom of Nuber than I have told you. Perhaps I understand why it is that God plainly directs me to that place, but I will not try to explain it. Nuber is a city of the damned, a place of greed and cruelty, smallness of the spirit, evildoing and blindness. So it may be that I go there to my death, and God's purpose in this may not be understood for a long time to come. I will demand nothing of you that is not freely given, and so God be with you.'

He said no more that day, and he did not preach at Fonda.

Sympathy and friendliness were strong in that lonely village, but cooled somewhat at Malachi's suggestion of an armed search party to rescue the ravished girls. He was talking to the mayor of the town, and the good man said nothing about resisting not evil, but pointed out that those bloody bandits would now be fifty or a hundred miles away in their own kind of country, by trails nobody knew. They were a familiar plague; it had happened before. Who could deal with it except the kind of police force no town nowadays can support? Be reasonable, man. Shortly thereafter the townfolk took up a collection to pay for the transport of Abraham's Army over Moha Water.

Here a maternally minded citizen intervened, protesting the exposure of these children to the perils of such a journey. Others before her had felt it, but this was a sensible woman with tact. She talked long and amiably with the Preacher while the two ferry captains were waiting on the tide, and then with his permission spoke to the children, praising their devotion, their hope of the New Jerusalem (a hope she shared), adding almost like an afterthought that if any of them felt unequal to the task, or wanted more time to think about it, why, she and some of her neighbors were prepared to give them shelter, or help for a journey back home if that was what they wanted.

Sitting on the pier with Malachi, Jesse heard him murmur: 'Bravo!' But he noticed the old man was gazing at the Preacher, not at this good Samaritan who looked as if she wanted to cuddle the whole company in her lap. 'We ought to stay with him, Malachi?' And Jesse studied the Preacher, trying to find what Malachi had been observing with surprise and respect.

'This woman is blessed,' said Preacher Abraham. 'Again I

163

say, you who wish to remain with her are released from your vows.' And when he asked for a sign from those who elected to leave him, more than half the company raised their hands, Philippa among them.

'He believes it,' said Malachi, 'even to the cup that will not pass. Yes, I think I ought to stay with him, Jesse, in what time he has left before death or disillusion. I have heard about Nuber too. Once or twice he has found it possible to talk with me. But you yourself are first with me: that is how I've always loved you.'

Jesse looked down at his feet. The grass sandals had never fitted; he carried them, like the old shoes, at his neck. 'It was to have been a city for the mues, among the rest.'

'You're not even a mue.' Malachi shook his shoulder. 'God, Jesse, I hope you'll marry some time and replenish the bloody earth with a pack of six-toed children. Think what it would do to the ski industry!'

'The what?' Jesse was bewildered.

'Never mind,' said Malachi, and kissed the top of his head.

Nuber, a city of wealth (which is always relative) and poverty (which is basic hell) surrounded by a dutifully toiling country-side with plantations of slave labor, felt in those years no foreign threat. Life could be a little relaxed. To enter the borders you had only to convince the commandant of the post that you nourished no pernicious design against the stability of the realm, and to convince him might cost no more than ten dollars. Malachi still had a mite more than that; or the band of Abraham's followers, less than fifty now, might even be admitted free.

The very location of the border posts was subject to the commandant's caprice. He might move his little establishment a mile or so down the road if something that way caught his fancy – a juicy melon patch, or a farm family with a good-looking daughter who might be more contented as a citizen of the Republic. (It is after all something of a distinction, Malachi remarked to Jesse; not every republic has a king for a dictator. And Jesse had been laughing some that day, a kind of half-choked outbreak, maybe a new Jesse trying to crack the chrysalis of a very solemn boy.)

To the camp at Trempa, a day's march from the nearest border post of Nuber, came an old peddler – at least he was dressed like one, and gnarled like a fellow often exposed to the seasons, but he never opened his shoulder-sack, nor paid much heed an anyone but the Preacher himself, beyond a few puzzled glances at Malachi. 'You ought to go back, Preacher,' he said. 'Oh, you ought to go back, let it pass from you. I come from Nuber and I know.'

'Who are you?' asked the Preacher.

'A tinker, an old man, a nobody. I come and go. I've been called Ahasuerus – in jest I suppose, for never did I despise Christ and his kindred; the old and slightly wise become used to jesting at their expense, it's only natural. You ought to go back. Oh, they are saying in Nuber, there's a wheel for you, you that condemn the wheel and wear that handsome symbol over your heart. Why, they've found a great steelbound wooden wheel, something maybe from an old-time farm wagon, I don't know.' He muttered and flexed his arthritic hands, tired from carrying the sack and from age. 'They are saying that if you come to preach your sedition at Nuber you shall carry the wheel on your back to the market place, and it shall be set up there for the multitude; and they speak of nailing your palms to the spokes. And oh, Abraham, there will be one to betray you and one to deny you, and one to judge you and wash his hands.'

'Why do they hate me?' asked Preacher Abraham.

'Because you speak of the good that all men dream of as if it could be real.'

At these words the Preacher was troubled, and when the peddler had received his blessing and gone away up the north road he came to Malachi and asked him: 'Why have you remained with me?' He shook back the hair from his shoulders, a young man's motion, but looked tired and old as he rubbed his fingertips over the frown that would not leave his forehead. The painted wheel on his tunic bore the dark appearance of blood. 'You have not faith, Malachi, yet you are faithful to promises, and have served me and my poor children with devotion. I watched you helping Jude care for Dinah at Coble, when she was dying. And in the weeks at Gran Gor, where the smallpox was, where so many died, you were tireless in caring for the sick, those of the town as well as our own. If only for these things I'm bound to love and respect you. And now it seems you are prepared to go with me, though I cannot ask it, even to the end of the journey.'

'Or perhaps I will deny you,' said Malachi Peters, smiling, and the Preacher presently smiled, in his own fashion. 'It's my belief that human beings choose their own ends, Preacher Abraham. There is no purpose under the heaven until living creatures on earth create it. And there must be few indeed who don't cherish a faith in some things, because all knowledge remains incomplete; even though faith is only the fantasy of things hoped for, the invention of things not seen. I have faith in the good will of myself and certain others, faith in the rightness of love and virtue and mercy. That faith will sustain me as it has in the past, while I live.'

The long weeks lay behind Jesse like a year of difficult growth. This was beginning autumn. The border post at Nuber stood only a few steps down the road. Tomorrow they would pass it, and that would happen which was to happen. Tomorrow would be the day that Nuber celebrated as the Day of Coming Forth, the day when according to their history and legend they came out from underground after the twenty-minute war and found that the Earth still lived. Jesse's memory brought him like a remote music the Gospel of Matthew: *Ye know that after two days is the feast of the passover, and the Son of man is betrayed to be crucified.*

Still and sleepless under his half of Malachi's blanket, Jesse gazed toward the south horizon where a few strong stars cut through the haze of the night. Malachi had said it would rain before daylight. A huge roadside oak spread over them, big enough to shelter most of the Preacher's little company, and Malachi had pegged a strip of canvas over their heads.

How did one learn the ways of earth and sun and sky as the old man knew them? It was more than observation. Observing the natural world, but also continually knowing himself a part of it. *He could speak like Saint Francis (though he doesn't) of 'my brother the sun.' Here am I, says he (or is it myself speaking for him?), a unique pattern briefly arranged on this earth for my only time to think and feel and see. So may it not be that what I do to and for myself and others is more important than what I believe? Belief governs what I do – yes, partly. Well, I can be mistaken about many things and still be happy if there is happiness, I can even be good. But I can never do evil without evil consequences, no matter how pure my intentions. Who taught me this? – I've discovered only a little bit of it just now. Why, Malachi. Malachi and the books . . .*

Tad will be taking good care of the books. He'd better!

He shut away the southern stars beyond his eyelids, and tried to measure the time since he had last attempted to pray as Preacher Abraham had told him it ought to be done: 'Relax, Jesse, and think of nothing directly, it's not a matter of words. Open your mind and give yourself to God.' He could not measure it – a long time, he knew. Maybe he had not attempted it since Dinah's death.

Senseless. *'As flies to wanton boys are we to the gods – they kill us for their sport.' Lear,* said Jesse's complex, accurate, toiling mind – *the Fourth Act, and spoken by Gloster after his blinding. 'I have no way, therefore I want no eyes; I stumbled when I saw . . .' But the true religious will have us believe God is merciful.*

A senseless death. Some hidden lethal thing, perhaps in Dinah's deformed bones, had stricken her with a sudden paralysis. For two days she could not lift herself, nor relieve her bladder, nor even breathe unless supported. Her twelve-year-old face remained sternly patient, asking no favors, but she could not hide the evidence of a racking pain. Then a fever when she no longer knew even Jude, and death. When it was over, the thing in Jude's face was not the appalled misery that Jesse had seen in Philippa, but hate, a hate that brooded and grieved and would not declare itself.

And while he yet spake, lo, Judas, one of the twelve, came, and with him a great multitude with swords and staves, from the chief priests and elders of the people.

Jesse sighed, in need of sleep. The Preacher's advice concerning prayer gave him nothing. *At the last came two false witnesses, and said, This fellow said, I am able to destroy the temple of God, and to build it in three days.*

And Jesse remembered the talk of Malachi, recent talk and that from long ago, when the first rumors of Preacher Abraham came to Melton Village. 'How often, Jesse, how often has Christ been crucified! The old grim story so many times enacted – for the poor human race has always longed for a Redeemer to take up the burdens that human people themselves alone must carry. Once he was a dying god on a spattered altar. This Preacher Abraham will make it plain that he must be crucified, and there will be those to do it as blindly as the rabble and the Roman soldiers. And maybe we learn a little, century by century; or sometimes we forget too much.'

Nevertheless tomorrow they would go into Nuber, the end already known, carrying the dream of the New Jerusalem, 'where the earth is so cherished that God will return –'

No, thought Jesse – *No. I have no wish to give myself to God, even if God lives. Human love is greater than divine love, for divine love* – he looked for the southern stars again but the rain had taken them, and was falling in light haste up there on the October leaves; with care he shifted the weight of his head on Malachi's arm – *divine love is at worst an illusion, at best a dream for some imaginary future time. Human love is here and now.*

Dean R. Koontz

THE NIGHT OF THE STORM

He was a robot more than a hundred years old, built by other robots nearly eight centuries after the end of human civilization. His name was Suranov, and as was the custom of his kind, he roamed the earth in search of interesting things to do. Suranov had climbed the highest mountains in the world, with the aid of special body attachments (spikes in his metal feet, tiny but strong hooks on the ends of his twelve fingers, an emergency grappling rope coiled inside his chest-area storage compartment and ready for a swift ejection if he should fall); his small, anti-grav flight motors were removed to make this climb as dangerous and, therefore, as interesting as possible. Having submitted to heavy-duty component sealing procedures, Suranov once spent eighteen months underwater, exploring a large portion of the Pacific Ocean, until he was bored even by the mating of whales and by the ever-shifting beauty of the sea bottom. Suranov had crossed deserts, explored the artic circle on foot, gone spelunking in countless different subterranean systems. He had been caught in a blizzard, in a major flood, in a hurricane, and in the middle of an earthquake that would have registered 10 on the Richter Scale, if the Richter Scale had still been in use. Once, specially insulated, he had descended halfway to the center of the earth, there to bask in pockets of glowing gases, between pools of molten stone, scalded by erruptions of magma, feeling nothing. Eventually, he grew weary of even this colorful spectacle, and he surfaced again. He wondered if, having lived only one of his two assigned centuries, he could last through another hundred years of such tedium.

Suranov's private counselor, a robot named Bikermien, assured him that this boredom was only temporary and easily alleviated. If one were clever, Bikermien said, one could find limitless excitement as well as innumerable, valuable situations for serious data collection both about one's environment and one's mechanical aptitude and heritage. Bikermien, in the last half of his second century, had developed such an enormous and complex data vault that he was assigned stationary duty as a counselor, attached to a mother-computer and utterly immobile. By now, extremely adept at finding excitement even through second-hand experience, Bikermien did not mourn the loss of his mobility; he was, after all, a spiritual superior to the ordinary robot. Therefore, when Bikermien advised, Suranov listened, however skeptical he might be.

Suranov's problem, according to Bikermien, was that he had started out in life, from the moment he'd left the factory, to pit himself against the greatest challenges – the wildest sea, the coldest cold, the highest temperatures, the greatest pressures – and now, having conquered these things, could see no interesting obstacles beyond them. Yet, the counselor said Suranov had overlooked some of the most fascinating explorations. The quality of any challenge was directly related to one's ability to meet it; the less adequate one felt, the better the experience, the richer the contest and the handsomer the data reward.

Does this suggest anything to you? Bikermien inquired, without speaking, the telebeam open between them.

Nothing.

So Bikermien explained it:

Hand-to-hand combat with a full-grown, male ape might seem like an uninterestingly easy challenge, at first glance; a robot was the mental and physical superior of any ape. However, one could always modify oneself in order to even the odds of what might appear to be a sure thing. If a robot couldn't fly, couldn't see as well at night as in the daylight, couldn't communicate except vocally, couldn't run faster than an antelope, couldn't hear a whisper at a thousand yards – in short, if all of his standard abilities were dulled, except for his thinking capacity, might not a robot find that a hand-to-hand battle with an ape was a supremely exciting event?

I see your point. Suranov admitted. *To understand the grandeur of simple things, one must humble himself.*

Exactly.

And so it was that, on the following day, Suranov boarded the express train going north to Rogale's Province, where he was scheduled to do some hunting in the company of four other robots, all of whom had been stripped to their essentials.

170

Ordinarily, they would have flown under their own power; now, none of them had that ability.

Ordinarily, they would have used their telebeams for communication; now, they were forced to talk to one another in that curious, clicking language that had been especially designed for machines but which robots had been able to do without for more than six hundred years.

Ordinarily, the thought of going north to hunt deer and wolves would have bored them all to tears, if they had been able to cry; now, however, each of them felt a curious tingle of anticipation, as if this were a more important ordeal than any he had faced before.

A brisk, efficient robot named Janus met the group at the small stationhouse just outside of Walker's Watch, toward the northernmost corner of the Province. To Suranov, it was clear that Janus had spent several months in this uneventful duty assignment, and that he might be near the end of his obligatory two years' service to the Central Agency. He was actually *too* brisk and efficient. He spoke rapidly, and he behaved, altogether, as if he must keep moving and doing in order not to have time to contemplate the uneventful and unexciting days that he had spent in Walker's Watch. He was the kind of robot too eager for excitement; one day, he would tackle a challenge that he had not been, by degrees, prepared for, and he would end himself.

Suranov looked at Tuttle, another robot who, on the train north, had begun an interesting, if silly, argument about the development of the robot's personality. He had contended that, until quite recently, in terms of millenia and centuries, robots had not had individual personalities. Each, Tuttle claimed, was quite like the other, cold and sterile, with no private dreams. A patently ridiculous theory. Tuttle had been unable to explain how this could have been, but he refused to back down from his position. Watching Janus chatter at them in a nervous staccato, Suranov was incapable of envisioning an era when the Central Agency would have dispatched mindless robots from the factories. The whole purpose of life was to explore, to store data collected from an individual viewpoint, even if it were repetitive. How could mindless robots ever function in the necessary manner?

As Steffan, another of their group, had said, such theories

were on a par with belief in Second Awareness. (Some believed, without evidence, that the Central Agency occasionally made a mistake and, when a robot's alloted lifespan was up, only partially erased his accumulated memory before refitting him and sending him out of the factory again. These robots, the superstitious claimed, had an advantage and were among those who matured fast enough to be elevated to duty as counselors and, sometimes, even to service in the Central Agency itself.)

Tuttle was angered to hear his views lumped with all sorts of wild tales. To egg him on, Steffan also suggested that Tuttle believed in that ultimate of hobgoblins, the 'human being.' At this, disgusted, Tuttle settled into a grumpy silence, while the other enjoyed the jest.

'And now,' Janus said, calling Suranov back from his reverie, 'I'll issue your supplies and see you on your way.'

Suranov, Tuttle, Steffan, Leeke, and Skowski crowded forward, eager to begin the adventure.

Each of the five were given: binoculars of rather antique design, a pair of snowshoes that clipped and bolted to their feet, a survival pack of tools and greases with which to repair themselves in the event of some unforeseen emergency, an electric hand-torch, maps, and a drug rifle complete with an extra clip of one thousand darts.

'This is all, then?' Leeke asked. He had seen as much danger as Suranov, perhaps even more, but now he sounded frightened.

'What else would you need?' Janus asked impatiently.

Leeke said, 'Well, as you know, certain modifications have been made on us. For one thing, our eyes aren't what they were, and –'

'You've a torch for darkness,' Janus said.

'And then, our ears –' Leeke began.

'Listen cautiously, walk quietly,' Janus suggested.

'We've had a power reduction to our legs,' Leeke said. 'If we should have to run –'

'Be stealthy; creep upon your game before they know you're there, and you'll not need to chase them.'

'But,' Leeke persisted, 'weakened as we are, if we should have to run from something –'

'You're only after deer and wolves,' Janus reminded him. 'The deer will not give chase – and a wolf hasn't any taste for

172

steel flesh.'

Skowski, who had thus far been exceptionally quiet, not even joining the good natured roasting the others had given Tuttle on the train, now stepped forward. He said, 'I've read that this part of Rogale's Province has an unusual number of – unexplained reports.'

'Reports of what?' Janus asked.

Skowski swept the others with his yellow visual receptors, then looked back at Janus. 'Well – reports of footprints similar to our own but not those of any robot, and reports of robotlike forms seen in the woods –'

'Oh,' Janus said, waving a glittering hand as if to brush away Skowski's suggestion like a fluff of dust, 'we get a dozen reports each month about "human beings" sighted in the wilder regions northwest of here.'

'Where we're going?' Suranov asked.

'Yes,' Janus said. 'But I wouldn't worry. In every case, those who make the reports are robots like yourselves: they've had their perceptions decreased in order to make the hunt a greater challenge for them. Undoubtedly, what they've seen has a quite normal explanation. If they had seen these things with the full range of their perceptions, they would not have come back with these crazy tales.'

'Does anyone besides stripped down robots go there?' Skowski asked.

'No,' Janus said.

Skowski shook his head. 'This isn't anything at all like I thought it would be. I feel so weak, so ...' He dropped his supplies at his feet. 'I don't believe I want to continue with this,' he said.

The others were surprised.

'Afraid of goblins?' Steffan asked. He was the teaser in the group.

'No,' Skowski said. 'But I don't like being a cripple, no matter how much excitement it adds to the adventure.'

'Very well,' Janus said. 'There will be only four of you, then.'

Leeke said, 'Don't we get any weapons besides the drug rifle?'

'You'll need nothing else,' Janus said.

Leeke's query had been a strange one, Suranov thought. The prime directive in every robot's personality, when he left the

173

factory, forbade the taking of life which could not be restored. Yet, Suranov had sympathized with Leeke, shared Leeke's foreboding. He supposed that, with a crippling of their perceptions, there was an inevitable clouding of the thought processes as well, for nothing else explained their intense and irrational fear.

'Now,' Janus said, 'the only thing you'll need to know is that a natural storm is predicted for the northern Rogale area early tomorrow night. By then you should be to the lodge which will serve as your base of operations, and the snow will pose no trouble. Questions?'

They had none they cared to ask.

'Good luck to the four of you, then,' Janus said. 'And may many weeks pass before you lose interest in the challenge.' That was a traditional send-off, yet Janus appeared to mean it. He would, Suranov guessed, prefer to be hunting deer and wolves under decreased perceptions rather than to continue clerking at the stationhouse in Walker's Watch.

They thanked him, consulted their maps, left the stationhouse and were finally on their way.

Skowski watched them go and, when they looked back at him, waved one shiny arm in a stiff-fingered salute.

They walked all that day, through the evening and on into the long night, not requiring rest. Though the power supply to their legs had been cut back and an effective governor put on their walking speed, they did not grow weary. They could sense their lessened abilities, but they could not grow tired. Even when the drifts were deep enough for them to break out their wire-webbed snowshoes and bolt those in place, they maintained a steady pace.

Passing across broad plains where the snow was swept into eerie peaks and twisting configurations, walking beneath the dense roof of crossed pine boughs in the virgin forests, Suranov felt a twinge of anticipation which had been missing from his exploits for some years now. Because his perceptions were so much less acute than usual, he sensed danger in every shadow, imagined obstacles and complications around every turn. It was positively exhilarating to be here.

Before dawn, a light snow began to fall, clinging to their cold, steel skin. Two hours later, by the day's first light, they crested a small ridge and looked out across an expanse of pine

174

woods to the lodge where it rested on the other side of a shallow valley. The place was made of a burnished, bluish metal, with oval windows, very straight-walled and functional.

'We'll be able to get some hunting in today,' Steffan said.

'Let's go,' Tuttle said.

Single file, they went down into the valley, crossed it and came out almost at the doorstep of the lodge.

Suranov pulled the trigger.

The magnificent buck, decorated with a twelve-point rack of antlers, reared up onto its hind legs, pawing at the air, breathing steam.

'A hit!' Leeke cried.

Suranov fired again.

The buck went down onto all four legs.

The other deer, behind it in the woods, turned and galloped away, back along the well-trampled trail.

The buck shook its huge head, staggered forward as if to follow its companions, stopped abruptly, then settled slowly onto its haunches and, after one last valiant effort to regain its footing, fell sideways into the snow.

'Congratulations!' Steffan said.

The four robots rose from the drift where they'd fallen when the deer had come into sight, and they crossed the small, open field to the sleeping buck.

Suranov bent and felt the creature's sedated heartbeat, watched its grainy, black nostrils quiver as it took a shallow breath.

Tuttle, Steffan, and Leeke crowded in, hunkering about the creature, touching it, marveling at the perfect musculature, the powerful shoulders and the hard-packed thighs. They agreed that bringing down such a brute, when one's senses were drastically damped, was indeed a challenge. Then, one by one, they got up and walked away, leaving Suranov alone to more fully appreciate his triumph and to carefully collect his own emotional reactions to the event in the micro-tapes of his data vault.

Suranov was nearly finished with his evaluation of the challenge and of the resultant confrontation, and the buck was beginning to regain its senses, when Tuttle cried out as if his systems had been accidentally overloaded.

'Here! Look here!'

Tuttle stood, Suranov saw, two hundred yards away, near the dark trees, waving his arms. Steffan and Leeke were already moving toward him.

At Suranov's feet, the buck snorted and tried to stand, failed to manage that yet, blinked its gummed eyelids. With little or nothing more to record in his data vault, Suranov rose and left the beast, walked toward his three companions.

'What is it?' he asked when he arrived.

The stared at him with glowing amber visual receptors which seemed especially bright in the gray light of late afternoon.

'There,' Tuttle said, pointing at the ground before them.

'Footprints,' Suranov said.

Leeke said, 'They don't belong to any of us.'

'So?' Suranov asked.

'And they're not robot prints,' Tuttle said.

'Of course they are.'

Tuttle said, 'Look closer.'

Suranov bent down and realized that his eyes, with half their power gone, had at first deceived him in the weak light. These weren't robot prints in anything but shape. A robot's feet were cross-hatched with rubber tread; these prints showed none of that. A robot's feet were bottomed with two holes that acted as vents for the anti-grav system when the unit was in flight; these prints showed no holes.

Suranov said, 'I didn't know there were any apes in the north.'

'There aren't,' Tuttle said.

'Then –'

'These,' Tuttle said, 'are the prints – of a man.'

'Preposterous!' Steffan said.

'How else do you explain them?' Tuttle asked. He didn't sound happy with his explanation, but he was prepared to stick with it until someone offered something more acceptable.

'A hoax,' Steffan said.

'Perpetrated by whom?' Tuttle asked.

'One of us.'

They looked at each other, as if the guilt would be evident in their identical, bland metal faces. Then Leeke said, 'That's no good. We've been together. These tracks were made recently, or they'd be covered over with snow; none of us has had a chance, all afternoon, to sneak off and form them.'

176

'I still say it's a hoax,' Steffan insisted. 'Perhaps someone was sent out by the Central Agency to leave these for us to find.'

'Why would Central bother?' Tuttle asked.

'Maybe it's part of our therapy,' Steffan said. 'Maybe this is to sharpen the challenge for us, add excitement to the hunt.' He gestured vaguely at the prints, as if he hoped they'd vanish. 'Maybe Central does this for everyone who's been sated, to restore the sense of wonder that –'

'Highly unlikely,' Tuttle said. 'You know that it's the responsibility of each individual to engineer his own adventures and to generate his own storable responses. The Central Agency never interferes; it is merely a judge. It evaluates, after the fact, and gives promotions to those whose data vaults have reached maturity.'

By way of cutting the argument short, Suranov said, 'Where do these prints lead?'

Leeke indicated the marks with a shiny finger. 'It looks as if the creature came out of the woods and stood here for a while – perhaps watching us as we stalked the buck. Then he turned and went back the way he came.'

The four of them followed the footprints into the first of the pine trees, but they hesitated to go into the deeper regions of the forest.

'Darkness is coming,' Leeke said. 'The storm's almost on us, as Janus predicted. With our senses as restricted as they are, we should be getting back to the lodge while we've still light enough to see by.'

Suranov wondered if their surprising cowardice were as evident to the others as it was to him. They all professed not to believe in the monsters of myth, and yet they rebelled at the thought of following these footprints. However, Suranov had to admit, when he tried to envision the beast that might have made these tracks – a 'man' – he was even more anxious than ever to reach the sanctity of the lodge.

The lodge had only one room, which was really all that they required. Since each of the four was physically identical to the others, no one felt a need for geographical privacy. Each could obtain a more rewarding isolation merely by tuning out all exterior events in one of the lodge's inactivation nooks, thereby dwelling within his own mind, recycling old data and searching for previously overlooked juxtapositions of seem-

177

ingly unrelated information. Therefore, no one was discomfited by the single, gray-walled, nearly featureless room where they would spend as much as several weeks together, barring any complications or any lessening of their interest in the challenge of the hunt ...

They racked their drug rifles on a metal shelf that ran the length of one wall, and they unbolted their other supplies which, until now, they had carried at various points on their functional body shells.

As they stood at the largest window, watching the snow sheet past them in a blindingly white fury, Tuttle said, 'If the myths are true, think what would be done to modern philosophy.'

'What myths?' Suranov asked.

'About human beings.'

Steffan, as rigid as ever, was quick to counter the thrust of Tuttle's undeveloped line of thought. He said, 'I've seen nothing to make me believe in myths.'

Tuttle was wise enough, just then, to avoid an argument about the footprints in the snow. But he was not prepared to drop the conversation altogether. He said 'We've always thought that intelligence was a manifestation, solely, of the mechanized mind. If we should find that a fleshy creature could –'

'But none can,' Steffan interrupted.

Suranov thought that Steffan must be rather young, no more than thirty or forty years out of the factory. Otherwise, he would not be so quick to reject anything that even slightly threatened the status quo that the Central Agency had outlined and established. With the decades, Suranov knew, one learned that what had once been impossible was now considered only commonplace.

'There are myths about human beings,' Tuttle said, 'which say that robots sprang from them.'

'From flesh?' Steffan asked, incredulous.

'I know it sounds odd,' Tuttle said. 'But at various times in my life, I have seen the oddest things prove true.'

'You've been all over the earth, in more corners than I have been. In all your travels, you must have seen tens of thousands of fleshy species, animals of all descriptions.' Steffan paused, for effect, then said, 'Have you ever encountered a single fleshy creature with even rudimentary intelligence in the manner of the robot?'

178

'Never,' Tuttle admitted.

'Flesh was not designed for high-level sentience,' Steffan said.

They were quiet a while, then.

The snow fell, pulling the gray sky closer to the land.

None would admit the private, inner fear he nurtured.

'Many things fascinate me,' Tuttle said, surprising Suranov who had thought the other robot was done with his postulating. 'For one – where did the Central Agency come from? What were its origins?'

Steffan waved a hand disparagingly. 'There has *always* been a Central Agency.'

'But that's no answer,' Tuttle said.

'Why isn't it?' Steffan asked. 'We accept, for answer, that there has *always* been a universe, stars and planets and everything in between.'

'Suppose,' Tuttle said, 'just for the sake of argument, that there has *not* always been a Central Agency. The Agency is constantly doing research into its own nature, redesigning itself. Vast stores of data are transferred into increasingly more sophisticated repositories every fifty to a hundred years. Isn't it possible that, occasionally, the Agency loses bits and pieces, accidentally destroys some of its memory in the move?'

'Impossible,' Steffan said. 'There would be any number of safeguards taken against such an eventuality.'

Suranov, aware of many of the Central Agency's bungles over the past hundred years, was not so sure. He was intrigued by Tuttle's theory.

Tuttle said, 'If the Central Agency somehow lost most of its early stores of data, its knowledge of human beings might have vanished along with countless other bits and pieces.'

Steffan was disgusted. He said, 'Earlier, you ranted about Second Awareness. You amuse me, Tuttle. Your data vault must be a treasure trove of silly information and useless theorizing. If you believe in these human beings – then do you also believe in all the attendant myths? Do you think they can only be killed with an instrument of wood? Do you think they sleep at night, in dark rooms, like beasts? And do you think that, though they're made of flesh, they cannot be dispatched but that they pop up somewhere else in a new body?'

Confronted with these obviously insupportable superstitions, Tuttle backed down from his entire point. He turned his amber visual receptors on the whirling snow beyond the window, and he said, 'I was only supposing. I was just spinning a little fantasy to help pass the time.'

Triumphant, Steffan said, 'However, fantasy doesn't contribute to a maturation of one's data vault.'

'And I suppose that you're eager to mature enough to gain a promotion from the Agency,' Tuttle said.

'Of course,' Steffan said. 'We're only alloted two hundred years. And, besides, what else is the purpose of life?'

Perhaps to have an opportunity to mull over his strange 'supposings,' Tuttle soon retired to an inactivation nook in the wall beneath the metal shelf where the guns lay. He slid in feet first, pulled the hatch shut behind his head, leaving the others to their own devices.

Fifteen minutes later, Leeke said, 'I believe I'll follow Tuttle's example. I need time to consider my responses to this afternoon's hunt.'

Suranov knew that Leeke was only making excuses to be gone; he was not a particularly gregarious robot and seemed most comfortable when he was unaddressed and left to himself.

Alone with Steffan in the lodge, Suranov was in an unpleasantly delicate position. He felt that he, too, needed time to think inside a deactivation nook. However, he did not want to hurt Steffan's feelings, did not want to give him the impression that they were all anxious to be away from him. For the most part, Suranov liked the young robot; Steffan was fresh, energetic, obviously a first-line mentality. The only thing he found grating about the youth was his innocence, his undisciplined drive to be accepted and to achieve. Time, of course, would mellow and richen Steffan; he did not, therefore, deserve to be hurt. How, then, to excuse oneself without slighting Steffan in any way?

The younger robot solved the problem, by suggesting that he, too, needed time in a nook. When he was safely shut away, Suranov went to the fourth of the five wall slots, slid into it, pulled the hatch shut, and felt all of his senses drained away from him, so that he was only a mind, floating in darkness, contemplating the wealth of ideas in his data vault ...

Adrift in nothingness, Suranov considers the superstition which has begun to be the center of this adventure: the human being, the man:

1. *Though of flesh, the man thinks and knows.*

2. *He sleeps by night, like an animal.*

3. *He devours other flesh, as does the beast.*

4. *He defecates.*

5. *He dies and rots, is susceptible to disease and corruption.*

6. *He spawns his young in a terrifyingly unmechanical way, and yet his young are also sentient.*

7. *He kills.*

8. *He can overpower a robot.*

9. *He dismantles robots, though none but other men know what he does with their parts.*

10. *He is the antithesis of the robot. If the robot represents the proper way of life, man is the improper.*

11. *Man stalks in safety, registering to the robot's senses, unless seen, as only another harmless animal – until it is too late.*

12. *He can be permanently killed only with a wooden implement. Wood is the product of an organic lifeform, yet lasts as metal does; halfway between flesh and metal, it can destroy human flesh.*

13. *If killed in any other way, by any means other than wood, the man will only appear to be dead. In reality, the moment he drops before his assailant, he springs to life elsewhere, unharmed, in a new body.*

Although the list goes on, Suranov abandons that avenue of thought, for it disturbs him deeply. Tuttle's fantasy can be nothing more than that – conjecture, supposing, imagination. If the human being actually existed, how could one believe the Central Agency's prime rule: that the universe is, in every way, entirely logical and rational?

'The rifles are gone,' Tuttle said, when Suranov slid out of the deactivation nook and got to his feet. 'That's why I recalled you.'

'Gone?' Suranov asked, looking at the shelf. 'Gone where?'

'Leeke's taken them,' Steffan said. He stood by the window, his long, bluish arms beaded with cold droplets of water which had been precipitated out of the air.

'Is Leeke gone too?' Suranov asked.

'Yes.'

He thought about this for a moment, then said, 'But where

would he go in the storm? And why would he need *all* the rifles?'

'I'm sure that it's nothing to be concerned about,' Steffan said. 'He must have had a good reason, and he can tell us all about it when he comes back.'

Tuttle said, '*If* he comes back.'

Suranov said, 'Tuttle, you sound as if you think he might be in danger.'

'In light of what's happened recently – those prints we found – I'd say that could be a possibility.'

Steffan scoffed at this.

'Whatever's happening,' Tuttle said, 'you must admit it's odd.' He turned to Suranov. 'I wish we hadn't submitted to the operations before we came out here. I'd do anything to have my full senses again.' He hesitated, then said, 'I think we have to go find Leeke.'

'He'll be back,' Steffan argued. 'He'll return when he wants to.'

'I'm still for initiating a search,' Tuttle said.

Suranov went to the window and stood next to Steffan, looked out at the driving snow. It had covered the ground with at least twelve new inches of white, had bowed the proud trees, and still it fell faster than Suranov had ever seen it fall in all his many journies.

'Well?' Tuttle asked again.

'I concur,' Suranov said. 'We should look for him, but we should do it together. With our lessened perceptions, we might easily get separated and lost out there. If one of us became damaged in a fall, he would most likely experience a complete battery depletion before anyone found him.'

'You're right,' Tuttle said. He turned to Steffan 'And you?'

'Oh, all right,' Steffan said. 'I'll come along.'

Their torches cut bright wounds in the darkness but did little to melt through the curtain of wind-driven snow. They walked abreast around the lodge, making a circle search. Each time they completed another turn about the building, they widened their search pattern. They had decided to cover all of the open land, but they would not enter the trees, even if they had not located Leeke by then. They all agreed to this limitation, though none – not even Steffan – admitted that half the reason

182

for ignoring the woods was based on a purely irrational fear of them ...

In the end, however, it was not necessary to enter the woods, for they found Leeke less than twenty yards away from the lodge. He was lying on his side in the snow.

'He's been terminated,' Steffan said.

The others didn't need to be told.

Both of Leeke's legs were missing.

'Who could have done something like this?' Steffan asked.

Neither Tuttle nor Suranov answered him.

Leeke's head hung limply on his neck, because several of the links in his ring cable had been bent out of alignment. His visual perceptors had been smashed, and the mechanism behind them ripped out through the shattered sockets. When Suranov bent closer, he saw that someone had poked a sharp object into Leeke's data vaults, through his eye tubes, and had scrambled his tapes into a useless mess; he hoped Leeke had been dead by then.

'Horrible,' Steffan said. He turned away from the scene and began to walk back toward the lodge, stopped abruptly as he realized that he should not be out of the other robots' company. He shuddered, mentally.

'What should we do with him?' Tuttle asked.

'Leave him,' Suranov said.

'Here to rust?'

'He'll sense nothing more.'

'Still –'

'We should be getting back,' Suranov said, shining his light around the snowy scene. 'We shouldn't expose ourselves.'

Keeping close to one another, they returned to the lodge.

9. *He dismantles robots, though none but other men know what he does with their parts ...*

'As I see it,' Suranov told them, when they were once again inside the lodge, 'Leeke did not take the rifles. Someone – or something – entered the lodge to steal them. Leeke must have come out of his inactivation nook just as the culprits were leaving. Without pausing to wake us, he gave chase.'

'Or was forced to go with them,' Tuttle said.

'I doubt that he was taken out by force,' Suranov said. 'In the lodge, with enough light to see by and enough space to maneuver in, even with lessened perceptions, Leeke could have kept himself from being hurt or forced to leave. However, once he was outside, in the storm, he was at their mercy.'

The wind screamed across the peaked roof of the lodge, rattled the windows in their metal frames.

They stood still, listening until the gust died away, as if the noise were not made by the wind but by some enormous beast that had reared up over the building and was intent on tearing it to pieces.

Suranov went on: 'When I examined Leeke, I found that he was felled by a sharp blow to the ring cable, just under the head – the kind of blow that would have had to come suddenly, from behind, without warning. In a room as well lighted as this, nothing could have gotten behind Leeke without his knowing it was there.'

Steffan turned away from the window and said, 'Do you think that Leeke was already terminated when ...' His voice trailed away, but in a moment he had found the discipline to go on: 'Was he terminated when they dismantled his legs?'

'We can only hope that he was,' Suranov said.

Steffan said, 'Who could have done such a thing?'

'A man,' Tuttle said.

'Or men,' Suranov amended.

'No,' Steffan said. But his denial was not so adamant as it had been before. He said, 'What would they have done with his legs?'

'No one knows what they do with what they take,' Suranov said.

Steffan said, 'You're beginning to sound as if Tuttle's convinced you, as if you believe in these creatures.'

'Until I have a better answer to the question of who terminated Leeke, I think it's safest to believe in human beings,' Suranov explained.

For a time, they were silent.

Then, Suranov said, 'I think we should start back to Walker's Watch in the morning, first thing.'

'They'll think we're immature,' Steffan said, 'if we come back with wild tales about men prowling about the lodge in the darkness. You saw how disdainful Janus was of others who'd made similar reports.'

'We've poor, dead Leeke as proof,' Tuttle said.

'Or,' Suranov said, 'we can say Leeke was terminated in an

accident and that we're returning because we're bored with the challenge.'

'You mean, we wouldn't even have to mention – human beings?' Steffan wanted to know.

'Possibly,' Suranov said.

'That would be the best way to handle it, by far,' Steffan said. 'Then, no second-hand reports of our temporary irrationality would get back to the Central Agency. We could spend much time in the inactivation nooks, until we finally saw the *real* explanation of Leeke's termination, which somehow now eludes us; if we meditate long enough, a proper solution is bound to arise. Then, by the time of our next data vault audits by the Agency, we'd have covered over all traces of this illogical reaction we now suffer from.'

'However,' Tuttle said, 'we might already know the *real* explanation of Leeke's death. After all, we've seen the footprints in the snow, and we've seen the dismantled body ... Might it be that men – human beings – really are behind it?'

'No,' Steffan said. 'That's superstitious. That's irrational.'

'At dawn,' Suranov said, 'we'll set out for Walker's Watch, no matter how bad the storm is by then.'

As he finished speaking, the distant hum of the lodge's generator – which was a comforting background noise that never abated – now cut out, and they were plunged into darkness.

With snow crusted on their chilled metal skins, they focused three electric torches on the generator in its niche behind the lodge. The top of the machine's casing had been removed, exposing the complex inner works to the elements; in the center of all that tangled wiring lay an obvious hole where some part or other should have been.

'Someone's removed the power core,' Suranov said.

'But who?' Steffan asked.

Suranov directed the beam of his torch to the ground.

The others did likewise.

Mingled with their own footprints were other prints similar but not made by any robot: those same, strange tracks that they had seen by the trees in the late afternoon, and which had profusely marked the snow all around Leeke's body.

'No,' Steffan said. 'No, no, no.'

'I think it's best that we set out for Walker's Watch tonight,'

Suranov said. 'I don't think it would be wise, any longer, to wait until morning.' He looked at Tuttle who was mottled by the snow which clung to him in icy lumps. 'What do you think?'

'Agreed,' Tuttle said. 'But I suspect it's not going to be an easy journey. I wish I had all my senses to full power.'

'We can still move fast,' Suranov said. 'And we don't need to rest, as fleshy creatures must. If we're pursued, we have the advantage.'

'In theory,' Tuttle said.

'We'll have to be satisfied with that.'

7. *He kills.*
8. *He can overpower a robot.*

In the lodge, by the eerie light of their hand torches, they bolted on their snowshoes, attached their emergency repair kits, and picked up their maps. The beams of their lamps preceding them, they went outside again, staying quite close together.

The wind beat upon their broad backs, while the snow worked hard to coat them in hard-packed, icy suits.

They crossed the clearing, half by dead reckoning and half by the few landmarks the torches revealed, each wishing to himself that he had his full powers of sight, and his radar, in operation again. Soon, they came to the opening in the trees which lead down the side of the valley and back toward Walker's Watch. They stopped there, staring into the dark tunnel which the sheltering pines formed, and they seemed reluctant to go any farther.

'There are so many shadows—' Tuttle said.

'Shadows can't hurt us,' Suranov said. Throughout their association, from the moment they had met one another on the train coming north, Suranov had known that he was the leader among them. He had exercised his leadership sparingly, but now he must take full command. He started forward, into the trees, between the shadows, moving down the snowy slope.

In a moment, reluctantly, Steffan followed.

Tuttle came last.

Halfway down toward the valley floor, the tunnel between the trees narrowed drastically. The trees loomed closer, spread their boughs lower. And it was here, in these tight quarters, in

186

the deepest shadows, that they were attacked.

Something howled in triumph, its mad voice echoing above the constant whine of the wind.

Suranov whirled, not certain from which direction the sound had come, lancing the trees with torchlight.

Behind, Tuttle cried out.

Suranov turned, as Steffan did, and both their torches illuminated the struggling robot.

'It can't *be!*' Steffan said.

Tuttle had fallen back under the relentless attack of a two-legged creature which moved almost exactly as a robot might move, though it was clearly a fleshy creature. It was dressed in furs, its feet booted, and it wielded a metal axe.

It drove the blunted blade at Tuttle's ring cable.

Tuttle raised an arm, threw back the weapon, saved himself – at the cost of a severely damaged elbow joint.

Suranov started forward to help, but was stopped as a second of the fleshy beasts belivered a blow from behind. The weapon struck the center of Suranov's back and drove him, totteringly, to his knees.

Suranov fell sideways, rolled, got to his feet in one well-coordinated maneuver, turned quickly to confront his assailant.

A fleshy face stared back at him from a dozen feet away, blowing steam into the cold air. It was framed in a fur-lined hood, a grotesque parody of a robot's face. Its eyes were too small for visual receptors, and they did not glow. Its face was not perfectly symmetrical as it should have been; instead, it was out of proportion – and it was puffed and mottled from the cold. It did not even shine in the torchlight, and yet ... Yet, there was obvious intelligence there – malevolent intelligence, perhaps even maniacal, but intelligence nonetheless.

Surprisingly, the monster spoke to Suranov. Its voice was deep, its language full of rounded, softened syllables, not at all like the clattering language the robots spoke to one another.

Abruptly, the beast leapt forward, crying out, and swung a length of metal pipe at Suranov's neck.

The robot danced backwards, out of range.

The demon came forward.

Suranov glanced at the others, saw the first demon had Tuttle backed almost into the woods. A third had attacked Steffan, who was barely managing to hold his own.

Screaming, the man before Suranov charged, plowed the end of the pipe into Suranov's chest.

The robot fell, hard.

The man came in close, raising his bludgeon.

Man thinks, though he's of flesh ... sleeps like an animal, devours other flesh, defecates, rots, dies ... he spawns his young in an unmechanical manner, though his young are sentient ... he kills ... he kills ... he overpowers robots, dismantles them, does (what?) with their parts ... can be killed, permanently, only with a wooden implement ... if killed in any other way, he does not die a true death, but springs up elsewhere in a new body ...

As the monster swung his club. Suranov rolled, rose up and struck out with his long-fingered hand.

The man's face tore, gave blood.

The demon stepped back, bewildered.

Suranov's terror had metamorphosed into rage, and he made use of that rage as he stepped forward and struck out again. And again. Flailing with all of his reduced strength, he broke the demon's body, temporarily killed it, leaving the snow spattered with blood.

Turning from his own assailant, he moved in on the beast that was after Steffan and, clubbing from behind, broke its neck with one blow of his steel hand.

By the time he reached Tuttle and had dispatched with the third demon, Tuttle had sustained one totally demolished arm, another smashed hand, and damage to the ring cable which, luckily, had not terminated him. The three of them, with any luck, would survive.

'I thought it was finished,' Tuttle said.

Dazed, Steffan said to Suranov, 'You killed all three of them!'

'They would have terminated us,' Suranov said. Inside, where they could not see, he was in a turmoil.

'But,' Steffan said, 'the prime directive from the Central Agency forbids the taking of life –'

'Not quite,' Suranov said. 'It forbids the taking of life which cannot be restored.'

'These lives will be restored?' Steffan asked, looking at the hideous corpses, unable to understand.

'You've seen human beings now,' Suranov said. 'Do you believe the myths, or do you still scoff?'

188

'How can I scoff?'

'Then,' Suranov said, 'if you believe that such demons exist, you must believe what else is said of them.' He quoted his own store of data on the subject: 'If killed in any other way, by any means other than wood, the man will only appear to be dead. In reality, the moment he drops before his assailant, he springs to life elsewhere, unharmed, in a new body.'

Steffan nodded, unwilling to argue the point.

Tuttle said, 'What now?'

'We continue back to Walker's Watch,' Suranov said.

'And tell them what we found?'

'No.'

'But,' Tuttle said, 'we can lead them back here, show them these corpses.'

'Look around you,' Suranov said. 'There are other demons watching from the trees.'

Tuttle looked, saw a dozen white faces on both sides, leering.

Suranov said, 'I don't think they'll attack us again. They've seen what we can do, how we have learned that, with them, the prime directive does not apply. But they're sure to remove and bury the corpses when we've gone.'

'We can take a body along with us,' Tuttle said.

Suranov said, 'No. Both of your hands are useless, and Steffan's right arm is uncontrollable. I couldn't carry one of those bodies all the way back to Walker's Watch with my power as reduced as it is.'

'Then,' Tuttle said, 'we still won't tell anyone about what we've seen up here?'

'We can't afford to, if we ever want to be promoted,' Suranov said. 'Our only hope is to spend a very long time in some inactivation nook, contemplating until we've learned to cope with what we've witnessed.'

They picked their torches out of the snow and, staying close to one another, started down toward the valley once more.

'Walk slowly and show no fear,' Suranov warned.

They walked slowly, but each of them was certain that his fear was painfully evident to the unearthly creatures crouching in the shadows beneath the pine trees.

They walked all that night and most of the following day before they reached the stationhouse at Walker's Watch. In that time, the storm died down and winked out altogether. The landscape was serene, white, quite peaceful. Looking at it, one felt sure the universe was rational. But Suranov knew, with a terrible, sick premonition, that – if he must believe in specters and other-worldly beings like men – he would never be able to think of the universe in rational terms again.

SCIENCE FICTION
STAR

Joanna Russ
| 0352398655 | **Picnic on Paradise** | 50p* |

Kilgore Trout
| 0352398469 | **Venus on the Half Shell** | 50p* |

SCIENCE FANTASY
STAR

W.W.
| 0352398523 | **Qhe: Prophets of Evil** | 50p |

SCIENCE FANTASY
TANDEM

Edgar Rice Burroughs
| 0426148401 | **Out of Time's Abyss** | 35p* |

THE FANTASTIC GOR SERIES
John Norman
0426144961	**Assassin of Gor**	45p*
0426167821	**Captive of Gor**	60p*
0426147952	**Hunters of Gor**	45p*
042617531X	**Marauders of Gor**	60p*
0426144880	**Nomads of Gor**	45p*
0426167740	**Priest-Kings of Gor**	50p*
0426124235	**Raiders of Gor**	40p*
0426143736	**Tarnsman of Gor**	35p*

PLANET OF THE APES
David Gerrold
| 0426147448 | **Battle for the Planet of the Apes** | 35p* |

John Jakes
| 0426147529 | **Conquest of the Planet of the Apes** | 35p* |

Jerry Pournelle
| 042614760X | **Escape From the Planet of the Apes** | 35p* |

George Alec Effinger
0426156757	**Escape to Tomorrow**	35p*
0426160371	**Journey into Terror**	35p*
0426151739	**Man the Fugitive**	35p*

Jane Gaskell
0426159667	**Atlan**	60p
0426164326	**The City**	45p
0426159586	**The Dragon**	45p
0426159314	**The Serpent**	60p

John Jakes
0426167074	**Brak the Barbarian**	45p*
0426167236	**Mark of the Demons**	45p*
0426167155	**The Sorceress**	45p*

Wyndham Books are available from many booksellers and newsagents. If you have any difficulty please send purchase price plus postage on the scale below to:

Wyndham Cash Sales,
123 King Street,
London W6 9JG

OR

Star Book Service,
G.P.O. Box 29,
Douglas,
Isle of Man,
British Isles

While every effort is made to keep prices low, it is sometimes necessary to increase prices at short notice. Wyndham Books reserve the right to show new retail prices on covers which may differ from those advertised in the text or elsewhere.

U.K. & Eire
One book 15p plus 7p per copy for each additional book ordered to a maximum charge of 57p.

Other Countries
Rates available on request.

N.B. These charges are subject to Post Office charge fluctuations.